D1824710

# THE SWORD OF LIGHT

## TALES OF THE MISPLACED
### BOOK FOUR

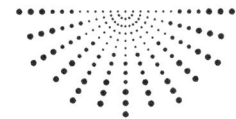

## ADAM K. WATTS

Copyright (C) 2023 Adam K. Watts

Layout design and Copyright (C) 2023 by Next Chapter

Published 2023 by Next Chapter

Edited by Graham (Fading Street Services)

Cover art by Lordan June Pinote

This book is a work of fiction. Names, characters, places, and incidents are the product of the author's imagination or are used fictitiously. Any resemblance to actual events, locales, or persons, living or dead, is purely coincidental.

All rights reserved. No part of this book may be reproduced or transmitted in any form or by any means, electronic or mechanical, including photocopying, recording, or by any information storage and retrieval system, without the author's permission.

# CHARACTERS

**Abaran:** *Urgaban* advisor to King Vegak of Pokorah-Vo.

**A'iwanea, Mama:** *Noélani* referred to as the Great Mother, primary goddess of the *Kajoran* people.

**Akajokira, Auntie:** *Noélani* daughter to Mama A'iwanea and Papa Mohanga. This is the goddess of protection for the *Kajoran* people.

**Akshira:** *Rorujhen* spouse to Farukan and mother of Barashan.

**Alénia:** A human woman living in the Shifara area. She is an expert with the long sword and seeks out any who are proficient to challenge them.

**Alex Stone:** Daruidai agent.

**Anazhari:** *Rorujhen* mare who agrees to become Mira's mount.

**Ancaera:** *Ashae* widow to Vaelir, whom she had married out of convenience to maintain control of her family estate of Shianri.

**Aputi:** King of the *Kajoran* people.

**Aradi:** Daughter to Duanna and mother to Nimué. The second *Baensiari*. Aradi brought the secret of witchcraft to Earth at the behest of her mother, who was also known as Diana.

**Arané-Li:** *Ulané Jhinura* Chamberlain in Su Lariano.

**Arduanna:** See Duanna.

**Arrosa:** *Wyl-Dunn* younger sister of Zoriaa and daughter to Tavarnin. Wife of Niall.

**Carmen Cansino:** This is a false identity used by Mira as a way of paying homage to Rita Hayworth, one of her favorite actresses.

**Chenosh:** *Qélosan* who is referred to by the *Bahréth* as The Envoy and granted status in their religion as an angel.

**Cirilia:** *Jhiné Boré* (Dryad) who lives on Earth in the heart of the small, wooded area near the Ramirez home.

**Corlen Veranu:** *Kajoran* that meets Nora on the island of Carabora.

**Deirdre Leland-Rinn:** Nora's biological mother.

**Dimétrian:** *Ashae* Master of the White Riders.

**Duanna:** Also known as the Great Mother of the *Uthadé* and is the namesake for Danu. She had many names, including Arduanna, Arduinna, Dunna, Dana, Danu, and Diana. She was the first *baensiari*. Mother to Aradi and many other gods of the *Uthadé*.

**Edrigun:** King of the *Wyl-Dunn* on Danu.

**Emma:** Shelby's younger sister from Earth.

**Farlen:** *Ulané Jhinura* who assisted in kidnapping Mira from Su Lariano not long after she first arrived.

**Farukan:** The *Rorujhen* formerly enslaved by the White Riders on Daoine. He serves Mira as mount and partner. Spouse of Akshira and father of Barashan.

**Felgor:** See Mouse.

**Gilglys:** *Ulané Jhinura* who assisted in kidnapping Mira from Su Lariano not long after she first arrived.

**Goibhniu:** Master *Uthadé* smith.

**Grace Ndané:** A witch and half-owner of Herbs, Antiques and Curiosities (HAC.) Mentor to her partner, Katya.

**Iratzé:** Queen of the *Wyl-Dunn* of Danu.

**Itara, Brother:** *Noélani* referred to as the *awa'ia* of the sun by the *Kajoran* people.

**Jack:** *Daijheen* who encounters Nora shortly after she first arrived on Danu and became her companion.

**Jakarael Abalaan:** See Jack.

**Jakeda:** *Urgaban* head chef at the Raven's Nest restaurant.

**Jill Ramirez:** Mira's foster-mother on Earth.

**Jimmy Doyle:** Homicide detective assigned to Katya's case.

**Jorge Cervantes:** Mira's biological Father.

**Karis Ulané Panalira:** Younger cousin of Neelu. Missing for many years. See Rispan.

**Kaiaru, Uncle:** *Noélani* referred to as the *awa'ia* of the sea by the *Kajoran* people.

**Kartahn Zeg:** *Bahréth* religious leader and necromancer. He has a more human appearance, but this is a glamour used to disguise his true nature.

**Katya Zahradi:** A witch and half-owner of Herbs, Antiques and Curiosities (HAC.) Apprentice to her partner, Grace.

**Kerbas:** *Wyl-Dunn* brother to Niall.

**Kirsat:** *Ulané Jhinura* friend to Mira from her military training in Su Lariano. Part of the original mission to Pokorah-Vo and who did not survive the journey.

**Kooras:** *Ulané Jhinura* friend to Mira from her military training in Su Lariano. Part of the original mission to Pokorah-Vo and who did not survive the journey.

**Korana, Sister:** *Noélani* referred to as the *awa'ia* of the moon by the *Kajoran* people.

**Laila:** *Impané* mage. Mother of Yormak.

**Laleya:** *Rorujhen* mare who agrees to become Grace's mount.

**Laruna:** *Ulané Jhinura* mage and magic instructor in Su Lariano. Became a fugitive when it became known she orchestrated Mira's kidnapping.

**Lélé Corana:** *Kajoran* ship captain.

**Luana Alaso:** *Kajoran* princess. Heir to the *Kajoran* throne.

**Luciana "Luci" Leon:** Social worker assigned to Mira and Nora for their foster care. She is also Mira's aunt, and formerly with the Daruidai.

**Lugh:** *Uthadé* who was half *Fu-Mo Ri* and a king at one time. Son of Duanna.

**Martin Laurent:** Nora's biological father.

**Mehrzad:** *Rorujhen* stallion who agrees to become Luci's mount.

**Merlain:** Also known as Merlin. A biological ancestor of Nora's.

# CHARACTERS

**Mira:** Mirabela Cervantes Ramirez. Nora's foster-sister.

**Mohanga, Papa:** *Noélani* referred to as the Sky Father, primary god of the *Kajoran* people.

**Mooren:** *Ulané Jhinura* assigned to accompany Mira and advise and protect her on her missions to Pokorah-Vo and Shifara. Holds the rank of Lance with the Su Lariano Palace Guard, which is equivalent to corporal.

**Mouse:** Also known as Felgor. Close *Ulané Jhinura* friend to Mira and Rispan since her early days in Su Lariano. Becomes manager for the Raven's Nest Restaurant.

**Neelu:** Neelu Ulané Pulakasado. *Ulané Jhinura* daughter to Queen Astrina. Mira's first friend in Daoine.

**Niall:** *Wyl-Dunn* groom to Arrosa.

**Nimué:** Daughter of Aradi and Oisin Rinn. A biological ancestor of Nora's. The third *baensiari*.

**Nora:** Leanora Leland. Mira's foster-sister on Earth.

**Ree:** Reelu Ulané Pulakaloso. Older sister to Neelu. Rispan's mother.

**Réni:** *Ulané Jhinura* Assistant Minister of Trade in Su Lariano. Assigned to accompany Mira on her first mission to Pokorah-Vo.

**Rispan:** Close friend to Mira and Mouse since her early days in Su Lariano. Is assigned to join her first mission to Pokorah-Vo.

**Rizina:** *Ulané Jhinura* bodyguard assigned to protect Mira when holding the rank of Bar, equivalent to private, with the Su Lariano Palace Guard.

**Sarpong Udu:** Homicide detective assigned to Katya's case. He is suspicious of Grace and does not like witches.

**Shahz Dega:** *Félbahlag* first mate to Lélé Corana.

**Shan:** God of the *Félbahlag*.

**Shelby:** Went to high school with Mira and Nora. Older sister to Emma. Learns how to use magic after seeing Nora do magic accidentally.

**Shéna:** Korashéna Ulané Sharavi. Last surviving member of the royal family of the *Ulané Jhinura* city of Su Astonil. Enslaved in Pokorah-Vo all her life until she was freed by Rispan.

**Shigara:** *Ulané Jhinura* Chief Healer for Queen Astrina in Su Lariano.

**Sophia "Sofi" Leon Cervantes:** Mira's biological mother.

**Tavarnin:** *Wyl-Dunn* father to Zoriaa and Arrosa.

**Tesia:** *Ulané Jhinura* master mage in Su Lariano. Friend to Neelu and daughter of Felora and Gylan. Trains Mira in magic and accompanies her on her mission to Shifara.

**Tony Ramirez:** Mira's foster-father on Earth.

**Unais Elizondo III:** King of the *Félbahlag* in Félbahrin.

**Zolat:** *Bahréth* who challenges Jack in Tyr Nya Lu.

**Zoriaa:** *Wyl-Dunn* priestess or keeper of the old ways. Eldest daughter of Tavarnin and sister to Arrosa.

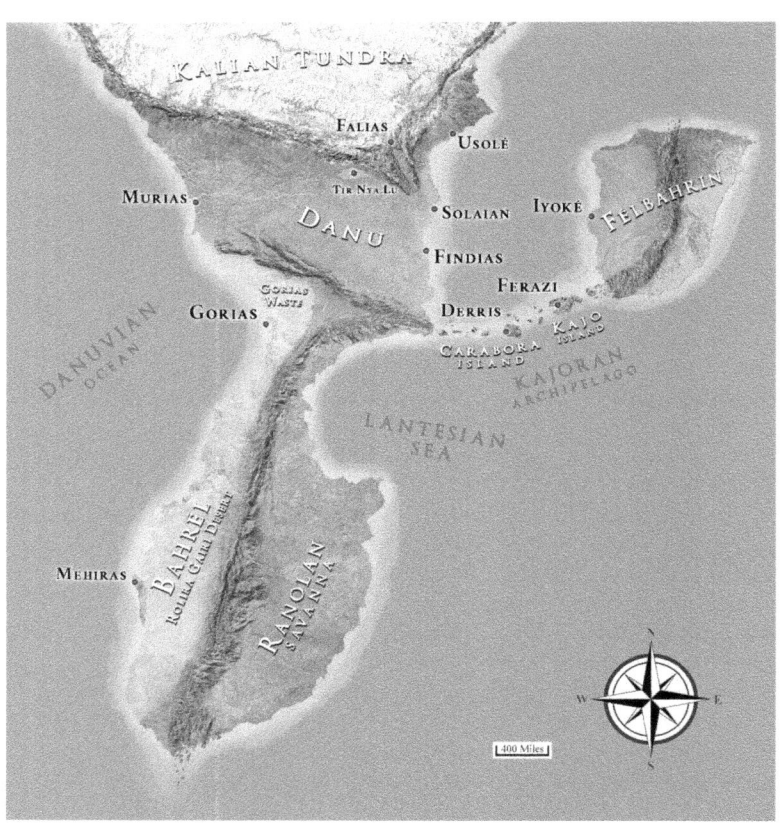

KALIAN TUNDRA

FALIAS

USOLÉ

MURIAS

TIR NYA LU

SOLAIAN

IYOKÉ

FELBAHRIN

DANU

FINDIAS

FERAZI

GORIAS WASTE

GORIAS

DERRIS

KAJO ISLAND

CARABORA ISLAND

DANUVIAN OCEAN

KAJORAN ARCHIPELAGO

LANTESIAN SEA

BAHREL

KOULKA GABRI DESERT

MÉHIRAS

RANOIAN SAVANNA

400 Miles

N
W        E
S

# CHAPTER ONE

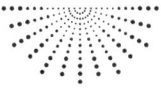

## NORA

"Hey! Here comes the Wicked Witch!" I heard Darek's sing-song voice clearly over the chit-chat in the lunchroom. "Nice wart!"

I felt the heat in my face as laughter erupted from other students around the room.

"Just ignore them!" Mira said from beside me. "They're jealous because they're stupid and you're not."

My embarrassment transformed to rage as I stormed to the lunch counter. Mira hurried to stay with me. Once again, just her presence had something of a calming effect on me. Mira was my foster sister. She was younger by two years. I'd only known her for about a year, but she was the only bright spot in my otherwise detestable life.

That wasn't fair. My foster parents do try. Jill and Tony were the best I'd had in a long line of disappointment. I'd been able to get closer to them than any of the other foster parents I'd had.

I couldn't tell them about the nightmares, though. I had them almost every night. I stopped trying to explain them a long time ago. As far as anyone knew, I hadn't had them for years. I hadn't even told Mira about them. But they were noted in a file somewhere. Not that they were all bad, but they weren't normal dreams.

The brain-drainers — excuse me, psychiatrists — I'd been sent to had just wanted to put me on drugs. They said it would stop me from having the dreams. Mostly it just made it harder to remember them and it didn't solve anything. Why was I having them? What was the cause? They couldn't answer that.

The last one had said something about a chemical imbalance, but by then I was old enough to wonder and ask questions like how they could tell there was an imbalance or what a normal balance would be. Their answers didn't sound very scientific and certainly hadn't been based on actual lab tests. So much for the experts. The pills just made me too foggy or too jittery to think or focus; my grades had dropped. I'd stopped taking those years ago, too. Since they thought the dreams had stopped, no one had given me a hard time about it.

There'd still been problems with my different foster families, though. I'd never really connected with them and always ended up moving on. Until Mira. She'd made a difference.

School? I hated school. I hated the other students for their cruelty. And I hated, once again, the large mole on the tip of my nose.

One more week and I would graduate. I only wished I had a real plan for what I would do then. Probably City College. I could take my classes online and not have to deal with students in-person. I could be anonymous.

Food selections made, we took our trays and looked for an empty table. I scowled when I saw that the only options were near the center of the room. I would have much preferred a dark corner somewhere. But I wouldn't give Darek and his cronies the satisfaction of slinking. Shoulders back and head high, I strode boldly to the center table and sat down with Mira following closely behind.

"Hi, guys! What's up?" A plain looking brunette sat down at our table.

"Hi, Shelby," Mira answered her. "One more week of school, then we're free for the summer!"

I glanced around; wherever Shelby was, her younger sister Emma usually wasn't far behind, but I didn't see her.

I pointedly looked around. "Where's your sister?"

"How should I know?" Shelby scowled at me.

Shelby's sister Emma was the smart one; they'd even bumped her up, so she was finishing her freshman year of high school at the age of thirteen. She didn't have many friends at the high school, so she was usually following her sister or Mira around. She even came over to the house sometimes to hang out with Mira. Or called her. Or texted. I felt kind of sorry for the kid, but for some reason I could never figure out, her older sister Shelby had always annoyed me. I wasn't feeling talkative, so I dug into the unremarkable lunch in front of me.

I had barely taken a few bites before something hit the side of my head. A paper airplane fell to the ground next to me. Muffled laughter identified the table of origin. Darek and his cohorts. I tried to hide my annoyance and continued eating, keeping the offenders in my peripheral vision. Even then, if not for Shelby's expression I would have missed the next launch that twisted in flight and flew straight toward Mira's face.

I raised my hand in defense and Darek's expression shifted from malicious glee to surprise as the airplane careened madly upwards and soared back toward him with a vengeance. He looked back at me, missing his chance to block the plane before it struck his right eye. Darek howled in pain and went to his knees, his hands covering his eye.

*What just happened?*

I watched as Darek's friends helped him from the room, heading toward the school nurse's office.

"That was weird," Mira commented.

"What happened?" Shelby asked.

"Serves him right." I shrugged. The airplane seemed to have a mind of its own, but they were hard to predict, anyway.

After we finished lunch, Mira and I headed down the hall and walked into the girl's room. I heard talking and giggles, but as soon as we stepped into the room, the half-dozen girls went silent, looking at me, and literally holding their breath. Mira went into one of the stalls and then the girls burst into laughter and fled, leaving me alone. I fumed silently. *I hate them!*

My reflection glared back at me from the mirror. I looked at it, seeing what everyone else saw. The red frizzy hair, the long-pointed nose with the huge mole. For a moment all of my anger focused on that mole. *I hate you! Just go away!* I spun away from the mirror and charged out of the room.

"Hey! Wait for me!" Mira caught up with me. Then she gave me an odd look. "Something's different."

I just shrugged, too annoyed to care what she was talking about. A few minutes later, we split up to go to our classes.

When I'd first met Mira, I wasn't sure what to make of her. I was sure she was fake and that eventually, she'd show her true colors and be just as selfish and spiteful as everyone else in my life had been. Or she'd just be stupid and let everyone treat her as a doormat and walk all over her. But I'd been wrong.

If Mira was anything, she was sincere. And compassionate. And definitely not stupid. Mira gave everyone the benefit of the doubt, which is more than I could say for myself. She would also allow for mistakes and give people second chances. I could understand that, but it wasn't something I could do. No, Mira was just a really good person. I couldn't even be envious of her or of how much people liked her. She deserved the admiration. I was lucky to have her in my life. She made me want to be a better person, but I could only really do that with her. The rest of the world could pretty much take a hike.

The rest of the school day was as bland and tasteless as my lunch had been. AP History and AP English. I'd taken both finals the day before. The grades weren't out yet, but I was pretty confident I'd done well. With the finals already done, there wasn't much left to do in class. My last class, and last exam, was geometry. That was another story. I'd never been as comfortable with numbers as I was with words, and then adding dimensions into it just made things worse. I struggled through the equations for the exam and just finished before the buzzer rang, sounding the end of the test and the end of the period.

"Leanora?" I heard Mrs. Riordan, the vice-principal, call to me as I stepped into the hallway. "Can I speak with you in my office for a moment please?"

I shifted my bookbag on my shoulder and moved to follow. "I go by Nora. Not Leanora."

"And not Lea?" Mrs. Riordan asked, trying to be friendly.

I barely managed to suppress the urge to roll my eyes. "No. Not Leanora. Not Lea. Not An. Just Nora."

"You look different." Mrs. Riordan observed me critically once we were in her office. "Did you change your hair?"

I looked at Mrs. Riordan to see if she was mocking me, but her expression seemed sincere. I shook my head, no.

"Alright. Can you tell me what happened in the lunchroom today?"

"What do you mean?"

"Darek said you threw a paper airplane and hit him in the eye."

"What?" I couldn't believe that jerk! "He was the one throwing paper airplanes!"

"How did he get hit in the eye?"

"I don't know… It just flew up and back at him like a boomerang. I never even touched it!"

"You didn't have anything to do with that?"

"How could I? Don't you have video? I thought the cameras they put up were supposed to help prevent bullying and stuff. What did the cameras show?"

"The cameras showed Darek throw two paper airplanes, but we lost the feed that would have shown him being hit."

"That's not my fault," I told her. "And it's not my fault if he doesn't know how to throw paper airplanes."

Mrs. Riordan tapped her index finger on her desk as she looked at me.

"We could see he threw two planes at you, if you got angry and threw one back—"

"I didn't throw anything!"

"But you're not concerned about his injury." It was not a question.

"Should I be?"

"That airplane cut the cornea of his eye. He'll be lucky if it doesn't permanently impair his vision."

"Maybe he'll be more careful next time." I was still mad he was trying to blame me for his stupid mistake.

"Maybe so." She paused. "When do you turn eighteen?"

"Last week." I was tired of the small-talk and the accusations. She should just let me leave.

"Oh? Happy birthday." She paused again. "Nora, I don't know what happened in there today and I'm going to drop it. You're not legally a minor anymore. But Darek *is* legally a minor for another two months. If you, as an adult, injured a minor, there could be severe consequences. Now that you're eighteen, you *are* legally an adult, and you have to behave with that level of responsibility. Now, I've kept you long enough. Enjoy the rest of your day."

The sudden dismissal surprised me. I collected my bag and headed for the door. Then I turned back, one hand on the door-knob. "I've finished all my finals."

"How did you do?"

"Probably all A's or close to it."

"Well done."

"What happens if I skip the last week?"

"Well, you'll still graduate. And since you're eighteen…" Mrs. Riordan shrugged. "There's not much we can do. I suppose that's up to you."

The few minutes in the VP's office had been long enough for me to miss the mass exodus of students leaving for the day. A few stragglers chitchatted here and there around their lockers or on the way to the parking lot. Posters were still up from the drama class's performance last week of *The Taming of the Shrew*. I'd thought about trying out for it. I'd even approached the door to the auditions when someone called out, "Hey! Here comes a shrew!" I just ignored the comment and walked past like I'd never intended to enter.

*One more week and then I'm done.*

I made my way to my antiquated Vespa to meet Mira and go home.

"Nora—"

"Let's just go." I got on, and Mira climbed on behind me.

The Vespa sputtered to life, and we took off. The three-mile ride was uneventful and the wind in my face from the ride calmed my nerves. When we reached the house, Mira held open the gate while I pushed the scooter through the side yard and into the garage through the side door.

"Nora?"

"What?"

"What happened to your mole?"

"What are you talking about?"

"It's not there."

"You're not funny." I didn't expect Mira to be mean. Had I been wrong about her?

"No… Look in the mirror." Mira pointed at the side mirror on the Vespa.

Annoyed, I bent over to examine my reflection. *What the—* my hand went to my nose. There was no mole! Just perfectly smooth skin! My reflection gaped back at me.

"It's gone!" I was ecstatic. I had hated that thing for so long!

"Yes." Mira nodded. "But how?"

"You don't have to always overanalyze things, little sis. Just be glad for me that it's gone."

"I am not overanalyzing. I'm just being practical. If something mysteriously changed on my face, I'd want to know why!"

7

"Yeah, yeah." I didn't care how; I was just glad it was gone. "Um. It fell off?" I frowned in thought, then shrugged. "Well, it was there after lunch. Hey! Mrs. Riordan said I looked different! It must have been before that."

"Wait a minute, I noticed something different earlier, too. When we came out of the restroom."

"You did?" I thought back. "I remember looking at it in the mirror. I was so mad about it. And at Darek."

"Strange how there is just no trace of the mole now. It's like it was never there."

"I just wanted it to go away."

"Girls," Jill's voice came from inside the house. "Is that you out there?"

"Coming, Jill," I called back. Then I turned to Mira. "What are we going to tell Jill and Tony?"

"You mean mom and dad?"

I couldn't help rolling my eyes in response. I wasn't ready for that. We went into the house from the garage and were stopped dead in our tracks by the rich and intoxicating odors permeating the house from the kitchen.

"Something smells good," I said.

"See, you *do* have keen powers of observation."

I gave her a mock scowl and continued into the kitchen. "What are you making?"

"Just a pot roast," Jill answered.

"Smells yummy!" Mira grinned. "I can't wait to taste it!"

"Yeah, what's the special occasion?" I asked. "The last time you made that was my first dinner here."

Jill put her hands on her hips and tried for a severe expression. "What? Can't a woman make a pot roast without a special occasion?"

"Maybe a normal woman," Mira teased. "But you, Mom? It's suspicious."

"Oh, hush!" Jill told her. "I just thought it sounded good. Now go do your homework."

"Mom," Mira reminded her, "there's only one week left of school. We don't have any homework."

"Oh, really? Well, if you hang out in the kitchen, I'll find some work for you to do!"

"No, no," I said as we hurried out, "we wouldn't want to get in your way."

I could hear Jill's chuckles as we went down the hall into Mira's room. Mira plopped down onto her bed, and I sat on a chair by the desk. A small chest sat nearby. Jill had given it to Mira two days before. It had belonged to Mira's biological mother and had some of her things in it, including the pendant Mira now wore and a couple of daggers that we discovered had been in a hidden compartment under the bottom. We'd tried taking the daggers to an antique shop to see if they could find out anything about them, but no luck.

"So." Mira grinned. "Wanna watch a movie?"

As always, I was infected by Mira's energy and good cheer. Over the past year that I'd been with the Ramirez family, my love of old movies had rubbed off on my new foster sister and Mira had embraced it with enthusiasm.

"Okay. What do you want to watch?"

"We haven't watched Gilda in a while?"

"Sure." I shrugged. "Who can get tired of Rita Hayworth? Right?"

"Exactly!"

We spent the next two hours rewatching the 1946, film noir movie without much side conversation. I turned it off once the final credits started.

"I'm glad they finally stopped being stupid with each other," Mira commented.

"Well, they have to do something stupid so they'll have a story," I said with a smirk.

Mira rolled her eyes. "Rita was so awesome. She could sing and dance and act. Of course, most of them did in those days.

But she was so glamorous, too. I can't believe she started as a flamenco dancer as a kid."

I nodded. "Glen Ford was pretty good, too. Maybe we can watch the original Big Heat this weekend."

"Girls!" we heard Jill call from down the hall, "time for dinner!"

We looked at each other and simultaneously said, "Pot roast!" We jumped up and headed down the hall.

Tony was helping Jill set the last of the food on the table and everyone went to their places. It was a cozy table, set for four. We didn't waste time helping ourselves and digging in. The carrots and potatoes were cooked perfectly, not too soft, not too hard. The beef was so tender it was falling apart.

"This is dreamy," I said.

Mira laughed. "It's dinner, not your date!"

"Beef is beef." I shrugged with a smile.

"Girls, please!" Tony rolled his eyes.

"Well, thank you." Jill beamed. "I'm glad you like it!"

"Seriously though." I looked at her. "What's the occasion?"

"Well," Jill began, "there is something to celebrate." She shared a look with Tony. "The legal stuff is finally over." She looked at Mira. "After six years of fighting, we can finally go through with the adoption. We've already signed the papers."

Mira gaped. "Really?" She jumped up, ran around the table, and was swallowed in a three-way hug with Jill and Tony.

I watched them with mixed feelings. I was happy for Mira, but I also felt a bit melancholy. I doubted I would ever have the home and family that Mira had found with Jill and Tony. Even if I did, would I trust it? Would I even deserve it? Not that Jill and Tony hadn't treated me well, totally the opposite. But Mira had been with them since she was ten. And Mira was, well... Mira. Everybody loved Mira. Including me.

As Mira made her way back to her chair, she looked at me and paused before she sat back down. "I'm sure they'd adopt you, too. If you want."

That was so Mira. She cared so much about others. About me. Before Jill or Tony could say anything, I put my hand on Mira's. "Sweetie, tonight isn't about me. It's about you. I'm really happy for you. You deserve a good life and all the wonderful things the world can give you. Congratulations."

"Thank you! You're the best sister, ever!" Mira gave me a hug before turning back to her dinner.

She spoke between bites. "Does this mean I'll have to change my last name?"

"That's up to you, Mirella," Tony answered, using his favorite nickname for her. "And if you want, you can even go Spanish style and just add Ramirez to the end."

"Mirabela Cervantes Ramirez," she mused. "I like it!"

After dinner, Mira and I helped to clear the table.

"Nora, can you help with the dishes while Mira takes her shower?" Jill asked.

"Sure." Not that I wasn't going to help anyway. I didn't want to be seen as a freeloader. Now that I was eighteen, they didn't have to keep me anymore.

"There was something I wanted to talk to you about," Jill said once Mira was out of hearing.

*Here it comes.*

"You're legally an adult now, so maybe—"

"You want me to move on." I didn't want to hear the excuses. "Fine. I'll be out tomorrow."

"No! That's not what I was going to say."

"I know. You were going to try to be nice about it."

"No! Would you listen to me please? I wanted to talk to you about adoption. About YOUR adoption."

"Oh, I get it." I turned to face Jill fully. "Mira's little comment made you feel guilty!" My breath was coming in panting double-beats of in and out between my clenched teeth.

"Stop it!" Jill took a deep breath. "We were planning to talk to you about this and we didn't know if it was something that you would want after turning eighteen. And you don't have to answer right now, you can take some time to think about it."

Before I knew what was happening, Jill wrapped her arms around me and held me tightly. "I know you've had it hard. You've been through a lot and gone through a lot of pain. And when you're scared or hurt you lash out, like you're doing now. Yes, Mira loves you. But that's not why we wanted to offer this to you. Not because of her, but because of you and who you are. Like what you said to her tonight at dinner. It shows who you are. We've seen that and we love you, too. We *want* to be your parents. Your family."

"No, I can't…" I was barely holding it together and tears were streaming down my face. I wanted to return the hug, but I just couldn't. "I don't know." I pulled myself from Jill's arms. "*I don't know!*"

"You deserve a good life, too."

Out. I had to get out. I ran for the front door past Tony's surprised face, and it slammed open in front of me. I ran through the door not knowing or caring how it opened or whether it closed. I ran for the nearby woods. It was my safe place.

I needed space. I needed air. I was panting and gasping; was I starting to hyperventilate? Why couldn't I get enough air?

I finally collapsed, sobbing, at the base of my favorite tree in the heart of the woods. *Had it been real? Did they really want me? And now I've ruined it! Just like I'd ruined it before with every foster family I'd ever had.*

# CHAPTER TWO

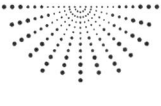

## NORA

"*N*ora?"

Mira's voice woke me into deepening twilight. I must have dozed off. Vestiges of a familiar dream clung to my mind as I sat up and looked around.

"There you are." Mira walked toward me. "You've been gone for a couple of hours. Jill was worried."

"I fell asleep." My mind felt clouded. I shouldn't be this tired and groggy. This wasn't just from the dreams.

"What happened?" Mira asked me.

"I… needed some air,"

"Okay," Mira answered, not understanding, but accepting what I had said. "It's getting cold. Are you ready to go back?"

"Yeah, give me a minute. Is Jill mad?"

"I don't think so, but you broke the front door. Tony went to the hardware store to get stuff to fix it. He was working on it when I left."

"The door?" I vaguely remembered going through it.

"It was practically ripped from the hinges. How did you do that?"

"No, I —" Things weren't making sense. "I didn't touch it. It just opened. I thought maybe Tony had left it open. I just needed to get some space, you know?"

Mira was shaking her head. "I heard you shout something in the kitchen, and then I heard the front door slam open. Tony says he was in the front room when you ran by."

"I don't know." I let out a heavy breath. "Let's go back. Time to face the music." I stood and brushed the dirt off my clothes.

"What —" Mira looked at me strangely. "What's that light coming from your hands?"

"What are you talking about?"

"Your hands. When you were brushing the dirt off. They were glowing or something."

I looked at my hands. They just looked normal.

"No glowing."

"No," Mira answered. "It was just for a moment."

I shrugged and started walking, but Mira stopped me.

"This wasn't the first time."

"What do you mean?" I asked her.

"Well, I didn't say anything because I wasn't sure. Remember when that paper airplane flew back and hit Darek? I saw some kind of weird light coming from your hand. And then in the restroom at school. I was in the stall and there was some kind of bright flash from the front and right after that we noticed that your mole was gone."

"That's crazy!"

"That's not all." Mira hesitated. "I also felt something at the same time, like, on my skin? I don't know how to describe it. But when I heard the front door slam open, I felt it again."

"You think I did something?" I asked her. "And it made my hands glow and gave you the creeps?"

"It didn't give me the creeps," Mira told me. "It's not a bad feeling or a good feeling, it's just sort of a sense of something."

"Whatever. How come I haven't noticed my hands glowing?"

"I don't know." Mira thought for a moment. "Try to do something."

"What do you mean?" I scoffed. "Is this some kind of Luke Skywalker shit? You think I used the force to get rid of my mole?"

"I don't know. Maybe. Something like that."

"Is this some kind of practical joke? It's not funny."

Mira shook her head. "No, I promise."

I held my hands up again and looked at them. "Nothing."

"So," Mira ignored me. "With Darek, it was probably just a reaction. But what about in the restroom?"

This all sounded like nonsense, but I didn't want to argue with her. Could there seriously be something to what she was saying?

"I was just really angry about Darek." I thought back. "And wishing I didn't have the mole on my nose."

"Somehow, your wish came true. But there has to be a way to do something without making you mad first."

"Maybe because I was just very focused on it?"

"Okay, what can you focus on here?"

I looked around and saw a sprout of some kind of plant where it had grown up through the loam of the forest floor. It had two leaves and wasn't more than about three inches tall.

"Do you think I could make that grow?" I asked her, trying not to sound skeptical.

Mira shrugged. "Try it."

I crouched in front of the seedling. I focused my attention on making it grow, holding my hands to either side of it.

"Nothing's happening," I said.

"Focus harder," Mira told me from where she stood on the other side of the little plant. "Make it grow."

I redoubled my efforts, pouring all of my intention and will into the little plant.

"Something's happening!" Mira exclaimed. "Your hands are glowing!"

I looked up at her.

"Don't stop!"

I tried focusing harder, but I still didn't see any glow and I couldn't see any change in the plant. Finally, I stopped.

"It's not working." I frowned. I wasn't disappointed, not really. After all, I couldn't just expect to suddenly be magical.

"Maybe that's not so easy to do," Mira suggested. "But your hands were definitely glowing."

"I didn't see my hands glowing," I recalled. "But I did see something else glow for a second."

"What?"

"Your pendant."

Mira looked down at her pendant in surprise.

"You know," I said, "none of this crazy stuff started to happen until after you opened that box."

"Let's try something," Mira said, taking off the necklace. "You put this on and try again. Let's see what happens."

I hung the pendant from my neck and crouched down to focus on the plant again. After a moment of heavy focus, a faint glow started to form around my hands, and I felt a sort of tingling on my skin. "Whoa!" I stood up. "I saw it!"

"I didn't see anything on your hands, but I did notice something with the pendant."

"Here." I lifted the delicate chain from my shoulders. "Take this back. That was freaky."

"Let's try something easier," Mira suggested.

"Later. I'm tired and I'm hungry again. Let's go back and see how much trouble I'm in."

"I'm sure it'll be alright," Mira said as we started walking back. "What do you think we should try next? Maybe something with you would be easier, like the mole."

"Maybe I could make my boobs bigger!" I joked.

Mira laughed at that. "You think that will be easy?"

"Probably not."

I thought about it as we walked, trying not to be too hopeful; if you don't expect too much, you won't be disappointed. "Maybe my hair?" I mused. "Maybe I could straighten my hair and I won't have to always look like I have a bird's nest for a hat."

When we got back to the house, Tony had a new door hung and was painting the frame.

"Hey, girls," he said. "We were about to send out a search party. It's getting late."

"We're back." Mira smiled. "No rescue needed!"

"Bummer." He made a face. "I was hoping for an adventure. Careful of the wet paint."

"I'm sorry about the door, Tony," I said. "I didn't mean to do that."

"Don't sweat it, Norie. Stuff happens."

"Hey! Just because I screwed up doesn't mean I'm going to let you call me Norie!"

He laughed. "That reminds me of something I say to Jill."

"What's that?"

"Yes, dear."

I rolled my eyes and went inside with Mira, carefully stepping over the paint spills on the canvas drop-cloth. We headed for the kitchen to see about some leftover pot-roast. We had just dished some up when Jill came in.

"Busted!"

Mira laughed. "You know I can never get enough of this stuff!"

"Yeah, I wasn't really worried about it going to waste."

"Jill." I couldn't meet her eyes. "I'm sorry I ran off like that. I just felt so… claustrophobic or something."

"Honey, it's alright. You just think about what I said and whatever you decide is okay. It's an open offer."

"Really?" I looked up. "Even after…"

"It would take a lot more than that to change anything, believe me." Jill smiled at me.

"Enough already," Mira piped in. "Let's eat!"

We were halfway into our food before Mira spoke again.

"Do you really want to try straightening your hair?"

"Maybe." I paused between bites, thinking about it. "This is pretty strange. Doesn't it scare you?"

"Not so far." Mira grinned. "Why? Are you thinking of trying something scary?"

"No. But what is this?" I lowered my voice. "Do you think I'm…"

"What?"

"Darek was just calling me a witch. Do you think maybe he was right?"

"Darek was just being a jerk, like always." There was no room for argument in Mira's tone. "If he was right about something, it would be a first."

"I bet that woman at the shop knows a lot more than she said."

"The one that freaked out about the knives?" The lady at one of the places we had taken the knives we found in the box of her mother's things had reacted strangely. "What was her name, Katya something?"

I nodded, my mouth full again.

"Maybe afterwards we can watch another movie? Maybe… *You Were Never Lovelier*?"

I had to laugh. "Another Rita Hayworth?"

"Yup, but this time with Fred Astaire."

We washed our dishes after we were done. With an exchanged look of determination, we went down the hall to the bathroom and closed the door behind us. I'd make a real effort. If it came to nothing, fine. We could forget about it and move on.

"You think you can do this without making your hair fall out?"

"That's not funny." I scowled at her.

"Sorry." Mira chuckled. Clearly, she was not.

I concentrated on my reflection, looking at the wild, kinky hair that fell to my shoulders from a part down the middle. It was so annoying. Remembering what I had done in the woods, I put the same kind of intention into my hair. I focused at the top, at the part, imagining the hair straightening.

"Something's happening," Mira told me. "I see a glow."

I kept my concentration on the hair at the part and slowly brought it down. The hair started to straighten! The effort I poured into my intention had me gasping for breath, but I didn't stop. The straightening continued to flow down from the part until it reached the tips. Finally, I relaxed, slightly out of breath.

"You did it!" Mira hugged me. "That was amazing!"

I examined my reflection in the mirror. My red hair now hung well below my shoulders; smooth and silky and straight!

"I want to try something else," I said with a smile. I was still trying not to be too hopeful, but my success so far was getting the better of me. It was hard not to be excited.

"What?"

"Just watch." I looked at my reflection. "I hope this works."

I focused my attention on my red locks. After several seconds, the hair began to slowly darken to the point it was raven black. I intensified my focus and highlights of blue, green, purple, and red began to flow down the length. When it stopped, I felt almost giddy with excitement.

Before I could say anything, a shimmering in the air appeared and began to expand near the tub in the small bathroom.

"What's—"

The shimmering formed a large oval. Vague shapes could be seen within it.

"Ah," it was a man's voice. "There you are."

He stepped out of the shimmering air, and it disappeared behind him. He was wearing an odd, red and gold robe and a cloth covered the lower part of his face. His eyes were not kindly. I grabbed Mira and we ran from the bathroom to Mira's room, closing the door behind us. I turned the lock, but I didn't know if that would help.

"Running?" We heard his voice. "No more of that."

In a panic, I looked around for something we could use to defend ourselves with. My eyes fell on the two daggers on top of Mira's dresser. I grabbed them and gave one to Mira as we turned to face the door. The man tried the knob and chuckled when it wouldn't turn.

"How droll." He kicked the door. When it didn't give, he kicked it again much harder.

"What's going on?" We heard Tony's voice coming down the hall.

Another kick and the door burst open.

The man stepped into the room with a grin. He looked back and forth between us and his gaze settled on Mira.

"Yes, you're the one."

He stepped forward and grabbed Mira with his left hand. Forgetting her knife, Mira struggled to pull away. The man started moving his right hand in a circular pattern and a shimmering appeared in the air. He started toward the shimmering, dragging Mira with him.

"No!" I shouted. I pulled the knife from the scabbard and leapt toward him, stabbing with the blade. The blade struck the gem of a pendant hanging from his neck and slid off to inflict a cut across his chest before it slipped from my hand. The gem splintered and the splintering mirrored in whatever was hovering in the air. He lost his grip on Mira as my weight against him knocked us all into the shimmering air.

We fell to the ground, and he pushed me away. We both got to our feet. I'd lost the knife and I looked around, quickly picking up a nearby stick about two feet long and holding it with both hands.

"You bitch!" he screamed. "What have you done?" He looked at the forest that now surrounded us, his hand going to the gash on his chest that was bleeding profusely down his robes. He moved his right hand in a circular gesture and when nothing happened, looked at his pendant and saw the cracks. Shock registered on his face.

He took an angry step toward me, but stopped when he saw that I stood ready with the stick. Then he looked at the woods around us and cocked an ear as if listening for something.

"Another time," he said and quickly strode off into the woods.

I took a good look around for the first time since getting back to my feet. It finally registered that I wasn't in Mira's room anymore. The trees didn't look quite like anything I had seen before. The sky wasn't dark like it should be, more like dawn. Or maybe dusk. Nearby, I could see walls of heavy stone.

"Mira?" I called. Only silence answered. Then a rustle of leaves.

"Nora? Is that you? What happened?"

A face showed between the leaves of a nearby tree. But it wasn't Mira.

"Emma?" That didn't make any sense. "Where did you come from?"

"I came by to talk to Mira about something," she said. "I didn't want to bother anyone, so I went around back to her window."

"You do that a lot?"

She shrugged, her eyes not meeting mine. "Sometimes." She looked back up at me. "But I heard some kind of a fight and looked in the window. I saw you attack some man who broke into Mira's room. The window was open, so I tried to come in and help, then… Where are we?"

That was a very good question.

Suddenly, there was a flurry of movement all around us and at least a dozen people erupted from the surrounding trees. They weren't like any people I'd ever seen before. They looked normal in most ways, but— pointed ears? The ears weren't the problem though. The problem was they were glaring at us over the points of the spears they held with obvious competence; the problem was that those points were all aimed at us.

# CHAPTER THREE

## NORA

*I* should have started scratching lines on the wall or something to keep track of the days. But I couldn't really tell how much time had passed since we'd been dragged from the forest and locked up in this cell. There were no windows, except the one on the door of this twelve-by-twelve room, and that one was usually closed. Emma had been full of unanswerable questions at first, but eventually I snapped at her and she'd withdrawn into a sullen silence.

I was pretty sure they'd been feeding us three times a day, and I think I'd had nine meals. Light seemed to come from glowing stones in the ceiling, and three times it had gone dark for an extended period of time. Three days was a likely guess.

They'd done something when we first got here, and I could see that my hair had changed back to normal. It was my normal red color again and curly. I had been worried my mole was back, but I'd felt for it with my hand, and it was still gone. A mirror would have been nice.

There'd been nothing to do besides thinking and sleeping, and we'd been doing a lot of both. I wasn't very good company for Emma, but I wasn't her babysitter. I had other things to think about. I'd been going over everything that had happened since

Mira opened that chest. One thing had become clear; the world was not what I'd thought it was. Magic was real. The sooner I wrapped my head around that, the better I'd be able to deal with it.

We should probably start exercising if we were going to be stuck here for very long. I didn't have any dreams the first night, but the last two nights had been really strange. Even stranger than my dreams normally were.

I didn't know where we were or why we were locked up, and nobody was telling us anything. They talked plenty, but we couldn't understand whatever language they were speaking. And they didn't understand English. Each day, someone new would show up and try to talk to us. I'd given up trying.

I needed to get out of here and find Mira.

"I do not understand the association with this Mira," a low voice sounded from the corner of the cell.

I nearly jumped out of my skin as I spun to face the corner. Emma's head jerked around to stare. There was a man standing there! Where did he come from?

"She is your sister but not your sister," he went on. "How can this be? It is not logical."

"Where did you come from?" I demanded. Then I realized. "You speak English!"

"I am come from *Sheobal*," he replied. "But I have not been there in some time. Of what use is this information to you?"

"What?"

"I said, I come from *Sheobal*—"

"How did you get in here?"

He cocked his head to the side and studied me. "That is your third question, yet you have not answered mine. This is not equitable." He turned and walked *through* the wall without another word.

What just happened? How did he do that?

*Magic is real*, I reminded myself. *Roll with it*. Maybe this guy could help me get out of here.

"Wait!" I called out. "I'm sorry! If you come back, I'll answer your questions."

After a moment, he stepped back through the wall. I took a moment to get a better look at him. He was at least six inches taller than me, maybe more. His hair was jet black, as were his eyes. He had a square face with a strong jaw. His shoulders were broad, and it looked like he had some solid beef under the loose robe he wore, though not too bulky. Emma looked back and forth between us, her eyes wide.

"You will answer my question?" he asked.

"Yes." I nodded. "I'm sorry, you startled me. You can't just show up like that."

"You are saying I cannot do what I did. This is not a rational premise. Will you answer my question now?"

"Um, yes. Could you repeat the question please?"

"Please explain this sister who is not a sister."

"How did—" I stopped myself before asking another question. I didn't want him to leave again. Not without taking me— us— out of here. "Mira and I are not regular sisters. We don't have the same biological parents. But both our parents died, and we were… assigned to someone else."

"Someone not your parent is functioning as your parent?"

"Parents, yes. Jill and Tony. They function as parents for both of us. So, Mira and I are sisters but we're not sisters."

"This is logical."

Why was he asking about Mira? Was she here someplace, too?

"And this is not your sister?" He indicated Emma.

"No."

Something seemed off with this guy, but if he could walk through walls, maybe he could help us.

"Do you know Mira?" I asked him.

"How could I know Mira? She is not here."

"Then how did you know about her?"

"Your thoughts. You broadcast them loudly. Why do you do this?"

"You read my mind?" I bit back what I was about to say and tried not to show my anger, but if he was inside my head he would know. What else was possible with magic? "What's in my mind is private. Don't do that."

"How else am I to learn of other beings?" He seemed confused.

"The same way the rest of us do. Talk to them."

"That is highly inefficient." He shook his head.

"And it's highly rude to read someone's mind without their permission," I snapped. I took a breath to calm myself before continuing. "It's an invasion of their privacy."

He just looked at me without saying anything.

"Promise me you won't do that again without permission."

He blinked slowly. "I will not attempt to enter your mind without permission. However, if you broadcast your thoughts, I cannot be blamed for hearing them."

*Broadcast my thoughts? How was I doing that?*

"Good enough." I frowned at him, thinking over what he'd said. "Why were you trying to learn about me?"

"I am come to learn of the beings in this realm," he said. "This one's thoughts are jumbled." He nodded toward Emma. "She is too young, and her mind has not learned sufficient focus. You are different from the other beings here and I was curious."

"Yeah, We're not from around here. Where *is* here, by the way? You said realm? Are we in a different country?"

"This world has had many names," he answered. "The most common name at this time is Danu."

"World?" Is this guy crazy? What exactly was going on here?

"Yes." He nodded. "What is the name of your world?"

"Earth."

"Earth." He seemed to think about that. "That is similar to your word for dirt or soil, yes?"

"Um, yeah. I guess it's not very imaginative. In some fiction

25

I've heard it called Terra. But I guess maybe that's just another variation of dirt."

"I have not studied your world yet. Did you also come here to learn of the people?"

"No, we kind of got here by accident." I looked at him. "I'm Nora. This is Emma. What's your name?"

"I am Jakarael Abalaan."

"Jaka what?"

"Jakarael Abalaan."

"Hm. How about I call you Jack, for short."

He looked at me in surprise. "That would be highly efficient!"

"Yeah, efficiency is good. You know," I looked at him sideways, hoping this would work, "it would be more efficient if we were to have this conversation someplace else."

"It would?" He looked around the cell. "How so?"

"The people here could come in at any time and interrupt us," I explained.

"That would be inconvenient."

"I agree." I nodded, keeping my face very serious. "They haven't been very concerned with things being convenient for people."

"Why have you not left?"

"It isn't as easy for us to come and go like you do." Obviously.

He tilted his head and looked at me, then glanced at the walls around us. "I see. These hold you."

He examined the door and then walked through it. I heard something slide and a thunk, then the door swung open.

"You can leave now?" he asked through the open doorway.

"It's a start," I said, stepping into the corridor. "But we should get all the way out of this place."

I looked both ways down the corridor and they looked the same. I signaled to Emma, and she rushed to stand just behind me. She started to say something, but I shook my head to keep her quiet.

"I don't suppose you know the way out of here?" I asked Jack.

He paused for a moment without moving, then pointed to the left.

"This passage leads to a central hub," he said. "From there we can choose from a number of exits."

"That works." I turned left and led Emma down the hall at a jog. There were doors on both sides, probably leading to more cells like ours, but I didn't stop to check.

When we reached what I assumed he meant by hub, I found a spiral staircase. Stone steps led up and down. I turned to Jack, expectantly.

"We are currently below ground level," he told me. "To leave this structure, we must go up."

"How far?"

"The most efficient exit would be at the top."

Great. I loved running upstairs. Almost as much as I loved a trip to the dentist.

We'd gone up two levels when I bumped into a guard entering the stairwell from a side passage. I shoved him back and quickened my pace up the stairs. I could hear him calling out behind us and the sound of more boots.

We made four more levels and the stairwell opened onto the top of a wide wall. About fifty yards away was what looked like the squat top of another stairwell. I looked the other way and saw the same thing. There were also soldiers that were starting to notice our arrival. The sound of boots preceded the half-dozen guards that erupted from the stairs behind us.

One of the guards strode forward, saying something to me that I couldn't understand. Emma moved behind me as the guard grabbed my arm angrily. There was a flash of movement and the guard's head flew from his body; the body crumpled to the ground. My eyes widened in surprise.

The other guards tried to prepare themselves, but Jack waded into them, his arms moving like machines, every strike inflicted massive damage until the group of guards were all on the ground, dead or injured. Emma looked like she might be going into shock.

The soldiers on the wall had called out a warning and more rushed out of the stairwells in response, brandishing sharp-looking weapons. Jack started to move past me to the closest soldiers. I shook off my shock and grabbed him.

"Jack! Stop!"

He glanced at my hand and then at my face.

"We just need to get out of here," I told him. "We don't need to hurt anyone!"

"They challenge," he said without emotion. "They attempt to interfere, and they challenge. *Daijheen* train all their lives to meet such challenges. A challenge must be met."

"No!" I shook my head. What had I started? "Not like that! These are people! They're just doing their jobs. They don't deserve this!"

He shrugged. "It is of no consequence. Physical constructs are replaceable."

"What? Physical constructs? You mean their bodies? They're *people*!"

The soldiers were in a ring around us now. I could see hatred in their eyes as they looked at us. They held their weapons at the ready but seemed hesitant to get close after what they'd seen Jack do. I could see one of them signaling to a group with cross-bows. Great.

"The being — the spirit — continues," he said. "Destruction of a body is not important. It's just a temporary physical construct to facilitate interaction with the physical universe."

"It's not that simple!" I shook my head. "You're trying to tell me it doesn't hurt anyone if you kill their… physical construct?"

"Well," he admitted. "There can be a certain degree of trauma involved in the sudden ejection from the construct, but—"

"Sudden what? How about we keep the trauma from sudden ejection to a minimum, okay? You can't justify killing people because the spirit will continue."

Just then, the guys with the crossbows fired. Jack waved his hand and the arrows, or whatever they were called for crossbows, turned into ash and lumps of melted slag in the air.

"You would have me ignore this challenge?"

"Yes!" What was wrong with this guy?

"They will view me as weak if I do not respond to the challenge."

"No one will see you as weak," I told him. "Besides, even if they did, so what? Who cares what they think?"

"It impacts one's status if—"

"Status?" I couldn't believe what I was hearing. "Only the weak care about other people's opinions." Let him chew on that.

He blinked at me, tilting his head to the side.

"Or are you saying you really *are* too weak to get us out of here without hurting anyone else?"

His eyes narrowed at that. "You pose an interesting equation. I would discuss this further."

Suddenly, his features began to shift. He grew about two feet in height and giant batwings sprouted from his back. His skin had turned dark red and black horns extended from above his forehead. Before I could say anything, he wrapped one huge arm around me and another around Emma. Then he leaped from the wall.

I was too scared to scream, but we didn't fall. Emma let out a soft wail and I could see tears streaming down her face. The enormous wings flapped, and we quickly left the soldiers behind. I glanced back and saw a walled city, similar to a fortress or something from medieval times.

Had we just been rescued by a demon? Or had we traded one jailer for another?

# CHAPTER FOUR

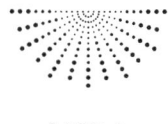

## MIRA

*I* let the portal from Daoine close behind me. I stood in the small clearing by the old tree at the center of the small woods near what I considered to be my true home. I took a deep breath and smelled the rich loam of the forest floor as I leaned on my staff. It was twilight, but I couldn't be sure if it was morning or evening. It felt more like evening.

It had been roughly two years since I'd been here. Two years of wishing I was here. Two years of missing my family. Two years of struggle and hardship. And loss.

Two years for me, anyway. I had no idea how much time had passed here. Much less. Only days or weeks. The spell that had sped up time in Daoine was gone. I'd seen to that. The spell had left its mark on me though; it had aged my body at least ten years. But I couldn't regret my time there. I'd learned and grown so much. I was so far from being the girl that had left earth two years ago.

There was still so much to be done in Daoine to ensure an equal voice for all races, but with the White Riders being disbanded and Mireygna no longer pushing the idea of separation and racial superiority for the Ashae. From what I'd overheard, it looked like the path would be much easier going forward. The coalition of races started by the *Urgaban* of Laraksha-Vo and the *Ulané Jhinura* of Su Lariano was growing. I'm sure there'd be bumps in their road ahead, but at least it should be a peaceful process. I'd done my part and kept all my promises. Now, it was time for me to take care of my own business.

I looked in the direction of home. Towards the house where I lived with Jill and Tony and Nora. They must be worried, not knowing what happened to me. How was I going to explain it? I chuckled, thinking of their shocked faces when they heard the story.

I'd let go of the *Ralahin* when I'd let the portal close, and I opened myself to it again and looked around. Flows of magic lit up around me in my Sight. It was similar to what I had Seen on Daoine, but somehow different.

There was something different about the old tree as well, something I wouldn't have noticed without my connection to the magic. I looked at it for a moment before I realized what it was. I wasn't alone.

"Hello," I said. "I can see you there. You can come out."

A figure slowly melted out of the tree. She was about four and a half feet tall. She looked similar to the *Ulané Jhinura* with what appeared to be Asian features and pointed ears, but her skin was a dark greenish brown. Her hair was long and black, and she had green eyes. She was what humans called a dryad or wood nymph. She was *Jhiné Boré*.

"I'm Mira," I told her, speaking in the common tongue of Daoine. "What's your name?"

"I am Cirilia." She seemed nervous.

"It's nice to meet you, Cirilia. I'm sorry I never noticed you here before."

That only produced a look of confusion on her face. She lived on Earth; did she even speak the common tongue?

"Is it better to speak in English?" I asked her, switching.

She gave an impatient shrug. "No, but how would you notice

31

me? You have never been here. I saw you arrive; it felt— was that truly Daoine on the other side?"

"I've been here many times. And yes," I nodded, "travel is no longer blocked to Daoine."

"If you had been here before, I would recognize you," she looked at me suspiciously.

"I was younger when I was here last," I told her. "Or at least, I looked a lot younger."

She looked at me more critically for a moment and then her eyes got big.

"You *were* here! With the other! The one who was trying to do magic!"

"Nora." I nodded. "I was here with Nora."

"But that was three nights ago! How are you so changed?"

*Three nights? Is that all?*

"It's been two years for me," I explained. "Plus, there was a spell that caused my body to age. I— That's why you can go to Daoine now if you want. The spell is gone."

She shook her head, and a smile curled her lips. "I cannot go to Daoine. My place is here." She put her hand lovingly on the trunk of the old tree. *Jhiné Boré* could not be far from the tree they were bonded with.

"There are probably others though, right? You can't be the only one here."

Her eyes grew suspicious again and she looked ready to run.

"Many were stranded here when the way became blocked," she said. "And many of those were hunted by humans. If any survived, they would be hiding, as I was."

That made me wonder if there were hidden communities around the world. And people walking around past them never knowing. Then something else occurred to me.

"You said three nights ago. Has Nora been back since then? The other girl?"

"Not that I saw, but later that night and through the next day, there were many humans in the woods. They went everywhere. Maybe she was among them."

That sounded like a search party. They must have been looking for me. I needed to get back and let them know I was alright.

"Thank you Cirilia," I told her, adjusting the straps on my small backpack. "I have to be going. I'll come back to see you another time."

"The one you call Nora," she called after me as I reached the edge of the clearing. "She is of the blood."

"Of the what?" I turned back, but she had gone. I had no idea what she'd meant. I shook my head and started walking.

By the time I reached the outer edge of the small woods, it was fully dark. I walked up the street towards home, my step quickening with anticipation. A white paper tacked onto a fence fluttered in the evening breeze and caught my eye as I walked past. I stopped short. Missing, it said. There were photos of me and of Nora.

*Nora's missing?*

Looking at the pictures, I realized I had another problem. The photos were me alright. There were two; one was from my sixteenth birthday, not long before I left. The other was a year older, from my *quinceanera* when I turned fifteen. I didn't look like that anymore.

How was I going to convince Jill and Tony I was me? They'd think I was just some crazy person. They might even call the cops.

This wasn't going to be as easy as I'd thought. I should take it slowly and test the waters. Besides, I needed to figure out what happened to Nora. But where could I go? I didn't have any money. The last time I'd seen my cell phone it was connected to the charger on my nightstand. It was probably still there, but at the moment, it may as well have been in Daoine for all the good it would do me.

If there were any *Ulané Jhinura* in the area… but even if there were, I wouldn't know how to find them.

Was there anyone who might be able to understand and who could help me? As I stood there, I absently put my hand on the hilt of one of my daggers. Then I let go and pulled my cloak around me, looking around; people didn't walk around armed like this here.

That reminded me of the day Nora and I went to the antique shops to see if they could tell us anything about the knives. The lady at the second place we went to seemed like she might know something. She practically threw us out when she saw them.

It had been two years for me, but I remembered where the shop was and started walking in that direction. I knew I was grasping at straws, but it was the best idea I had.

It took me an hour of walking to get to the place. I recognized the sign: Herbs, Antiques and Curiosities. HAC, she'd called it. I reached the door just as she was flipping the sign to *closed*. She met my eyes and hesitated. I must have looked a bit odd with my cloak, pack, and staff. With a smile, she opened the door.

"I suppose a few more minutes won't hurt," she stepped aside and swept her arm to invite me in. "I'm Katya. What can I do for you?"

"Hi, Katya." Now that I was here, I wasn't sure how to proceed. "You probably don't recognize me, but I was here the other day asking you about something."

"The other day?" She looked at me, studying my face. "No, I don't recall it. What were you asking about?"

"These," I said, drawing my cloak aside so she could see the knives at my waist.

Her eyes got big, and she took two steps backwards.

"*Those* I remember, *You* I do not." There was no missing the fear in her eyes.

She moved her hand in a pattern in the air and my pendant let me see that she was working magic. I reached for the *Ralahin* immediately and saw that she had erected some kind of a protective barrier around herself. It was in a sort of odd, geometric shape. I hadn't seen magic used this way.

"Interesting," I mused. Her eyes got bigger.

"What happened to the young girl who had those knives?" she demanded.

"She—" I shrugged, looking away and letting the cloak fall back into place. "She went someplace where time moved faster and came back looking older."

She just looked at me, taking in what I'd said. I waited as she studied my face.

"You're saying that was you?" she asked me.

I nodded absently, still studying her barrier. The magic seemed somehow different than what I was used to. "I only just got back."

"Why come here? Why not go home?"

"And tell my parents what?" I snapped. I drew the magic out of her barrier, and it collapsed.

"How did you do that?" She looked really frightened now.

I sighed. "I've been gone a long time. I learned a few things."

A figure rushed in through a doorway in the back of the shop. I could see her working magic and she was flinging some spells in my direction. I threw up a shield instantly and they bounced off.

"Stop!" I held up my hands in a gesture of peace. "I'm sorry, I didn't mean to scare you. I really just need some help." I looked at Katya. "I *was* going to go home, but then I realized what would happen."

The woman who'd come from the back glared at me. She was a few inches taller than I was, with ebony skin and sharp, delicate features. Her black hair was gathered into a tight bun on the back of her head. "Don't trust her!" she said to Katya. "She's dangerous!"

Moving with the *Ralahin*, I flitted to just behind the woman, my dagger at her throat. Fast as I had been, the flow seemed sluggish in some way I couldn't define.

"I'm more dangerous than you know," I told her. I stepped back and re-sheathed my dagger. "But only to my enemies. As far as I know, you're not my enemies." She spun away and looked at me with narrowed eyes.

"How did you move so fast?" Katya was stunned.

"Moving with the *Ralahin*? It's one of the things I've learned."

"*Ralahin*?" the second woman asked. "I don't think I've heard of that."

"It's the *Ulané Jhinura* word for magic," I explained.

"The what?"

"*Ulané Jhinura*." Non-comprehension showed on both of their faces. "Sprites?"

"You mean like Tinkerbelle?" Katya was looking skeptical.

"No." I shook my head. "That would be like the *Pilané Jhin*. Pixies."

The two exchanged glances before the second woman spoke again.

"These are creatures from fairy tales," she said. "Few believe they ever existed."

"Oh, they exist all right," I said. "I don't know how many are still around on Earth, but there are some at least. Right after I got back, I ran into a—" I stopped myself. That wasn't my secret to tell. Instead, I looked at the other woman. "We haven't been introduced. I'm Mira."

"I'm Grace," she hesitated. "Are you some kind of a witch? A sorcerer?"

"I don't really know what those labels mean," I told her. "I'm more familiar with *mage*."

"Well," Katya began. "Witches usually start as just a regular person with an interest in spiritual philosophies. But sometimes they have a natural ability to use magic and that draws them to witchcraft. There are a lot of different types of witches, and they use different means of casting spells, mixing potions and the like. A sorcerer has innate magical abilities and doesn't need to use spells, grimoires, or anything to work magic. Though they can learn to use them if they want."

"This isn't a classroom, Katya." Grace arched an eyebrow at her.

"That doesn't fit with what I learned." I shook my head. "I certainly didn't have any natural ability, but I don't need spells to use magic."

Katya started to answer but Grace held up her hand.

"You said you came here looking for help," she said. "Before we agree to help you, we're going to need to hear your story."

"That's going to take a while." I smirked. "Got any goblin grog?"

Katya looked alarmed. "Any what?"

"Booze," I told her. "Preferably something strong."

"That we have." Grace nodded. "Katya, make sure the front door is locked and meet us in the backroom. I'll pour."

# CHAPTER FIVE

## MIRA

*I* only meant to give them the highlights, but the further I got into my story the more I found myself talking more about my friends on Daoine and everything that had happened to us over the last two years. It started out light-heartedly, talking about some of the mischief Rispan got us into during our training, and Katya and Grace laughed about it with me.

I didn't go into detail on everything, and some parts were hard to tell. The telling of it was therapeutic, though; I needed to tell it.

The loss of my friends from military training, Tarana, Kooras and Kirsat, was hard enough. I still felt so raw about Mooren. And then as I told it, I heard Farukan's final words in my head again and I had to stop and refill my glass while I composed myself. Tears flowed freely as I described Laila's sacrifice.

"You've faced more in two years than most people face in a lifetime," Grace said to me.

"But here, it's only been a few days!" Katya pointed out.

"And now you're back." Grace nodded.

"Now I'm back. Yes." I shook my head. "Back to where a few

days ago I was sixteen years old. But now I'm eighteen years old in a body that's more like thirty."

"At least all of that is over." Katya patted my hand gently. "You can get back to your life and your family here."

"It's not over," I told her. "My sister is missing, and I can't go to my parents because they'll never believe I'm me! And I still don't know who that man was that tried to grab me in the first place, or why my mother had these magical things! There's only more questions and more problems to solve."

Katya glanced at Grace, who nodded.

"You can stay with us until you get everything sorted," Katya said.

"Sorted…" I looked up at her. "I don't even have a plan."

The next thing. Do the next thing. That's what I always did; push forward and do the next thing. But what was the next thing? I didn't know.

Nora. Find Nora first. Go from there.

"I need to find my sister," I told them. "She might be in trouble."

"Do you know where to start?" Grace asked me.

"No." I shook my head. "I have no idea." Then I looked at the two of them "You used magic. Are you witches? Sorcerers? Wizards?"

Katya snorted. "Wizards aren't much more than ceremonial witches with a superiority complex. We're witches, but Grace is the strong one. She can do a lot more than I can. I think she's really a sorcerer, but she doesn't want to admit it."

Grace frowned at her.

"Do you know of some way we can use magic to find my sister?" I asked them.

Grace drummed her fingers on the table while she thought. "I don't know. I can look into it. You'll need to give me a couple of days."

"What if that guy comes back in the meantime?" I asked her.

"I think you might be a bit harder for him to handle than the last time." Katya smirked.

She had a point.

"I think he homed in on the daggers," I told her. "I have them warded now, so they're invisible, magically speaking. When I'm ready to ask him some questions, I can drop the wards, but finding Nora is my first priority." That got me thinking. "I wonder if I can home in on Nora the way he homed in on the daggers."

"I was thinking something along those lines," Grace said. "I don't know how it's done, so I can't say for certain whether it would work."

"How did you take down my shield earlier?" Katya asked. "I've never seen it done like that."

"It wasn't tied in place." I shrugged. "I just pulled out the end and drew the magic out of it, so it unraveled."

"Pulled it out and sent it where?" Grace asked.

I shook my head. "I didn't send it anywhere. The magic was drawn in to create the barrier and I just released it."

"But," Grace glanced at Katya, "when a spell is created, magic is drawn out of nature and formed into the spell. If you just let it loose... isn't that dangerous?"

"That's not what I see when I look at magic." I frowned. "It's more like the other way around; nature comes from magic. Not magic from nature."

"When you look at magic," Grace repeated. "You can see magic?"

I looked back and forth between them. "You can't?"

She shook her head. "We can see spells sometimes, depending. If they are fully formed. But not raw magic."

"Oh," that surprised me. "Hmm. Here." I took the pendant from my neck and handed it to her. I opened myself to the *Ralahin* and, drawing in some of the magic, I wove a flow around the glass I'd been drinking from and lifted it from the table. "You should be able to see something with the pendant. That's one of its properties."

Grace nodded, watching raptly. She reached out and took Katya's hand.

Katya gasped in surprise as the physical contact lent her the same ability. "That's what magic looks like?"

"Some of it," I said. "Sometimes. The pendant only lets you see magic that's being worked. But you can get an idea of what I'm talking about. Magic flows through all things. Actually." I remembered something I'd seen, "it's kind of similar to that painting… Van Gogh… Starry Night? Magic flows through everything, kind of like the way the flows look in that painting. Anyway, one of the first things I learned was how to see it."

"What does it look like?" Katya asked.

I shrugged. "It's hard to describe. Like the air is full of streams of glitter? But not just the air; everything."

"Then I suppose vampires *can* sparkle," Grace mumbled. "I stand corrected."

"What?" I asked her.

She shook her head. "Just an old argument. Never mind."

"Vampires are real?"

Grace shook her head again. "Couldn't say. I've never met one." She looked at me. "I know you're thinking that finding your sister is the first thing you need to do, but I think you're wrong." At my look, she went on. "Think of your parents, girl. They must be worried sick! You have to let them know you're alright. When you disappeared… You said you saw posters up, so it must have been reported to the police. And the police are spending time looking for you instead of doing other important things."

She was right. I wasn't thinking. It was irresponsible of me to ignore that whole situation. But that didn't give me a path forward.

"How?" I asked her. "I'm not disagreeing with you; I just don't know how to pull that off. If I show up looking the way I do, they won't even listen, and I could end up in jail or locked up in a mental ward."

"If your only obstacle is your appearance," she smiled, "we can help you with that."

"How?"

"A glamour. It's a type of illusion magic," Katya piped in. "It's not that hard. Even I can do it a little. Especially since you don't need to radically change how you look. And with your ability with magic, you should be able to hold a glamour for a longer time."

"I'm not familiar with using magic that way." I frowned. "How long will it take to learn?"

"Not long." Katya grinned.

Grace threw a serious expression at me. "You're going to talk to your parents tonight."

An hour and a half later, Grace and Katya dropped me off in front of the house. Bringing a five-foot staff in a car was awkward, so I'd left it at their shop for now, along with my backpack. To anyone looking at me, I was the same Mira who had left here a few days ago. It was late evening, and the lights were on inside. They hadn't gone to bed yet.

"If there's a problem, or if you need anything," Grace had told me, "just call us."

"And we'll see you soon." Katya gave me a hug. "We're going to help you get through this."

I watched their taillights disappear around the corner and then I walked up to the door. Should I knock? Just go in? I tried the door, but it was locked. Taking a deep breath, I knocked.

After a few moments, Tony opened the door. His eyes got big when he saw me and suddenly, I was picked up off my feet in a giant bear hug.

"Mirella! Where have you been?" He was squeezing me too tightly for me to answer. "Jill! Jill!"

"What's going on?" I heard her voice from behind him as he put me down and stepped aside.

"Hi, mom." It was all I could get out before I was running to her. Then tears were streaming down both our faces as we wrapped our arms around each other.

"We've been so worried, Mirella," Tony was saying. "We were afraid we might not see you again. What happened?"

"Where's Nora?" Jill asked. "Isn't she with you?"

"We need to call the police and tell them you're back," Tony said.

I pulled back from Jill and looked at them both.

"Before we call anyone," I said. "I need to tell you guys what happened. You're going to have a hard time believing it, but I'm not crazy."

"Where's Nora?" Jill asked again.

"I don't know."

Tony closed the door. "What do you need to tell us, *mija*?"

"It's a long story," I said. "So, we should sit down. But first I want to show you something." I walked over to the mantle over the fireplace. Jill had several candles set up, mostly for decor. "In order for you to believe my story, you're going to have to believe something else first." They both looked at me in confusion. "Magic," I told them. "You have to believe in magic." Using my connection to the *Ralahin*, I lit each of the candles one at a time, pointing to each as I did it.

"How did you do that?" Jill asked.

"I told you," I answered. "Magic. *Real* magic."

Tony strode forward to look at the candles. "This is no time for jokes, *mija*. It's not like you."

"It's no joke," I told him. "It's real."

I drew flows of magic in and wrapped them around Tony, then I carefully lifted him off the floor. His eyes grew wide, and I was afraid he might panic.

"What's happening?" He flung his arms out to try to hold onto something, but nothing was close by.

"Don't be afraid," I told him. "You're safe." I set him back onto the floor. "I had to show you it was real. That I'm not crazy or something."

"So, you're some kind of *bruja* now?" he asked me. "A witch?"

I shook my head. "Not exactly. Let's sit down and I'll explain everything. But please believe me."

I headed for the dinner table and Jill stopped me again and held me close for a moment.

"Tell us whatever you need to, honey," she said. "*You're* safe."

We sat at the table and Jill put the water on for some herbal tea. "Are you hungry?" she asked. "I made some ceviche today."

"Yes!" Jill's ceviche was the bomb. I also knew she tended to get busy in the kitchen when she was feeling stressed. If she'd made ceviche without some kind of party, she was stressed. I felt bad about making her worry.

She dished up a bowl for me and I had to take a few bites before starting on the story.

"It started with that box," I said. "The one with my mother's things in it. Wait here, let me get it."

I went to my room. Tony had fixed the door and I could see the fresh paint. It seemed so long since this had been my room, my inner sanctum. I looked around. It was a nice room. Sweet, even. But not quite what I would want, now. I just wasn't that little girl anymore. I grabbed the small chest and brought it back to set it on the table. I sat down at the table and looked at them.

"There were some things in the box. Magical things. Some of them were in a hidden compartment. This was the first thing I found." I held up the pendant I wore. "And then there were two of these." I pulled one of the daggers from my waist and set it on the table. "They're magical." I opened the chest. "What we didn't know was that the box was warded." I pointed to the markings on the inside. "This kept the magic items hidden. When we took them out, they weren't protected anymore. Someone sensed them, and evidently, they wanted them."

"I checked that before I gave it to you." Jill frowned. "I didn't see any knives in there."

"There's a false bottom in the box," I told her. "There was no reason for you to suspect it."

The water was hot, and Jill made the tea. The warm cup felt good in my hands, and the tea went down nicely over the spiciness of the ceviche. It was almost feeling like home again.

"I've been on another world," I told them. "And time moved faster there than here. For me, I've been gone a *lot* longer than just a few days."

I gave them everything. I didn't hold back. They deserved to know it all. When I got to the part about Neelu saying she would teach me to flit, Tony interrupted.

"Did she teach you? How fast can you move?" he asked.

I grinned at him, standing up. Then suddenly I was standing behind him with my hands on his shoulders. Then I was behind Jill. Then I was back in my seat.

"Wow!" Tony laughed. "Maybe you should try for the Olympics!"

I shook my head and went on with the story.

"That sounds like you, all right." Jill smiled when I told them about what happened when I first met Rispan. "You were never afraid to stand up to bullies. And that poor boy!"

"Actually," I told her, "I didn't know it at the time, but he didn't need my help. Rispan and Mouse became like brothers for me. I hope you can meet them sometime. But I'm getting ahead of myself."

I hesitated when I got to the part where I was kidnapped, when I killed the two kidnappers. Would it change how they felt about me? This was the first time I killed anyone. But it wasn't the last.

Jill gasped when I told about the first one, Farlen. I'll never forget their names. Farlen was the first man I'd killed. His partner, Gilglys, was the second.

"It was self-defense," she said, gripping my hand. "You didn't have any choice!"

"Mom, dad." I looked at them both. "This wasn't the worst situation I've been in. I need you to be ready for that."

They exchanged glances and then nodded at me to continue.

At one point, Jill interrupted with a mischievous look. "And when will we get to meet this Mooren?"

I hadn't expected the question and I just gaped at her.

"I know you." Jill grinned at me. "There's something in your eye when you talk about him."

I felt a catch in my breath. I tried to clamp down on my emotions but felt the tears starting down my face. I'd been doing so well up to then, but her question caught me completely off guard. Would it ever stop hurting?

"Easy, *mija*." Tony wrapped his arms around me, my body shuddering with quiet sobs. "Take a breath."

After a couple of minutes, I nodded. Wiping my eyes, I went on with the story. I told them of our success in Shifara, and then of how Mooren died and my capture and enslavement. And the fighting.

"That time," I said, not meeting their eyes. "That part of it… It was… bad. And I hated them. So, I killed as many of them as I could, whenever I could. I killed a lot of them."

I wasn't going to give them the details, but they needed to know that things had happened, that I had done things, and I wasn't the same person they knew.

"I can't imagine what it was like," Jill told me. "What you were going through. But you can't look at what happened there in terms of our laws and culture here. It's just not the same."

"You're still you, *mija*," Tony said. "You're still our little girl."

I saw the shock on Jill's face when I told them about Farukan's death, but I didn't pause in my story. I continued through to the end. About what happened with the time spell.

"When we were in the spell," I said, "it aged us. That spell was strong enough to speed up time for a whole world. What it would do to a body that was standing directly in it… Laila was able to pull most of the effects onto herself; she became so old… It's the only reason I'm still alive, and that I was able to succeed. She sacrificed herself. But… the spell… it aged me, too. It aged my body. I'm… I'm not a little girl anymore."

"You look the same to me," Tony observed.

"I was wondering about that," Jill commented. "It sounds like you were there for a long time. You said it was longer than a few days for you."

"I was there for close to two years. I don't really look like this anymore. Before I came here tonight," I explained. "I used magic to look like what you would remember. I was afraid that if you didn't recognize me, you wouldn't believe me. But I don't want to hide anything from you. You deserve the whole truth."

"Show us," was all Tony said.

I nodded. I dropped the glamour spell and looked at them both to judge their reaction.

"You still look like you," Jill assured me. "A little older, sure. But still you."

"If I hadn't heard the story first." Tony nodded. "I see what you mean. But I know you. I still see you. You'll always be our little girl."

I breathed a sigh of relief.

"Come on." Jill gave me a mock scowl. "Did you really think any of this would change that?"

"Well." I shrugged. "It's not exactly in the job description."

"It's crazy." Tony shook his head. "A few days ago for us, you were a sixteen-year-old in high school. Now, you're a veteran. A hero. I'm proud of you, *mija*."

That made me feel a little better. "Thanks, dad."

"What about Nora?" Jill asked. "If she didn't go with you, where is she?"

"I don't know. I don't think I was supposed to end up where I did. Something went wrong with the portal. I thought she'd be *here*, but then I saw the posters saying we were both missing."

47

"I'll call the police first thing in the morning," Tony said. "Tell them to stop looking. We'll need a story for them; they won't believe all this. But we still have to find Nora."

"We can tell them me and Nora had an argument," I suggested. "I got mad and took off for a few days, but I'm back and sorry I worried everyone. Nora got mad and took off, too. But she's eighteen. She can come and go as an adult."

"Works." He nodded. "And if they ask what you argued about?"

"Boys," Jill suggested. "No need for details. Just say she said it was too embarrassing to talk about."

"If they ask, I'll say the same thing," I agreed. "I can put that disguise back on, so I'll look younger if I need to. But meanwhile, like you said, I need to find Nora."

Tony opened his mouth to speak and then stopped. Then he shook his head. "You're all grown up now, too. You've been living as a grownup since you left. That's two years for you. Give us a minute to adjust, okay?"

Jill looked at him and then back to me. "I thought we'd have more time before having to cut the apron strings. That's going to be harder than this whole magic business! I'm not ready for this!"

"That reminds me of an old saying." Tony gave her a wry smile. "Man makes plans; the universe laughs."

# CHAPTER SIX

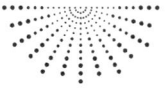

## NORA

"Where are you taking us?" I yelled to him. I didn't know how well he would be able to hear me. The wind was buffeting my ears as we flew, and I could barely hear my own question. He glanced down at me, though.

"We go to a place no one goes," he called back. "No one will interrupt us there."

I started to ask him how far it was but stopped. It really didn't matter; I wouldn't be able to stop him, and we had nowhere else to go, anyway. I could only hope that wherever it was, we would be safe. But at this point, I had no way of knowing.

I watched as the ground went by far below us. Farmlands and forests, rivers and hills. The city we had left got smaller in the distance and eventually disappeared over the horizon behind us. In the distance, I saw what might have been a herd of wild horses. I couldn't estimate how fast Jack was going, but he seemed to be covering a lot of ground very quickly. I doubted birds could travel this fast, so it must have been more than just wings that propelled us.

The ground below transitioned suddenly from green, verdant hills to a stark and desolate landscape where nothing grew. It was barren dirt and rock of what appeared to be the dried bed of an inland sea. Occasional swirls of wind moved dust around like a fickle decorator. I'd never seen anyplace that looked so inhospitable.

Eventually we arrived at the ruins of a large city on what must have been an island. He landed at the top of a broken tower that had once been much taller. I could see remnants on the ground below us. As soon as he put us down, he changed his shape back to how he'd looked when I first met him. Emma collapsed onto the ground and hugged her knees to her chest. She was clearly terrified, and I should probably be doing something to make her feel better, but that wasn't something I knew much about. Mira was good at that kind of thing; not me.

"What is this place?" I asked Jack.

"From what I have been able to determine, this was a city called Tir Nya Lu," he answered. "Some stories may also refer to it as Tanelorn, there is some confusion on that point. A terrible war was fought on this world centuries ago. The city was devastated at some point and after the war the people left this world. This wasn't pertinent to my research."

"But who did they fight against? And what about the people who—" I didn't want to think about what he'd done to them. "The people where we just came from?"

"No, no." He shook his head. "The current inhabitants of this world came later. The *Ande Dannu*, *Dannu Fé*, and the *Wyl-Dunn*. You and I met at Solaian, which is the capital for the *Ande Dannu*."

"Sounds like you've learned a lot," I commented. "I don't suppose you know how I could go home? To Earth, I mean."

"That has not been part of my research."

After seeing what he did to the people at that last place, I wasn't sure I wanted him to know how to get to Earth. I didn't trust him; killing was too easy for him. Just because he'd gotten me out of a jam didn't make him my friend. I'd had people help me before who turned out not to be friends.

I looked at the city around us, what was left of it anyway. It must have been really beautiful at one time. I tried to imagine it as being on an island, with green hills and trees.

"So, this is where you live?" I asked him.

"I come to this place to consider what I have observed," he acknowledged.

"How long have you been *observing*?"

"I am seeing a third generation come into adulthood."

"Wow!" I wasn't sure whether I should be impressed. If what he was saying was true, he was older than he looked. "I suppose you understand the people here pretty well by now."

He scowled at me. "I do not. They confound understanding at every turn. They react illogically. They make choices that cannot succeed."

"That sounds pretty normal." I shrugged. "By the third generation, you should be used to it."

"How can this be normal?"

"Dude, you've been watching these people for three generations and you're still expecting them to be totally logical? How is *that* logical?"

"Why should I not expect them to be logical?"

"Look." This guy wasn't as bright as he thought he was. Was I really going to have to lead him by his nose? "You have observed a general pattern of behavior for three generations, right?"

He nodded.

"Is it logical to expect that pattern to suddenly change?" I shook my head. "Expecting the pattern to suddenly change… That's just denial of reality because you don't like it. You're not going to understand anything with that approach." I glanced at where Emma was still huddled. I didn't really have any room to talk about human interaction and understanding.

"There is no fault in my method!" he snapped.

I shrugged again. "How well did you say that was working out for you?"

His skin started to shift to red and his hands half-formed into claws. I needed to remember it might not be a good idea to poke the demon. I held myself still as he calmed down.

"I don't mean to change the subject," except I did, "but is there a better place for us to talk than up here on this tower? And where do you sleep? Where do you eat?"

"Eat?"

"Yeah, you know. Food?"

"There is no food here."

"Jack," I told him, "I don't know about you and how you live, but I'm a regular person. So is Emma. We need food and water to survive. And sleep. Probably very similar to what you've been *observing* around here for three generations."

He blinked at me slowly for a few moments, then pointed to a nearby building.

"That is a library," he said. "You may wait there. I will see to your physical needs."

With that, he turned and leapt from the building, changing to his other form. His huge wings carried him quickly away. I looked at the library building and felt a little overwhelmed as I tried to figure out the best way to get there. I knew things would look differently once we were on the ground, so I tried to memorize our relative position. The library was one of the only places in the area that still had a roof.

"Come on," I said to Emma. "Let's get down from here."

She eyed the broken stairwell nervously. "Can't he just fly us down?"

"He probably could have. But he didn't. Don't worry, I'll help you." I tried to sound more confident than I felt.

"I know you don't like me." Her eyes were downcast.

"It's not personal," I told her. "I don't like most people." Ouch. That probably wasn't going to help. "What I mean is; I don't dislike you. I just don't get close to people very easily, that's all. I'm not like Mira. I guess we're opposites in that way."

"You like *her*, though," she looked up at me. It seemed like the talking was helping her.

"Mira? Most people do." I shrugged. "It's hard not to."

She thought about that for a moment, then looked at the stairs. "Are you sure that's safe?"

I just chuckled at the question.

"What's so funny?"

"I haven't been sure of anything since we got to this world."

She got to her feet and walked over to the stairwell, peering down into its depths.

"I'm pretty sure I can climb down that," she told me.

I didn't think it would be a good idea to mention that my real worry wasn't climbing down, but with whether the structure was stable enough not to collapse while we were doing it.

Making our way down was nerve-wracking; the stairwell was as broken as the rest of the tower. The stones seemed to have settled in place though and didn't move as we crawled over them or had to drop or jump from one to the next. It really would have been nice if Jack had put us on the ground before he left. I shook my head. It probably didn't even occur to him.

Getting over the pile of debris outside the tower was another challenge. I slipped a couple of times, and had to help Emma, but we made it without any serious injury. I went to jump off the last piece of broken rock onto the ground and my feet slid out from underneath me from the loose grit on the surface. I landed unceremoniously on my butt.

"Are you alright?" A voice called from nearby.

I looked up to see a man with dark hair and a goatee. He wore an expression of concern on his distinguished features. Something about his skin seemed odd, almost shiny.

Emma made the last jump with a lot more agility than I'd managed it.

"I'm fine." I stood up and brushed the dirt from my pants, embarrassed that he'd seen me fall. Just for a moment as I was looking down, his features seemed to shift slightly. "Where'd you come from?" I looked at him more closely. "I thought this place was deserted."

"It is, mostly." He nodded as he walked toward me. "I'm sort of a caretaker here. But I keep a low profile when the *Daijheen* comes. He is gone, yes?"

"*Daijheen*?" I asked. "You mean Jack?"

"Jack is the one you came with?" I nodded. "He is a *Daijheen*. I believe you call them demons."

"How come you speak English?" I asked him. "So far, only Jack has been able to understand me."

He shrugged off my question. "A translation spell. Easy enough if you know how to do it. How is it that you are traveling with the *Daijheen*? Are you his servants? His slaves?"

"Servants? No." I shook my head.

He looked at me. "His mistress?"

"What? No! We just met the guy. There was a… disagreement with some people. More of a misunderstanding. Anyway, he got us out of there and brought us here."

"Out of where?"

I shook my head. "He told me what the place was called, but I don't remember. Something about *Ande Dannu*? They couldn't understand us."

He nodded, thinking. "That sounds innocent enough. I was afraid there had been force. Or even violence. That would not be unusual for one of his kind."

My eyes fell when he said that. There had been violence. A lot of it. He noticed my reaction.

"Ah." He nodded again. "There *was* violence. Not surprising. And now you are stranded here, and you cannot escape him."

There was nothing I could really say to that. I didn't know that what he was saying was exactly true. But I didn't know it wasn't, either.

"I can help you," he said. "But I will need you to help me, too."

"How can you help us?" Emma asked.

"I can make sure you get wherever it is you want to be," he told us. "But my first priority is to safely send this… demon… back to where he came from, so he can't hurt anyone else here."

"Why don't you just talk to him?" I asked. "Explain it so he'll understand."

"*Daijheen* don't typically react well when you imply they have been wrong."

Jack *had* seemed about to lose control when I'd challenged his methods earlier.

"And how many more would be injured, or worse," he went on, "while we were trying to teach him to be something he's not?" Something about him seemed indistinct, but as he talked, I was struck with how distinguished he looked. "Violence is simply part of their nature; they can't be blamed for it. But they can be removed from where they are a danger to others. Will you — I'm sorry, what's your name?"

"I'm Nora. This is Emma."

"Nora… Emma." He nodded. "I am Kartahn Zeg. Nora, will you help me to send him home? To where he belongs and where he won't be a danger to anyone?"

"You're not going to hurt him?"

"Absolutely not," he said firmly. "That would be against *my* nature."

"What exactly would you need me to do?"

"I only need you to keep him occupied," he told me. His features shifted slightly in the heat and for a moment I thought I saw scales. His smile reassured me as he continued. "I can ensnare him with magic and then send him home, but I need to be fairly close to him in order to do it. He will sense my presence unless his attention is on something else. I bear him no ill will, but I must protect the people of this land. You have no idea the damage he has caused. If you help me, you will save much heartbreak and many lives. In return for your help, I can also send you both wherever it is you need to go."

What he proposed sounded reasonable, and we certainly had

no other way to get back to Earth. Jack didn't know where it was. And what Kartahn Zeg said about Jack fit with my own thoughts; I wasn't sure I wanted him coming to Earth any more than Kartahn Zeg seemed to want him to be in this world.

"And you aren't going to hurt him?"

"Upon my oath." He nodded. "No harm will come to him. When do you expect him to return?"

I shrugged. "I don't know exactly. I think he went to get some food and water. We're supposed to wait for him in the library."

"The library?" He seemed to perk up at that. "What library?"

I looked at him. "You said you're the caretaker here, right?"

He nodded. "I was curious which one you meant. There are several libraries in the area. This city was once rich in knowledge and books of learning were in high esteem. For example, I usually prefer to do my own studies there." He pointed to a large building nearby. "Is that where you are to meet him?"

"No." I shook my head. "That's not the one he mentioned."

"Ah." He nodded again with a smile. "Very well then. Why don't you lead the way to where he told you to wait, and I'll keep an eye out in case he returns before we are ready."

I took Emma's hand and started off down the rubble-strewn street along the path I had scoped out from the tower. I still didn't understand how it was that nothing grew here. Jack had said this place had been abandoned after a war. Had something happened in the war to just completely eradicate plant and animal life here? Did nuclear fallout even do that?

As we approached the library, I could see the remains of statues that once stood on either side of the steps. They were of some sort of animal, but not enough was left for me to know if it was anything I'd be familiar with. Parts of the ornate carvings that had been the elaborate facing of the building remained, and I could only imagine how magnificent it had looked before all the damage.

One of the double doors to the building leaned on the frame to one side, the other lay on the ground. I could see the effects of wind and rain as I stepped into the entryway. Beyond the entry, another door to the interior was still functional and I pushed past it to the library proper. There were several floors and there were rows and rows of shelves, all full of books. The very center was open to the ceiling far above.

Light shone down through a skylight that, amazingly, was still intact. There were tables and chairs for readers, same as I would expect for any library. Other than dust, the interior, and the books, seemed untouched by whatever had ravaged the city outside. There must be a treasure trove of information here. Though I doubted it would be in English, so it wouldn't do me any good.

"What do we need to do?" I asked him.

He pointed to a table and chair in the center of the room. "Go ahead and have a seat there. That will be our focal point. I'll get everything ready."

I sat down with Emma and watched as he walked around the room, depositing pinches of some powdery substance from a bag he pulled out of the satchel that hung over his shoulder. He made three circuits around the room, mumbling words I couldn't understand. Each time, he drew powder from a different bag.

"What is that stuff?" Emma asked him.

"These are needed for the spell," he answered. "To hold him in place so that I can send him where he needs to go."

He walked to where we waited.

"One more thing," he said. "You will be in the snare with him, and he may become angry. You will want to be shielded so he can't hurt you."

"You think he'd hurt me?"

"Perhaps, perhaps not. But a little precaution would be prudent."

That sounded reasonable. He drew some leather straps from his satchel.

"We simply place these on your wrists and ankles," he said.

"When I activate the spell, this will give you a protective shield that he won't be able to penetrate."

They appeared to be leather bracelets and anklets. I didn't see how they would help, but I still didn't understand how magic worked. I let him put them on us, and again he mumbled words in some language I'd never heard before. Then he stood back, apparently satisfied.

"Now we just need to wait," he said. "I'll stay out of sight. When he comes in, just talk to him, and let him approach you. I'll take care of the rest."

Kartahn Zeg retreated to the back of the library and disappeared behind a row of shelves. I settled down to wait for Jack. I wished he had given me some idea how long he'd be gone. I looked up again at the skylight, marveling that it had survived. When I'd looked at the library from the tower, it hadn't been clear what I was looking at.

That's when I remembered that the other buildings in the area hadn't had a roof. How could that other building have been a library that Kartahn Zeg used for study if it didn't have a roof? Something wasn't right here. I started to look around for him, but then I heard a sound from the front. I turned to see Jack coming through the door.

"I have brought you a selection of food," he announced. He seemed very pleased with himself as he walked toward me with bulging sacks over each shoulder.

"Jack," I called. "Wait—"

He was already a half dozen steps into the room when a network of lines sizzled into existence around the three of us. Suddenly, I was jerked into the air by the leather straps on my wrists and ankles, the straps pulling me painfully in four different directions. I heard a cry and turned to see Emma hanging in the air and being pulled in four directions like I was.

Jack dropped the bags and his shape started to shift.

"Ha!" I heard Kartahn Zeg's voice. "Snared!"

Jack launched himself at the magical cage and rebounded.

"You cannot keep me for long necromancer!" Jack growled at him. "You will not feast on me this day!"

"Do not resist, *Daijheen*," Kartahn Zeg cackled. "Witness!"

He made a motion with his hands and the straps pulled harder. I screamed in pain and surprise.

"You have given your protection for these, have you not? They are under your aegis?"

Jack looked stunned; his eyes locked on me.

"Release them!" Jack demanded.

"What would happen to you if someone under your protection was killed?" Kartahn Zeg laughed. "That was foolish of you. Such a simple act that creates a mortal bond."

"Release them!" Jack said again, his voice more of a growl.

"Swear by your power that you will not oppose me and I will leave you all alive," the oily sound of Kartahn Zeg's voice made me queasy. How could I have listened to him?

"I swear it," Jack growled.

"The words, *Daijheen*!" Zeg demanded. "Say the words!"

"You first! I do not trust you."

As Zeg laughed, his features blurred and his skin took on a shiny, scaly appearance. "Very well. I, Kartahn Zeg swear by my power that if you do not oppose me, I will leave you all alive."

Something happened when he spoke the words and I felt invisible ripples of something wash over me.

Jack glared at him before he spoke. "I, Jakarael Abalaan, do swear by my power that I will not oppose you this day."

I felt the sensation of invisible ripples again as he finished the words.

"Oh, very good!" Zeg could barely restrain his glee.

"I see your true face." Jack glared at him. "I know you."

"It won't help you." Zeg shrugged smugly.

Whatever was holding us up let go and we fell to the floor. Zeg walked across the room to Jack, moving his hands in a strange pattern and speaking in that odd language again. Jack stood unmoving, then he arched back, a scream erupting from his lips as something similar to electricity erupted from him and flowed to Zeg. He looked like he was in intense pain.

"Jack!"

Then whatever was happening stopped and Jack fell to the floor.

"Thank you for the gift, *Daijheen*." Zeg grinned at him with a mock bow. "You were all too easy!" He strode out the door without a backward glance.

I rushed to where Jack was struggling to his hands and knees.

"Jack? Are you alright? What happened?"

"I had no choice." He shook his head. He looked at me and I saw the accusation in his eyes.

# CHAPTER SEVEN

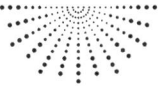

## NORA

"Why would you betray me?"

That stopped me. "I didn't know he was going to do that! I'm sorry, I was wrong!"

Once again, I had screwed something up. Why should I be surprised?

He shook his head as he slowly got to his feet. "It doesn't matter. It is done. And now the necromancer has my power."

"Your power? What do you mean? What just happened?"

"He has stolen my power; the power of a *Daijheen*." He sighed. "He has taken my essence, and now I am no more than you or any mortal. I knew he was hunting me. I should have warned you. The folly is my own. And now we are trapped in this lifeless place."

"What do you mean trapped?"

"We are hundreds of miles from anyplace," he answered. "Without my power, we cannot survive the journey across the waste. The only food or water we have is what I brought just now."

"Is there anyone we can call for help?" Emma asked.

He shook his head. "No."

"Why can't we get across this waste without your power?" I went back to his earlier comment. "Is it really that far?"

"If I could fly over, we could be across it very quickly," he said. "But on foot, we don't have enough water."

"Maybe we can find a way to carry more."

"There is no more water here to carry," he explained. "There has been no water here since the devastation occurred."

"Then staying won't be any better than going," I pointed out. "We'll run out of water either way." We needed more options. There had to be something. Maybe with magic? "I can use magic. Maybe we can do something with that."

"What can you do?" He looked up at me.

"I don't really know," I admitted. "I only just found out I could use magic a few days ago."

He just looked at me.

"What? We should at least try something." He was starting to piss me off. "I'm not just going to give up."

He shrugged dismissively. "Then don't give up."

"I thought you didn't want to look weak?" I snapped at him. "How do you think it looks when you give up?"

"And I thought you said it was weak to care what others thought?" He didn't even glance at me as he spoke.

I knew Emma and I couldn't make it alone; we didn't know the way. Even if we made it across, We didn't speak the language. We needed him. But how could I get him out of this apathy he seemed to have sunken into?

"Look," I told him. "Let's have some dinner. Then we'll get a good night's sleep and figure out what to do in the morning."

He gave a noncommittal grunt and didn't bother to look at me. I didn't want to think about the part I had played in his condition, so I focused on my hunger.

One at a time, I went to the two large bags Jack had dropped after coming into the room and brought them to the table. They were both pretty heavy. There was a lot of food and as soon as I opened the first bag, I was almost overwhelmed by the aromas.

It's a good thing I wasn't a vegetarian. Not that there wasn't any fruit, but it was mostly meat. It was all cooked and some of it was still warm.

Emma took one look, and she was ready to dig in. She must have been even more starving than I was.

There were several roasted birds; I'd guess they were small chickens, but I didn't know if they had chickens here. There was also a big haunch of some red meat. There were several containers of liquid, like leather bags. I checked them, and they all seemed to be alcoholic.

"I thought you said you brought water?"

He just shrugged. "Close enough."

"Is it juice?" Emma asked.

"Juice for adults," I told her. "You're too young."

"But I'm thirsty," she pouted. "I've had wine before. Is it wine?"

I scowled at her. She would need some liquid. Didn't alcohol dehydrate you? What if it was the only thing available to drink?

"Fine," I said. "Just don't have too much."

Everything was tossed into a couple of burlap sacks, which didn't strike me as particularly sanitary, but I was too hungry to care. There were also some blankets and a few other items Jack had evidently assumed would be helpful. I found a dark green cloak and put it on. Evenings could get a bit chilly, and the cloak would help me to stay warm, though it was a bit big for me.

I followed Emma's example and started digging into one of the roast chickens with my bare hands. It had been rolled in herbs I wasn't familiar with, and the taste was incredible, though it was also very spicy. I washed it down with gulps of whatever kind of wine was in one of the leather bags.

"Aren't you going to eat?" I asked him.

His eyes rested on the chicken in front of me before he sighed and got to his feet. He pulled out a chicken for himself and sat down across from me at the table.

"Where did you get all this food?" Emma asked him.

"There was a large camp to the north." He still sounded depressed, but at least he was talking. "They seemed to have plenty."

"It's a lot of food. Was it expensive?" I didn't even know what they did here. Did they have some form of money? Did they use a barter system?

"I do not understand this concept."

"Expensive? You know, like the value."

"Food is needed for survival." He furrowed his brow. "Survival is high value, yes? This is expensive?"

"No." I shook my head and washed down another bite. "Expensive is about what you have to give or pay for something. Was it a lot?"

He still didn't look like he knew what I was talking about.

"Jack, you did give them something in exchange for all this, didn't you? You didn't just take it?"

"You wanted food. I obtained food."

I looked from the food in front of me and back to Jack. "You didn't kill anyone did you?"

Emma paused and looked at her food in horror.

"As you indicated previously, answering a challenge without killing is much more difficult. A much higher level of skill is required. Yet I succeeded."

"You stole this food."

"Possession was contested. I won."

"No! That's not—" I found myself fumbling for words. "How can you watch people for three generations and still not understand? They weren't... contesting possession. They *owned* this stuff. They put in the work to raise or gather and cook it, and you walked in and just took it away. You can't do things like that."

"Again, you say I cannot do what I have done. Your thought process is flawed."

"It means you're not *supposed* to do it," I explained. "It means it's not acceptable. And in this case, it means you owe a debt to these people! If you could fly, we'd be going back there right now. I swear, you're like a child raised by... mushrooms!"

"Mushrooms?"

"I was going to say wolves, but that would be an insult to wolves."

His eyes narrowed at me, but before he could say anything, several people were rushing in through the front door. They looked similar to the people who had put me in that cell. They wore armor and had sharp weapons pointed at us.

Jack lurched up from the table and charged the nearest one. He swung his arm and struck the side of the man's head. His mouth dropped open in shock and pain when his hand rebounded from the man's helmet.

"*Gyajhan*!" the man snarled at him. He swung the butt end of his spear into Jack's jaw and Jack collapsed unconscious on the ground. All eyes turned to me.

I held my hands up, trying to appear as un-threatening as possible. "I don't suppose any of you speak English?"

The man who had knocked Jack out stepped toward me. "*Gyajhan*!"

"No!" In a panic, I tried to push back from the table and the chair fell over, tripping me, and I scrambled to move away from the man coming toward me. Emma had ducked under the table.

"Kerbas! *Bor*!" another voice called out and the man stopped advancing toward me. "Surrender yourself, thief, and this will be less painful for you."

"I'm not a thief!" I told him. "But I surrender!"

"We shall see what you are," he answered. Then he spoke to the others in a language I didn't understand, giving them some sort of instruction.

Two of them grabbed hold of Jack and started dragging him out of the room. Others loaded the food back into the sacks. The man near me pulled out a leather strap and pointed to my hands. I'd seen enough movies to guess this was their form of handcuffs and I let him tie my hands together. He motioned to

Emma, and she crawled out from under the table and let him tie her hands as well.

Arrested. Again.

But at least this time they had someone we could talk with. That was an improvement over last time. Plus, if these guys had followed Jack so easily, maybe they'd be able to get us out of this place. How had they done that? Did they sprout wings, too?

The man led us outside to where about a dozen others waited. These people all seemed very capable. And deadly. Then I saw something else that made me pull up short, causing our captor to turn and look at me.

"Wow!" Emma was clearly more excited about what we were seeing than I was.

There was a huge bird. A bunch of them. They looked like a bird from the front, anyway. The head was definitely like a bird, some sort of raptor, like a hawk or an eagle. And they had immense wings and talons that looked like they could tear a person in two with one swipe. But behind the wings was the body and back legs of an animal. And a tail. It looked like the body of a huge lion, but with the head and wings and claws of a giant bird in front.

I'd heard of something like this from stories. It was a griffin. And they had saddles on them. One of them was looking at me like it thought I might make a good snack. Then it opened its beak, and I heard a coughing sound that might be a laugh.

They were tying Jack's unconscious body over the hindquarters of one of the griffins. Before I knew what was happening, the man that was leading us grabbed me with both hands and threw me bodily through the air to land behind the saddle of the griffin that was watching me and then lashed me in place. He was much stronger than I would have given him credit for, especially given his height. Then he lashed Emma next to me and climbed into the saddle in front of us. I felt the muscles of the griffin bunch and we were launched into the air.

It was dark out, but the sky was clear, and a moon showed

overhead. It wasn't like the normal moon, the one orbiting Earth I mean. But it was big and bright, I could make out shadows on the ground below. Still, I thought it was a bit dark to try to navigate anywhere.

I don't know how long we flew. I was used to having my cell phone with me to check the time, and I was regretting not owning a watch. It had to be more than an hour, though. At least I'd been able to eat something before they showed up.

I expected some kind of town or city, but we landed in a large camp. There were no permanent buildings, but there were a lot of very sturdy looking tents. I could see torches burning around the camp for lighting. Our guard, I guess that's what he was, pulled us off the griffin and led us to a tent. He removed the leather strap from our wrists. I wanted to ask questions, but since the guy didn't speak English, there wasn't any point. He pointed inside, and I nodded, and we went in.

The tent flap closed behind me and we were immersed in darkness. I turned around and led Emma right back out of the tent. No way were we just going to sit in the dark in some tent. He had started to walk away and turned sharply at my reappearance. His eyes narrowed and he pointed back at the tent. I shook my head, pointed to the tent and then to my eyes. Then I folded my arms across my chest.

There was a laugh from nearby and I turned my head and saw the man who had spoken English to me earlier. His beard was down to his chest, and he appeared to be somewhat older than the other one. He was looking at my guard.

"Kerbas, *jha hisé dzara ri debaru nya valod.*"

"*Va jhari chazan.*" The man scowled back.

"What are you saying?" I asked the older one.

"I was telling Kerbas here that you might be afraid of the dark," he grinned at me, "but he doesn't think that's his problem."

"What language is that? Who are you? Who are these people?"

"So many questions," he laughed. "We mostly use the common tongue; you should learn it. I am Tavarnin and we are the *Wyl-Dun*."

"*Suri chazan gru*," Kerbas spoke to him. "*Su gorimal so dza*." Then he turned and stormed away.

"He seems awfully cheerful," I said. "What's his problem?"

"Well." Tavarnin shrugged. "It *was* his brother's wedding feast that you and your friend raided earlier."

"I didn't raid anything!" I bit my tongue before I said anything else. It wasn't the time, and I needed to keep a cool head. Jack had screwed up, and he wasn't going to be capable of getting us out of trouble. And I didn't have Mira's natural charm or calming influence. Well, she calmed me, at least. I can't speak for others.

"There's been a misunderstanding," I told him in a more rational voice. "I'm sure we can resolve everything if we can have a conversation with the right people."

"Oh, it will be resolved all right." There was a coldness behind his apparent joviality. "We generally resolve thieves by cutting off their hands and leaving them in the Scourge."

"The Scourge?" I asked him. Then the rest of what he'd said sunk in. Cutting off their hands?

"The ruins where we found you are at the heart of it."

We were distracted as the griffin carrying Jack landed. Then someone was helping him down. He was conscious but seemed shaky.

"Now he's here," Tavarnin said gruffly. "We can get to it. This way."

We went where he pointed, and a couple of the others were guiding Jack. Our destination looked to be a large tent at the center of the camp. As we approached, one of the guards outside the entrance glanced at us and ducked inside. He was back outside the tent when we got there and nodded us in.

Several people, *Wyl-Dunn*, as I assumed from what Tavarnin had said, were inside the tent. One man wore a circlet on his head and glanced over at us with a bored expression. He picked up a goblet from a table and sat in one of a pair of ornate chairs that rested on a slightly raised section of the floor. He asked Tavarnin something, but I assumed it was more of that common tongue language. I didn't understand what he said, but Tavarnin nodded in reply.

"On your knees before the king and queen," Tavarnin said, and he pushed us down roughly.

Jack had been brought in next to me and was forced onto his knees as well. He still didn't look like he was totally aware of his surroundings.

A woman was talking to me. She also had a circlet around her head. I assumed this was the queen.

"I'm sorry," I answered. "I don't understand you."

She raised an eyebrow at me and then went to a small chest at the side. She rummaged around for a moment and held up a ring to the king. He nodded, the bored expression still showing. She tossed it to him. He caught it out of the air and slipped it onto a finger. She found a second ring and placed it on her own finger. Then she glanced at Tavarnin expectantly.

"She speaks in this way," he told her.

She nodded and turned to me. "What is your name, thief?"

I paused to remind myself to stay calm. "I am Leanora Leland," I told her. "Most people call me Nora. This is Emma. A… friend." Somehow, those rings must make them able to communicate with me in English. "And I understand how things must look, but we are not thieves."

"Were you not discovered with food purloined from the wedding feast of Niall and Arrosa?" she asked me. "And not simply with it, but eating it?"

"We were brought food to eat," I answered, trying to sound as cool and formal as she was. "We were not present when it was acquired."

"But you knew it was stolen."

I shook my head. "Not until later."

"You at least knew that your companion was a thief, did you not?"

"No, I—" I glanced at Jack. His eyes still weren't focusing well. "He's not really a thief either. He doesn't understand how things work. I tried to explain it to him when I found out—"

"Then you did know it was stolen?"

"Not at first!" Calm down. "Not at first." I took a breath. "We were in the ruins, and I told him I would need food and water. He told me he would get some and to wait for him. He came a few hours later with food. I only found out while we were eating that he hadn't paid for the food. I told him he had a debt for taking it. He didn't understand. He's not from this world. I guess his people do things differently."

"It matters not what they do where he is from;" she arched her eyebrow at me. "It matters what he does when he is here. What type of creature is he?"

"He's a *Daijheen*, whatever that is."

She laughed. "You can't lie to me, girl. If he were a *Daijheen* we could not have taken him so easily."

"I'm not lying!" It was really hard to stay calm with all of these accusations flying at me. "Another man came. He said his name was Kartahn Zeg. He tricked me. He stole Jack's power. I don't really know what that means, but that's probably why."

The queen glanced at the king, who had looked up with a little more interest when I mentioned Kartahn Zeg. The queen went to where Jack knelt and looked into his eyes. I could tell Jack was trying to focus and failing. Then she went and sat in the chair next to the king's.

"Kartahn Zeg is known to us," she said. "If he has acquired the power of a *Daijheen*, this is troubling, but that discussion is for another time. I accept your explanation of what has occurred." She glanced at the king before continuing. "It is my judgment that you two are innocent of the crime that was committed earlier this day, and you were in no way party to it.

The one you call Jack is guilty. He shall be clipped and left in The Scourge."

"Clipped?" The term confused me.

The two men on either side of Jack shifted position. One held him in place and the other drew a sword and pulled Jack's arm straight by the hand.

"No! Wait! He didn't mean it! He's like an infant! He didn't understand! He won't do it again, I promise!"

The queen made a halting motion with one hand and the man with the sword froze.

"You will take him as your burden?" she asked me. "You will teach this… infant how to behave in a society with rules?"

"Yes! I'll do it!"

She nodded. "Very well. We shall just clip one side and leave him to you. He will be your responsibility. This is the judgment of King Edrigun and Queen Iratzé."

The sword flashed and Jack's right arm was severed mid-forearm. He was screaming and then his scream cut off as he passed out.

# CHAPTER EIGHT

## MIRA

*T*he next two days were frustratingly slow. Tony called the police department first thing to let them know I wasn't missing, and they told him they'd send someone around to take a statement.

There were still a few days of school left, but Jill called in and let them know I wouldn't be coming. Finals were all finished, so it wasn't a problem. The last week of the school year was mostly coasting, anyway. I was supposed to go back for my junior year in September, but we'd cross that bridge when we got to it. Holding an illusion of myself at a younger age wasn't something I wanted to try for more than a couple of hours at a time, let alone a whole school year, and somehow, I didn't think I'd fit in without it.

Mostly I was spending time with Grace and Katya at their shop. I still needed to take my driver's test. I figured I could hold the illusion spell long enough for that, so I needed to get it scheduled soon and get my license. Meanwhile, I couldn't even drive Nora's scooter, so I called a Hitch each morning to get to the shop. It was cheaper than a regular taxi service, but you never knew what you were going to get.

On the second morning, I brought my mother's chest with

me. I hoped to spend some time going through the contents to see what I could find out about my parents. When I got there, I bumped into Shelby as she was coming out of the shop. I was surprised to see her there.

"Shel—" I caught myself before I said her name. "Shalom," I said instead, pretending that was what I had intended to say all along.

She looked at me with a confused expression. "Do I know you? You look familiar."

"I don't think so." I pretended to study her face. "But I come here sometimes. Maybe you saw me here before."

Her eyes narrowed with suspicion. "What's your name?"

"Carmen," I blurted. "Carmen Cansino. And you?"

"I'm Shelby," she said, her expression unchanging. Before she could say anything else, I moved past her.

"Well, have a good morning, Shelby!" I smiled at her. "It was nice to meet you!" Then I was inside, and I walked straight to the back.

Katya was behind the counter and smiled as I approached.

"What was she doing here?" I asked.

"She was looking for some candles and a few other things, why?"

"I know her from school."

"Do you think she recognized you?"

I shook my head. "I don't think so. She just surprised me, that's all."

"Well, it seems she has an interest in witchcraft."

"Really?" I looked at her. "Why do you say that?"

"From the things she bought. They weren't random."

The office in the back was part workshop, separate from the large stockroom. I went through to where Grace sat at her large desk. Her laptop had been shunted to the side and she had several thick books spread out in front of her. She glanced up when I came in and then leaned back in her chair as I plopped down into the one across from her after putting the box on a side table.

"Still nothing," she said. "Not even a clue."

"Good morning to you, too." I gave her a cheeky grin.

She rolled her eyes at me. "Yes, yes. Good morning. Some of us have been up for a while."

"Did you have your coffee yet?"

She shook her head. "I didn't want to risk spilling on the books. I still have not found anything that will help to find your sister. Not if she is on another world."

We had tried a simple location spell the previous day but came up empty. The spell should have given us at least a direction if she was anywhere on the planet, alive or dead.

"I thought of another option," I told her. "If we can find the man who tried to take me, maybe he knows something about where she might be. Plus, I need to find out why he was after me in the first place."

"It's risky," she answered. "We don't know how powerful he is."

"True." I nodded. "But I took on Dimétrian."

"With help, as I recall from your story."

That was true. Laila had given me an extra boost of power.

"Even so," I told her, "he's probably not done with whatever he was up to. The longer we wait, the more prepared he'll be. Maybe we can tempt him to come out from wherever he's hiding. Otherwise, he might end up catching me by surprise."

"Risky," she said again. "But so is doing nothing. What do you propose?"

I pulled the white-handled dagger out from inside my jacket and set it on the desk.

"Bait," I said. "Right now, this is shielded, but if I take that off, this thing shines like a magical beacon. Anyone looking will sense it. That had to be how he found me last time."

"You said something about this before."

"Yes." I nodded. "And the more I think about it, the better it sounds."

"You don't think it's too obvious? That he might suspect something?"

I leaned forward onto the desk. "I was worried about that, too. But if we only give him glimpses, like we're trying to hide it and not doing so well, it might entice him to move faster, before he's ready."

She cocked an eyebrow at me. "Has playing the tease always come so naturally to you?"

It took me a moment before I realized what she meant, and I felt my face heat up. "No! That's not what I meant!"

"Isn't it?" She laughed.

"Whatever." This was not a subject I felt comfortable with. "Do you think it will work or not?"

"The plan holds some promise," she nodded with a smirk.

"When do you want to start?" I asked with a grin and picked up the dagger.

"You can start by putting that back down," a voice spoke firmly from behind me.

I jumped up from the chair and spun around to see a man standing in the doorway next to Katya. Katya's eyes were large, and I could see she was scared. I connected to the magic, but he spoke again before I could do anything.

"I wouldn't try that if I were you," he said.

He made a quick motion, and something tightened around my arms and pulled me back into my chair, unable to move my arms or legs. I turned my head to look and Grace seemed to be in the same condition. I looked back at the man as he walked Katya to another chair and sat her down.

"Now then." He pulled a chair to the corner and sat where he could see all of us, crossing one leg over the other. "You've changed a bit since the last time I saw you, but you can't hide from me. Time for some questions."

Was this the same man who tried to grab me before? The one who was responsible for sending me to Daoine?

"You don't look the same either." If this was the same man, he'd been wearing some kind of robes before. Now, he was dressed in a gray business suit.

His eyes traveled from one of us to the next, then settled on the dagger that was on the desk. Then he saw the bourbon and poured himself a glass. Resuming his seat, he took a mouthful of the amber liquid. After a moment, he swallowed it.

"Very nice." He nodded. "Where were we?"

"You were going to give us some answers!" I glared at him.

"Ah, no." He smiled. "You have that backwards. You're going to answer some questions for me, and you'd better hope I like your answers. Though I suppose there's not much chance of that. But I warn you; do not lie to me." He reached over and picked up the dagger. "What did you do to the owner of this knife?"

The question made no sense. "It's mine," I told him. "I'm the owner."

"Possession of something does not make you the rightful owner." His eyes narrowed at me. "How did you get it?"

"That's none of your business!"

"Oh, but it is." The invisible binding started to squeeze tighter, and I could barely take a breath. "It is very much my business. I really need you to answer my question."

"What's the big deal?" I asked, gasping for breath. "I got it from my mother!"

"Is that so?" He cocked his head to the side. "And where can I find your mother? Is she at home?"

"You can't."

"Tell me!" The binding got even tighter.

"She's dead!" I really hated it, but I forced the words out through my clenched teeth. "My parents died years ago. So, you're out of luck!"

"You think I'm stupid? I've seen your parents. I've been watching your house."

The bindings stopped squeezing so tightly.

"I know how to find her," he said.

"You're not as smart as you think!" I snapped. "Jill isn't my real mother. Not biologically."

His expression changed and he stepped forward to study my face carefully. Meanwhile, I was trying to get a sense for this binding he had on me. I was hoping to get hold of the end so I could unravel it, but it was somehow slippery. Then he nodded and the binding fell away completely. He started to say something, but I didn't wait. I lunged from the chair, landing a palm strike up under his chin with all the force of my body behind it. His head snapped back, and he collapsed unconscious on the floor.

Grace jumped up from her own chair. "Nicely done!"

The three of us worked together to lift him into a chair. Then I drew in flows of magic to form a binding to hold *him* in place. Two could play at that game. Then I tied off the end so he wouldn't be able to unravel it.

"He's secure." I nodded to Grace and Katya.

"You really are a force to be reckoned with, aren't you?" Grace looked at me appraisingly. "I know you told us you'd had some training, but you knocked him out with one blow! Impressive."

I didn't really think about it in those terms. My training in Su Lariano with the *Ulané Jhinura* had been really good. But then the experience when I'd basically been Dimétrian's personal gladiator had taken things to a new level, and *that* was something I didn't care to dwell on.

There was a groan from our captive, and he blinked and looked around. He started to move and discovered that he couldn't.

"Somehow," he said to himself, "I don't think this part is going to make it into the report."

I didn't know or care what he was mumbling about. "Now you're going to answer some questions from me," I told him. "Let's start with who are you and why are you after me?"

"Sure." He smiled. "Agent Alex Stone of the Daruidai. And I'm working a cold case on a couple of missing agents."

"Mira." Grace's voice held a note I hadn't heard before. "You need to let him go. Right now!"

"What?" I looked at her. "No! I need more answers!" I turned back to him. "Where's my sister? Where's Nora?"

"Your sister? Oh, you mean the girl who tried to stab me the last time we met?"

"Where is she?"

"Last time I saw her, she was on Danu," he said. "She shattered my power source and it split that portal into a kaleidoscope of destinations. We ended up in the forest on Danu. I had the devil's time getting back."

"What's Danu?" It sounded familiar. "Isn't that where the *Ashae* came from? You left her there?"

"She wasn't exactly friendly." He cocked his head. "*Ashae*? How do you know of them? We haven't had contact with them for centuries."

"That's where your portal sent me!" I told him. "I was there for two years!"

"Mira!" Grace was more insistent. "Release him! He is Daruidai!"

"What's that?" I asked. "Some kind of a druid?"

"Not exactly," Alex answered. "Druids came much later."

"Mira!" Grace cut in.

"Fine!" I undid the knot and his binding unraveled.

"Much better." He rubbed his jaw. "You pack a wallop."

I looked at Grace. "Care to explain?"

"I've only heard whispers," she said. "They've been confused with other orders in history, like the Knights of Malta, Knights Templar. Even the Masons. Or fictionally, like the Talamasca. But none of those were the real deal. Daruidai are like police for the magic world. But not just the police. They are also judge, jury and executioner."

"You make it sound a lot worse than it is," Alex spoke dismissively. "But we digress. This has all been an unfortunate misunderstanding." He looked at Grace and pointed to the bourbon. "Do you mind?"

She nodded. "Though it's a bit early in the day."

"Never." He poured himself another glass, glancing at me. "Your natural parents were Sofia and Jorge, yes?"

I nodded. Jill and Tony had always been open with me about my birth parents, what little was known of them.

"They were Daruidai, like me." He took a sip of his bourbon. "They went missing about seventeen years ago. If I was to make a guess, I'd say that's about the time your mother was pregnant. Something they never mentioned to me."

"You knew my parents?"

"Quite well." He nodded. "Or so I thought."

"What happened to them?"

"That's what I'd like to find out. Those daggers showing up is the first clue I've had in a long time."

"Wait." I held up my hands. "This is all too much."

"Why do you look so much older than you did a few days ago?" he asked. "You said you were with the *Ashae* for two years—"

"No." I shook my head. "I was with the *Ulané Jhinura*, but—" I shook my head again. "One thing at a time. We need to get Nora. We have to make sure she's safe. Then we can talk about all this other stuff."

He sat there for a moment, considering. "Fair enough. But I only know where she *was*. I couldn't say for certain where she is now."

"And you can get us there?"

"Us?" He looked surprised. "No. There is no us. Give me a few days to look into it and I should be able to have her back in no time."

"A few days? I know first-hand what it can be like on a strange world. A few days could mean the difference between life and death. A few days isn't good enough, Stone."

"All I have is a starting point," he told me. "Tracking her down from there could take some time."

"Then I guess we'd better get started."

"You're not going," he insisted. "This is no place for a civilian."

"Are you talking about the one who took you down a few minutes ago?"

"Well," he hedged. "That was—"

"That was a small example of some intensive training and experience I've had over the last two years," I told him. "I've been through more than you can imagine. And if you think for one second I'm not coming with you to find Nora you are sadly mistaken. Am I making myself clear?"

He looked over at Grace. "Can you talk some sense into her?"

Grace shook her head. "I've heard her story. You are better off *with* her than arguing with her."

He looked skeptical. "She hasn't had the training for something like this. She'd probably just be a liability. If things get complicated…"

"She literally saved an entire world," Grace told him. "Can you say the same thing?"

I glanced at her and then back to him. "I had some help." I shrugged. "So, what's the plan?"

He raised an eyebrow at me. "Fine. Don't say I didn't warn you. The Danu realm doesn't allow free travel. They have alarms in case someone goes there without authorization."

"So, what happened when you and Nora went there last time?" I asked. "There was no authorization for that, right?"

"Correct." He nodded. "That was an accident. And that's why I left before the *Ande Dannu* showed up."

"*Ande Dannu*?"

"Most people just call them Fae."

"Fae?" I looked at him. "As in *Loiala Fé*?"

He shrugged. "It's possible there's a connection to the term. In this realm they are divided into the Summer and Winter Courts. Known as Seelie and Unseelie Fae, respectively. And then there's the *Wyl-Dunn*, Wild Fae, but they're nomadic and we don't talk to them much. Well, with any of them really. They aren't very friendly with humans. And they're pretty strict about illegal border crossings."

"And you left Nora there to be arrested or whatever?"

"To be fair, she had just tried to stab me," he pointed out. "If she hadn't struck my pendant by mistake, I would probably be dead."

"If you'd tried talking to us instead of just trying to drag me off maybe she wouldn't have tried to stab you."

He pursed his lips. "Water under the bridge. Hindsight and all that. We will need to go in through one of the transfer gates they have set up. It's sort of like going through immigration at the airport, or a border crossing. We can go there and make inquiries. Hopefully, she hasn't gotten into too much trouble in the meantime."

"That doesn't sound so complicated."

"It shouldn't be," he admitted. "But they tend to take offense very easily. Best to let me do the talking."

"Fine." I nodded. "When do we leave?"

"I'll need to take care of a few things first." He checked his watch. "How about we meet back here at two this afternoon?"

I didn't like the delay, but I nodded. He left to take care of whatever it was he needed to handle, leaving me feeling restless with nothing to do.

# CHAPTER NINE

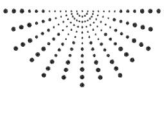

## MIRA

*T*here was a small clear space in the stockroom. I pushed some boxes and a few pieces of antique furniture to the side and made the space larger. I pulled my *renki* out of my backpack and changed. Then I ran through my unarmed forms to get loosened up. It also gave me something to focus on. It was a cramped space, but I made do. It was my first workout since I got back, and it felt good to stretch my muscles.

There wasn't enough space to go through the forms with my staff, but I was able to work with my daggers. While I didn't want to inflict serious injury, history had shown me that it was best to be ready for any situation. Back on Daoine, I had started to develop my own forms for going back and forth between open-hand combat and knife-work. I'd gotten fairly proficient at having a blade suddenly appear in one or both of my hands, and just as quickly disappear back into its sheath.

It wasn't quite as smooth as I wanted it to be. Yet. But I was getting there.

"Nice moves." Alex was standing in the door from the front of the shop.

I'm sure he meant it as a compliment, but I didn't care. I wasn't looking for status or approval. I knew how good I was.

And I knew how good I wasn't. I also knew that when push came to shove, I could use magic to move faster and not many would be able to defend against that.

"Ready to go?" I asked him.

"Have you ever had to use them against a real opponent?"

"Yes," I replied flatly.

He waited, expecting me to elaborate. When I didn't, he shrugged and went on.

"Yes, I'm ready." He pointed to my sweaty *renki*. "Do you want to change first?"

I nodded and went into the restroom. After a quick sponge-bath with a washcloth to clean off the sweat, I changed back to my regular clothes. I did keep the belt with the daggers strapped on, though.

"I'm ready," I said as I stepped back into the room. Then my cell phone went off. It surprised me; I'd been without one for two years. I looked at the screen. It was Jill.

"Hello?"

"Hi honey, I wanted to let you know that I just got a call from Ms. Leon, the social worker. I told her you were at the shop, and she said she was going to swing by there and talk to you."

"What for?" I hardly ever had to talk with her.

"Well, you did go missing for a few days. She was probably notified."

"Right."

"Anyway, I don't think her office is very far from you. So be ready."

"She's coming today?" I shook my head. "I'm not going to be here!"

"Mira, I know you've been taking care of yourself for two years, but now that you're back, you have to remember how things work here. You need to talk with her."

"Right." I sighed. "I'll be here." After I got off with Jill, I turned to Stone. "You're going to have to go without me."

"No problem." He didn't try to hide how happy he was

about the news. "I'll come back by and let you know what I find out."

He left through the front, and I went and sat down in the office. I'd worked out the story with Jill and Tony, so I should be fine talking to Ms. Leon. I ran through the details in my head one more time. Then I stood up, thinking I should probably change into something else before she got here. Grace was standing in the door.

"Mira, there's someone here to see you." Her voice was neutral, and I suspected she was ready in case this person turned out to be an enemy. "She said her name is Luciana Leon."

"Sorry," I said. "I should have told you someone was coming. Jill just told me a few minutes ago."

"Hello, Mira." A dark-haired woman stepped past Grace and into the office. "It seems like such a long time since I've seen you." She looked me up and down. Then she turned to Grace. "Do you mind if we use the office for a private talk? We shouldn't be very long. I've already cleared it with Mrs. Ramirez."

Grace glanced at me before answering. "Certainly. Let me know if you need anything." Grace glanced at me again like she was trying to tell me something, but I didn't know what it was. Then she left us alone.

"Now then." Luciana Leon closed the door and went to sit in one of the chairs. She was in her forties but looked younger. She also looked like she might be one of those female body-builders, but not the really bulky kind. She indicated one of the other chairs. "Why don't you have a seat?" She spoke with only the slightest accent. She probably could have carried the conversation out just as well in Spanish, if not better.

"Hi, Ms. Leon." I sat down. "I'm sorry to have been such a bother. Everything is really okay."

"Call me Luciana," she said. "Or better yet; Luci. You had Mr. and Mrs. Ramirez very worried," she looked at me seriously. "What happened?"

"Oh, it was just a silly argument with Nora, and I got mad and—"

"Yes, yes," she interrupted. "I've heard the story. I want to know what really happened."

Her eyes looked pointedly at the daggers in my belt.

"Oh, this?" I tried to think fast. "It's part of a costume. I know it's way early for Halloween, but I like to plan ahead."

"Costume," she repeated. "And I suppose part of that costume is to make you look older."

I gaped. The illusion spell! I'd forgotten it!

"It seems your past is catching up with you," she was shaking her head. "I had hoped for a couple more years."

I froze as her words sunk in. "What are you talking about?"

"Where is Leanora?" she asked.

"Don't ignore my question!" I lurched to my feet, one hand on the hilt of a dagger.

"I'm not your enemy, girl." Her voice was calm. "Sit down."

I studied her for a moment before sitting back in the chair. But my right hand still rested on top of the black hilt.

"Your parents came to me nearly seventeen years ago," she told me.

"Came to you? Are you Daruidai?"

She shook her head. "I was raised in it. But I have not been active with them for a very long time."

"Why did they come to you?"

"They were hiding. They were being hunted and they wanted to keep you safe. Your mother was barely showing at the time. I have some connections. I was able to give them new identities and it worked for several years."

"Then... I don't even know their real names?"

"Oh, when they died, they got their true identities back. I thought that if it was known that they were dead, the hunters would stop." She cocked her head. "And they did. At least, they did for a while. Something changed. What happened? And where did you get those knives?"

"They were in the bottom of the chest." I shrugged. "The one with my mom's things. There was a hidden compartment."

"Ah," she nodded. "I had told Mrs. Ramirez to give it to you when you turned eighteen. Opening that box must have triggered something." She saw the surprise on my face. "Where do you think she got it? That sort of thing isn't normally passed on like that through the system. I promised your parents that I would make sure you were okay if anything ever happened to them. I thought the Ramirez family would be good for you. Was I wrong?"

"Wrong? No! They've been wonderful!" I thought about what she'd said. "I suppose I should thank you. I couldn't have asked for better parents."

"I am glad to hear it," she nodded. "So, when Leanora's file came across my desk—"

"Nora," I corrected her. "She doesn't like to be called Leanora."

"When Nora's file came across my desk, I asked Mr. and Mrs. Ramirez if they would take her in as well, as a favor to me."

"Why?"

"Putting all my eggs in one basket, I suppose."

"That's usually a bad idea," I pointed out and she laughed.

"True, but it made it easier to keep track of you both."

"I still don't get it. Why did you want to keep track of both of us?"

"Leanora— Nora is not... She is not fully human." She looked at me, putting a hand on my arm. "I don't know what you have discovered about your past so that might sound crazy to—"

"In three days, I spent two years on another world and aged even more," I interrupted her. "I've been through— Assume I know a lot."

She sat back in her chair, looking me over again. "Very well. There were some red flags about Nora's case. When I spoke with her I was able to confirm it. Nora is only partly human. I wasn't able to determine what all she was, but I thought that with your family history… if you were together, you might be able to support each other if anything ever came of it."

"You mean like her spontaneously being able to use magic?"

She looked at me sharply. "That would qualify. Mira, where is Nora?"

"I think she's on Danu," I told her. "Alex Stone has gone to check and see if he can bring her back."

"Alex Stone?"

"He's a Daruidai."

"They are involved already? That was fast. If Nora is on Danu, they should be able to bring her back." She looked at me. "Mostly, the Daruidai serve the common good, but there are internal politics… factions that have their own agenda. Do not trust them too fully."

"Is Stone in one of these factions you're talking about?"

"I don't know," she shook her head. "I don't know him, but you can be sure he will follow orders. That's what they do. Mira, there's a reason I am no longer with them. And there's a reason your parents didn't go to them when they were being hunted. Some among them are not what they seem."

"That's reassuring."

"These two," she dipped her head toward the front of the shop. "Grace and Katya. Witches?"

I nodded.

"They seem like good people."

"They are," I told her. "You probably heard; the adoption is finally going through. Someone had been fighting it."

She nodded.

"Why would someone fight it?"

"I don't know." Her eyes went to the floor in thought. Then she looked back up at me. "Meanwhile, the most important thing," she said, standing up, "is to have people around you that you can trust. That you can rely on." She pulled out a business card and scribbled some numbers on the back before handing it to me. "This is my cell number. Don't put it in your phone. Memorize it and then throw this card away. Call me if you need anything."

"You're leaving? But I have a lot of questions."

"They will keep for now. You'll hear from me soon." She paused on her way out. "Maybe best for now not to mention my name to the Daruidai. Well… unless they start giving you trouble. I still have a reputation as an inquisitor. It's kind of like a detective and a lawyer in one."

"Why would they give me trouble?"

She shrugged. "No reason. They probably won't."

After she left, I called Jill to let her know how it went and that she could be more open with Ms. Leon. Luci.

"Oh, good!" I could hear the relief in her voice. "Well, I made some chicken enchiladas for dinner. They'll be ready when you get home."

That set my mouth watering. At the same time, if Jill was cooking, she was probably stressed.

"I might be late, but I have a line on Nora," I told her. "Someone is checking it out for me. I'll explain more tonight."

"And you're sure you're alright? I know you've been taking care of yourself, but we are here for you if you need anything."

"I know you are, mom. And you have no idea how much that means to me."

"We might not be able to do magic, but we can still help."

I laughed. "I don't need you to do magic, mom. I just need you guys to keep being who you are."

Twenty minutes later, a voice spoke from the door and broke into my thoughts.

"You're brooding."

"Hi Grace. No, I'm not brooding. I'm just thinking about everything that I've found out since coming back." I told her what I'd learned from Luci.

"That's quite a lot," she nodded. "Especially with everything Alex Stone told you."

"But there are still so many questions." I frowned. "It's like every answer turns into two more questions."

"And there's the brooding," she smirked.

"Yeah, yeah." I let out a deep breath. "I think it's time I really looked at everything in that trunk." I tipped my head to where it still sat on the side table. "There has to be a clue or two in there."

I walked over to the chest and opened it. Grace stood next to me and ran her hands over the markings on the inside.

"These form a powerful warding spell," she said. "It would definitely hide anything inside the box."

"The daggers were under a false bottom," I told her.

I removed enough of the contents that I could raise the edge of the bottom to show her what was underneath. There were two empty sockets where I'd removed the daggers. The third was slightly larger and occupied. This was the one I hadn't been able to pull out so easily.

"Can you hold this up?" I asked her. "I want to see if I can get that out."

With her holding up the edge of the false bottom, I tried to get hold of the last object. It was a bit awkward, but I managed to grasp it well enough to pull it up. It was much heavier than the daggers had been. As more of it became visible, I could understand why. The part I was pulling up was the pommel of a larger grip than what the daggers had. Once more was visible, I could get a better hold of it, and it became much easier. It kept coming. It was a two-handed sword in a sheath.

"This is different from the daggers," Grace said once we had it laid out on the desk to examine it. "There are some similarities to the metalwork of the sheath, enough to suggest a similar origin, but they were not made as a set."

The sword had a two-handed grip, wrapped in dark-brown, woven leather. There was an engraved metal separator in the middle, dividing the top and bottom portions of the grip. The crosspiece arms were slightly scalloped, and also had engravings. The pommel was rounded and would fit nicely in the palm of one hand when using it to leverage a faster swing.

I picked it up and drew it from the sheath. It was double-edged, as would be expected in a two-handed sword. The first third of the blade from the hilt had more engravings, which gave way to what was called a Fuller groove. This was used to try to keep the blade from becoming too heavy and didn't extend into the last several inches of the blade; making it too thin there would weaken it and you would risk shattering the blade on impact.

I took a two-handed hold and went into a fighting stance. The balance was perfect. Looking at the sword with my *Ralahin*-enhanced vision, it became so bright it was hard to look at.

"There are some very strong and complex spells imbued in this thing," I told her. "I don't know what they do. But this doesn't give us any answers. It's just another random puzzle-piece." I re-sheathed the sword and leaned it in the corner of the room out of the way.

I felt frustrated. I didn't need more questions; I needed to start getting some real answers. Grace could see it in my face.

"Why don't you go home," she suggested. "Get some rest. Tomorrow we can go through the other things from the chest together. Katya and I may not be Daruidai, but we might know enough to recognize something that would be of help to you."

"That sounds like a good idea." I thought for a moment. "Maybe I'll just take it easy tonight. Go home early and just spend some time with Jill and Tony. We can worry about all this other stuff tomorrow."

Just then, Stone walked in, and he was clearly agitated. He marched across the room and helped himself to the whiskey.

"First, something's destabilized the gateways; the fixed portals," he said after he'd taken a swallow. "They've been there for centuries. It worked, but it was tricky. That sister of yours."

He scowled at me. "I had to do some fast talking to get out of there, they were going to arrest me as soon as I brought her up."

"Why? What happened?"

"They're pretty pissed. It seems she broke out of jail and murdered a bunch of guards. If they find her, she'll be executed."

# CHAPTER TEN

## MIRA

"That's crazy!" I snapped at Stone without thinking. "Nora wouldn't do that."

"I don't know." He shrugged. "She did try to stab *me*."

"Get over it," I told him. "She was protecting me, and you were an intruder in our house. That's different. She's not a murderer."

"Whatever the case." He held up a hand. "We'll get no help from the *Ande Dannu*. In fact, you'd better hope they don't find her before we do."

"How can we find her if they won't even let you in?"

"There's always the Winter Court," he said. "And worst-case scenario, we could try the Wild Fae, but they're harder to get hold of."

"Okay, so let's try the Winter Court, whatever that is," I answered. "Can we go tonight?"

He was shaking his head. "Things with the Winter Court don't happen very quickly. You're going to have to be patient."

I held back a hasty answer, taking a breath. "Did you find out anything else?"

"Evidently, someone helped her escape," he answered. "Once they got outside, whoever it was sprouted wings and flew away with her to the west. No one has seen either of them since."

"Wings."

He nodded.

"Like a pixie?" I asked. "A *Pilané Jhin*?"

"No, evidently this person was pretty big."

"And not a dragon?"

"Dragon?" He scowled and shook his head. "No, it sounded like he or she had a general humanoid shape, but with wings. I wasn't able to get any details, though."

"Are there many races that are that big, humanoid, and have wings?"

"There are a few. Hopefully, your sister will be safe with this one until we can find her."

"But we don't know that."

"Well." He shrugged. "It seems that whoever it was helped her escape the holding cell. That sounds like they might be friendly."

"Not everyone that helps you out of a tight spot is your friend," Grace pointed out.

"True. But there's nothing we can do about that for now. I'll reach out to the *Dannu Fé*, the Winter Court, and see if they know anything or if they'll let me in to look around." His eyes found the open chest. "What's that?"

"Just some private things of mine," Grace spoke up.

"In a warded chest?"

"It had my grandmother's book of spells," she answered easily. "You know how some people can be, hunting down old grimoires. They think they'll find some world changing spell."

He nodded, his eyes still on the box.

"That's some pretty powerful warding for an old spell book," he said. "Did you draw those markings?"

"Oh, no," Grace shook her head. "I found the box at an estate sale several years ago."

"Was there anything in it?" He looked at her curiously.

"Not when I bought it. But you know how estate agents are; everything gets hauled out of every corner and gets a price tag."

"Where did you get it?"

Grace frowned. "It's been a while. I might have a record someplace. Is it important?"

"No, just curious."

I didn't know why Grace thought we shouldn't tell him the truth, but I was suddenly very conscious of the sword leaning against the wall in the corner and I didn't want him to see it and start asking more questions.

"Then you'll let me know as soon as you hear anything?" I asked him.

He tossed back the rest of his drink and stood up. "Yes. But be patient. It may take a few days to even make contact with them."

"How do I reach you in the meantime if I need anything?"

He fished in the inner pocket of his coat and pulled out a leather case. He extracted a business card from the case and handed it to me. I looked at it. It simply read *Alex Stone, Extraordinary Investigations*, and a cell number.

"Extraordinary Investigations?" I asked him.

He shrugged. "It covers a lot of situations."

Once he was gone, I went to the chest and closed it. Then I looked at Grace for an explanation.

"He seems trustworthy, but—" she gave her head a small shake. "You have already been warned about the Daruidai. Maybe it would be better not to show them all your cards. At least for now."

"Fair point," I acknowledged. "Thanks for watching out for me."

"Go home," she told me. "I'm going to do some research on the sword. Maybe I can find something out for you."

I took a Hitch back to the house and had a pleasant dinner with mom and dad. I didn't tell them what Stone had told me about Nora. There were too many unknowns, and it would just make them worry even more than they were already. As soon as I had definite information, I'd bring them into the loop.

It was nice to just relax and enjoy mom's enchiladas and their easy company. I tried not to look at Nora's empty chair. We fell into our familiar pattern, but there was also an unspoken tension about that empty chair. I still wore my daggers; after everything that had happened over the last two years, I felt uncomfortable without their familiar weight at my side. Both mom and dad noticed them, but they didn't say anything. After dinner, dad brought out some cards and we played a few hands of double-canasta. Dad almost always won, but we gave him a challenge sometimes.

I was just about to get undressed to take a shower when my cell rang. I looked at the caller ID before answering.

"Hi Grace. What's up?"

"The sword is gone!"

"What? Gone?"

"I was at my desk and suddenly a woman was there. It was like she stepped out of a window of water in the air. She took the sword and disappeared."

"It's gone?" I repeated. My mind was spinning.

"And Mira," she added. "She was glowing. And so was the sword. And I swear the grip and sheath had turned white instead of brown."

"Who—"

"Just a minute," Grace stopped me. "Katya? Are you alright?" I heard sounds of something breaking in the background. "Who are you? What do you want?"

I hadn't tried it since I'd gotten home, but I pulled the *Ralahin* to me. It came slowly and I had to really pull to bring it in. I focused on the workshop where I'd spent the afternoon working out and ripped a portal into the air. As soon as it appeared, I jumped through.

I could see several figures in dark robes. Their faces were covered by some kind of black mask. One of them held Katya in a magical binding. Others were throwing magical attacks at Grace, who was standing by the door to the office. I had to be careful what I used to avoid hurting Grace or Katya. I threw a fireball at the one holding Katya. As soon as it struck, Katya fell to her knees, the binding no longer holding her. I sent a lightning bolt to strike the ones attacking Grace.

Grace ran to Katya and helped her to her feet. The attackers were also recovering and turning their attention to me. I put up a shield, and Grace and Katya retreated to the office. I fell back to the office behind them as our attackers started a coordinated attack on my defenses.

I couldn't fight them effectively and protect Grace and Katya at the same time. We had to get away from them. I opened another portal back to my bedroom.

"Go through!" I yelled.

Grace went through. Katya was close behind and I jumped to follow. Suddenly Katya stopped and she rushed back to grab the chest. We went through the portal at the same time, and I closed it behind us. Katya staggered forward and fell to the ground. I could see a thick ice shard sticking out of her back and blood soaking into her shirt. One of the attackers must have struck her at the last second. The wound looked bad; she was going to need to get help right away.

I heard a blast from the front of the house. Could they have followed us? We weren't safe here! I thought fast.

"Mom! Dad!" I shouted down the hall. "Come fast! Run!"

Their bedroom was at the end of the hall, past mine, and they both stepped into the hallway with confused looks on their faces.

"*Mija?* What's—"

"No time!" I cut him off. "In here! Now!"

As they rushed to obey, I could see shadows moving in the front room of the house. I was already drawing in the *Ralahin*, focusing on the only other safe place I could think of and that I knew well enough for a portal.

"Go through!" I yelled as soon as the portal formed. I had put up a shield at the end of the hall and could feel the magical bludgeoning it was receiving.

Dad saw Katya on the floor and picked her up, stepping through the portal with mom right behind him. Grace grabbed the chest and followed. I jumped through right behind her and closed the portal.

We were in my suite in Su Lariano. Before I could say anything, the front door burst open and a half-dozen guards charged in, weapons drawn.

"Send for a healer!" I yelled at them.

"Mira?" It was Bar Rizina, one of my old bodyguards. She glanced at Katya and then turned to another guard. "The healer! Now!"

The guard disappeared down the hall. The door to the second bedroom opened and two figures stepped through.

"Hey, Mira. Back already?" He took in the scene and turned to the person next to him. "See, I told you she was the one that always found all the trouble."

"Rispan?" I looked at him. "Shéna?"

Probably for the first time since I'd met him, Rispan's face reddened with embarrassment.

"Yeah, about that," he said. "I take it you didn't come back for the wedding?"

# CHAPTER ELEVEN

## NORA

"What did you do?" I rushed to Jack's side. The guard was already binding the arm to slow the blood loss.

"He will survive," Queen Iratzé told me. "Our healers will see to him for now, and they will show you how to take care of him until he is recovered."

"Recovered? You chopped off his arm!"

"Hand. As prescribed by law," she nodded. "Now, we need to discuss this Kartahn Zeg. And other matters."

"But—" I turned back to Jack.

A woman had appeared and signaled to the guards. They picked Jack up from under his arms and followed the woman out of the tent with Jack's feet dragging on the ground.

"Come," Iratzé said. "Sit." She indicated some stools that sat next to the table of food.

Emma clung to my side, and I led her to the table.

I tried not to think about what had just happened with Jack. I didn't think he'd deserved to have his arm cut off. Then again, Jack had been pretty violent as well. We'd seen a lot of blood in the past day. How could this seem so normal?

"How is it that you have a *Daijheen* as a companion?" King Edrigun spoke for the first time since we'd entered the tent.

"He found us in a cell," I answered. "I talked him into helping us get out."

He looked at me sharply. "Why were you in a cell?"

I shook my head. "I don't know. The people there… I think Jack called them *Ande Dannu*… they couldn't understand us. We couldn't understand them. Jack was the first person we could talk to since we got here. I didn't even know where "here" was. Jack said this is called Danu?"

"How did you come to arrive at a place you didn't know?"

"There was this man," I told him. "I think he was after my sister, Mira. He showed up in our house through this weird window-thing that appeared in the air. He tried to drag her into one and I jumped on him. The next thing I knew… I wasn't at home anymore. Emma had been near me, and she came with me somehow, but Mira didn't. The man took off, and those other people came, and they put us in the cell. Me and Emma. We were there for days. Then Jack walked in. Through the wall. *Through* the wall. Who does that?" I shook my head. "And then he was reading my mind and asking me these weird questions." I was rambling, and I couldn't stop. "And I said I could answer better if we talked someplace else if he could get us out. So he opened the door and we went up the stairs and…"

My words trailed off. I couldn't describe the rest; what Jack had done. I'd never seen violence like that before.

"I don't imagine the *Ande Dannu* simply let you walk out," the king commented.

I shook my head, still not able to find words or meet their eyes.

"I can guess what happened when they tried to stop a *Daijheen*."

It was all my fault. If I hadn't been so impatient; if I hadn't asked Jack to get us out, those people would still be alive. I could feel the tears on my face. In my mind, I could see the bodies falling as Jack charged into them.

"I didn't know!" I looked up at them. "How could I? I tried to stop him, but it was too late. I'm sorry!"

I squeezed my eyes shut and clenched my teeth together. I could feel the nails biting into my palms as I balled my hands into tight fists. I would not cry. Crying was for the weak, for the victims. I refused to be a victim. Never again. Plus, I had to stay strong for Emma. There was no one else to watch out for her here. Like it or not, I was going to have to take care of her.

"And Kartahn Zeg?" Edrigun prompted.

My eyes snapped open to look at him. "He showed up after Jack left to get food. Who is he?"

"He is a necromancer—"

"He is a madman!" Iratzé interrupted him.

"If he could succeed in his ambition," Edrigun suggested. "It would be a great accomplishment."

"If?" Iratzé shook her head. "But he cannot. You know this."

The king nodded. "I believe you are correct."

"What's he trying to do?" I asked her.

Iratzé studied me a moment before answering. "What do you know of the cycle of life and death of these bodies we wear?"

"Um." I shrugged. "Not much?" Then I remembered what Jack had said. "The spirit goes on, right? Jack said something about that. Something about the body being a temporary physical construct."

"A *Daijheen* would know," she nodded. "What you identify as yourself is a combination of the physical and the non-physical. When the body is shed, the non-physical essence continues. After some period, short or long, another body is taken, and another combination is born. A *Daijheen* is like a necromancer; they both can feed from the energy of other beings. They can even feed on the very essence of other beings. But a necromancer can do something else; they can take stolen energy and reanimate a body that has been shed. Kartahn Zeg believes he can reunite the essence of the dead gods with their slain bodies and bring them back to life. Then he believes he can steal their power and become a god himself."

"We don't know that part for certain," the king amended. "But we suspect it."

"But," something didn't make sense. "Didn't you say this essence thing gets a new body? What happens to that body if the essence is taken back?"

"If he could actually do it? The new bodies would probably die over a short period of time," Iratzé answered. "But when the essence takes a new body, any connection to the shed one is severed. The cycle of life has always been thus."

"So, what happens if he brings the bodies back to life without that… essence?"

"They would simply become mindless, soulless monsters," she told me.

"But mindless monsters that were once the bodies of gods," Edrigun added. "They would be very dangerous."

"And now this necromancer has the power of a *Daijheen*." Iratzé shook her head. "It may be enough for him to make the attempt."

"That sounds pretty bad," I admitted. "But… gods… are gods even real? That's just stories, right? Maybe there's nothing to worry about."

"Those we call gods were real," Iratzé said firmly. "How do you define what it is to be a god?"

"I don't know." I shrugged. "Creator of the universe. All knowing. All powerful."

"I have heard some say this defines godhood," she nodded. "But there are other concepts. Cannot gods also have limitations? Perhaps, these things are simply relative. Perhaps, simply to be far beyond us in power or knowledge is enough. I won't quibble over esoteric definitions; for practical purposes, these people were gods. Let academics argue philosophy from the safety of their libraries and universities. It is we who must face these monsters should they rise."

She clearly had strong opinions on the subject, and I was in no position to argue. Then again, she'd seemed to have strong opinions about everything so far.

"You mentioned a sister," Edrigun changed the subject. "Where is she?"

"I don't know. She wasn't around when I got here. I guess she's still at home, wondering where I am. I don't suppose you know how to send me home?"

"Knowledge is not the question." Iratzé cocked an eyebrow at me. "Just because one *can* do something does not mean they *should*. The Summer and Winter Courts become very irritable regarding unauthorized travel to and from other realms."

"Relations with the Courts can be a bother," Edrigun agreed. "This would not be a good time. You could always petition one of the Courts directly. Normally I would suggest the Summer Court, but after your recent experience there, I wouldn't recommend it."

"Then what—"

I heard a commotion sounding from behind the tent and then someone started playing some lively music.

"It seems the celebration has resumed," Edrigun smiled at Iratzé.

Kerbas stepped into the tent, the expression on his face the happiest I'd seen it so far. He scowled as soon as he saw me and Emma, but turned his attention to Edrigun and Iratzé. He spoke to them in whatever language it was they used and King Edrigun nodded. Edrigun stood and offered his arm to Iratzé, who joined him with a smile.

The royal couple started for the entrance and Edrigun paused. He said something to Kerbas that made the man's eyes widen and I heard an eruption of laughter from Tavarnin. With a grin, Tavarnin pulled a ring off of his finger and tossed it to

Kerbas. He made some admonition to Kerbas and followed the royal pair out.

"Tavarnin!" I called after him. "What am I supposed to do?"

"Whatever I tell you to do." Kerbas glared at me. "Not more. Not less."

I glared right back at him. "You think I'm some kind of a slave?"

His eyes narrowed. "I think you are a criminal who has been given a chance she does not deserve."

"And I think you're a jerk!" I told him. "You don't know anything about me!"

He ignored my comment and was apparently deep in thought for a moment.

"You must attend the celebration." Kerbas nodded to himself. Then he looked at me sharply. "But be warned; you must show courtesy and respect." He put his hand on the hilt of the knife at his waist. "Any offense will have dire consequences for you."

"Um." I knew nothing about their culture. What if I did something wrong by mistake? "Maybe we should just stay here."

"I must attend. Therefore, you must attend."

Before I could say anything else, he grabbed us by an arm each and pulled us out of the tent. We went around to the back and there were more people than I could count. There was a cleared space in the middle and there were a lot of people engaged in some kind of stylized dancing that involved a lot of posing, turning, clapping, finger-snapping, and foot stomping, as well as cheering and whistles from dancers and onlookers.

The musicians were to one side. There was something that looked like a panpipe that competed with some sort of violin for the melody. There was also a harp, and one man was beating on the head of a drum with his palms and fingers. There was also a jingling sound and I saw that a number of people had small bells on bracelets around their wrists that they would shake in time to the music, sort of like a tambourine.

Everywhere I looked, wildflowers were strewn, spread, or hung for decoration.

"What's all this?" Emma asked.

"Wedding celebration," he answered absently, looking around for something. Evidently, finding what he was looking for, he grinned. Then he frowned at us. "Stay close to me at all times. Do not leave my side."

Then he was pushing through the crowd, and we had to struggle to keep up with him. He arrived at what I assumed must be the happy couple, and embraced the groom. They slapped each other's backs and then the groom turned to the nearby table. He picked up a wide, short cup that had flat handles extending from each side. He took a swallow from whatever was inside and handed the cup to Kerbas, who also took a swig. Kerbas then handed the cup to the bride. She took a drink as well.

Then the bride saw me and Emma standing next to Kerbas. She held the cup out to me and Kerbas seemed to hold his breath, waiting for my reaction, tension etched in his expression.

"This is my brother Niall and his bride Arrosa," he told me.

Unsure of what I should do, I smiled at her and took a drink. I don't know what I was expecting, but I'd snuck a sip of straight vodka once and it was very similar, but this was even stronger. I choked and handed the cup back. The groom laughed and made some comment to Kerbas.

"What was that?" I asked, wiping my mouth with the back of my hand. I noticed that the bride and groom were both barefoot.

"Cheenya," Kerbas answered, his eyes had relaxed, and he was scanning the dancers. "It is a traditional drink for many celebrations."

Suddenly, several men rushed forward carrying a chair. It looked like it was one of the ones from Edrigun and Iratzé's tent. They grabbed Niall and lifted the chair into the air with him on top. The music and dancing continued as they paraded him around the crowd. Then they brought him back to the front and put him down facing the crowd and everyone went silent.

A voice sounded through the night, singing words I couldn't understand. The musicians joined in, but in contrast to the rowdy music from before, this was almost ethereal. The clear soprano voice rang pure and strong. The singer stepped forward as she sang. A large medallion, maybe eight inches across, hung from her neck by a chain. I could see intricate designs on it, but I couldn't make out any details.

Kerbas drew us a few steps to the side as the woman approached Niall and Arrosa. She stepped between them and turned so that she was also facing the crowd. She held out the medallion in both hands as she sang. Niall and Arrosa both placed a hand on the medallion. There was something about the song; it felt like it was taking hold of me.

"What is she singing?" I whispered to Kerbas. "What's that song?"

"An old tradition," he answered in a low voice. "It is part love song and a song of promise. But it is also a sort of prayer, invoking the Great Mother and asking her blessing for the couple."

"The Great—" My question died on my lips as light started emanating from the medallion.

The singer didn't stop, and the light intensified. The song pulled me, and I took an involuntary step forward. Kerbas and Emma both looked at me in surprise and I saw that I was glowing, too. The song filled me; somehow, it was familiar. I was walking toward them and I was singing. *What's happening to me?* But I wasn't singing the same words she was; it was different. It seemed like I should know the meaning. And I was singing a harmony. My hand lifted to rest on top of theirs and the light became even more intense; from the medallion and from me.

Suddenly, it was like I was in two places at once. I could see the bride and groom, and the singer, but I was also in a room. There was a desk and a pretty black woman sat behind it looking at me in surprise. There was light coming from the corner of the room. I stood by the singer and Niall and Arrosa, yet at the same time I walked to the corner of that room, toward the source of light. The woman at the desk turned her head to watch me. What was the light coming from? I reached out and took hold of it. As soon as my fingers wrapped around whatever it was, the vision of the room faded. I was back with the song, with the singer, one hand on the medallion and something heavy in the other. The song reached its final long note. As it ended, I could feel my knees giving out and I was falling.

# CHAPTER TWELVE

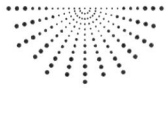

## NORA

*I* opened my eyes to see the canvas roof of a tent above me.

*What the actual frick just happened?*

"Good morning."

I turned my head to find the source of the voice. It was the singer, or whatever she was, from the reception. Morning? My eyes went to the entrance of the tent, and I saw sunlight peeking through the cracks around the cloth door.

"What happened?" I asked her.

"Are you alright?" I could hear the worry in Emma's voice. She was sitting on a nearby chair next to a table of food.

"I think so," I assured her, then I looked back to the singer.

"You gave the blessing of the Great Mother to the newly-weds," the woman answered. "You touched them with her power. And you produced the Sword of Light."

*Sword?*

"Okay. How did I do all that, exactly?" I sat up. My hand rested on something very soft, and I looked down to discover I was on a bed of furs.

"You are asking me?" Her brow furrowed. "You do not know? I had assumed you were a High Priestess."

"Yeah, not so much." I shook my head.

"What are you saying?" Emma was looking at me strangely.

The woman blinked a few times before answering me. "Perhaps you have some connection to the Great Mother you do not know of," she suggested. "The prayer song and the Joining Cup could have invoked the connection."

I thought about that for a minute. "What kind of connection?"

She shrugged. "I cannot say for certain. It would most likely be a connection through blood or through spirit."

"I'm not following you."

"Through blood," she explained, "would simply be that you are a distant descendent. Through spirit would mean that in a previous incarnation, you had a very close relationship to the Great Mother or someone very close to her. There may be other possibilities as well, but one of those seems most likely if you have no knowledge of it."

Neither explanation helped me to get my head around what had happened.

"Pardon my discourtesy," she said. "I have not introduced myself. I am Zoriaa. I am what some would call a priestess. At least, I fulfill that role. But I am simply a keeper of the old ways. I am also the eldest daughter of Tavarnin, whom I believe you have met."

I nodded. "I'm Nora."

I heard the sound of a double clap from outside the tent.

"Enter," Zoriaa called.

Kerbas walked in, apparently with something to say to Zoriaa, but as soon as he saw me awake, he refocused his attention on me.

"Why did you not tell us who you were?" he demanded. "What is the purpose of your deception? To test us?"

I just looked at him. I had no idea what he was talking about.

"Kerbas!" Zoriaa scolded him. "Do not be rude."

He turned to her and started a reply, but she cut him off.

"And do not make assumptions! She is not aware of her connection to the Great Mother. There has been no deception."

He looked at her and then back to me.

"Yeah." I nodded. "What she said."

He gaped at me and turned back to her. "No deception? Yesterday she feigned ignorance of our speech, today she speaks it plainly. How is this not deception?"

"Perhaps yesterday she *was* ignorant of the common tongue," she answered him. "Today is a new day."

"What's this common tongue thing you're talking about?" I asked.

Zoriaa looked at me. "The common tongue is what we have been speaking this morning."

"What? No, we—" I stopped as I actually listened to my words. I knew what I was saying, but the words weren't what I was used to. No wonder Emma was looking at me that way. "What's going on?" This was really starting to freak me out.

"Relax." Zoriaa evidently saw my anxiety. "Something has awakened within you. This is just one part of that. Old knowledge coming to light."

"What do you mean old knowledge?" I could feel my chest getting tight and I was gasping.

Zoriaa came to my side and put a hand on my shoulder, squatting down to look me in the eyes. "Take a breath. Slowly. In and out. In. And out."

I focused on her and struggled to get control of myself. Mira could always calm me down so easily. I wish she was here with me. She'd make sense out of all of this. She was always so good at seeing the big picture; how things fit together. What would Mira do?

Mira always said that when you didn't know what was going on or when you were confused, just do the next thing. Whatever that was. It didn't matter how small, just do it. Alright. Breathing first. I closed my eyes and took a few breaths.

ADAM K. WATTS

"Okay," I said after a moment. "I'm okay." I took another breath. "What do you mean old knowledge?"

"You recall I said there were two main possibilities?" she asked me. "And that one of them had to do with a previous incarnation?"

"What, now you're going to tell me I was Cleopatra or the Queen of Sheba in a past life or something?"

"I do not know who those people are," she answered. "But your new ability to speak the common tongue indicates that in some previous life, you knew it. You being here, combined with what happened last night, has simply caused that knowledge to resurface."

I looked over at Emma. "She's saying that I was someone in a past life that spoke this language," I explained to her in English. "And that somehow I am remembering the language."

Emma's eyes got big. "That's so cool!"

That wasn't the response I expected.

"Who were you?" she asked.

"I don't know." I shrugged. I looked at Zoriaa and switched languages. "Who am I supposed to have been?"

She shook her head. "We may never know. Curiosity is natural, but who you are now is always more important than who you *were*. Past lives are ended; they are done. This is your life now. Old duties and responsibilities, old debts and identities, they are nothing more than dust. They are no longer yours."

"That is mostly true," Kerbas interjected. "But who someone was can also be very important." He looked at her. "She brought the Sword of Light, Zoriaa! It has been lost for centuries! If she is the Keeper—"

"There is time enough for that," she interrupted him.

"That duty does not get left behind!" he insisted. "If she *was* one, then she must *be* one."

She nodded acceptance. "But we cannot assume she is."

"I don't know what's going on," I said. Whatever they were

110

talking about was starting to freak me out again. "I just want to go home!"

Kerbas looked at me but spoke to Zoriaa. "I'll need to report this. There will be questions."

"Who was he talking about?" I asked Zoriaa after he left. "This Keeper person?"

"There has always been a sort of… custodian for the Sword of Light. And there has always been a hero or king to wield it. A champion."

"And what, the custodian polishes it?"

She laughed and it was a soft, musical thing. "The custodian protects it and chooses the champion."

"And the champion uses it? Like a loan? Then they give it back?"

"Eventually," her face took on a sad expression, "all champions fall."

"Wait… So, if I'm this custodian person, I have to pick someone to be a champion, and whoever I pick will get killed?"

"We do not know that you are the custodian, but you brought the sword," she nodded to my side and I saw a sword lying next to me on the bedding. "But I should tell you; for now it will be assumed that you are the custodian. Or the champion."

I put my hand on the sheath and a calming warmth came over me. The prospect of the sword and having other lives was somehow less scary.

"Tell me more about the sword."

"The earliest mention is when it was wielded by King Nuada," she told me. "He carried it for many years. When he fell, it was passed to Lugh. There are stories of other champions… some here and some in the land of Eire or beyond. Siegmund. Artur. And the sword has been called by many names, but always it was also the Sword of Light. It is known as one of the four treasures of the *Uthadé*."

"And if I'm this custodian, that's why I was able to do that blessing thing last night and sing that song with you?"

Her brow furrowed. "I cannot say for certain how this happened. The answers lie within you. If you wish it, I can help you to find them."

"Yeah, I don't know what that means."

"I could help you to look back," she explained. "To sift through your past lives to find your connection to the sword, or to the Great Mother."

"What are you guys talking about now?" Emma asked me.

"She wants to help me look through my past lives to find out who I was," I told her. "Or what my connection to everything is."

"Can she do me, too?" She was practically bursting at the seams. "I want to know who I was! How does it work?"

I scowled at her enthusiasm, though the last question was a valid one.

"How does this looking back thing work?" I asked Zoriaa.

"I would join with your mind, with your soul. Together we would make the journey."

"You want to take a trip inside my head? How 'bout I take a raincheck for now?" She gave me a confused look. "Let's save that decision for later," I clarified. "I don't understand the question well enough yet."

She nodded, then indicated the side table. "You should eat. We can talk more later."

I looked back at the table of food and realized I was famished. It was a simple fare of fruits and cheeses, but I dug in. I glanced over at Emma.

"I already ate," she told me.

I nodded as I chewed. Then I remembered what my last meal had been and started feeling guilty about Jack.

"Where's Jack?" I asked Zoriaa. "The guy that was with me." I couldn't quite call him a friend.

"He is still with the healer. Once he has sufficiently recovered, responsibility for him will fully transfer to you. That may be delayed given your new… situation."

"Well? What have you found?" a voice spoke from the entry. It was Iratzé. "Is it true? Is she *baensiari*?"

Zoriaa shrugged. "I saw what you saw. More than that is not known."

Iratzé didn't look happy with the answer. "Find out."

"Yes, my queen." Zoriaa tipped her head.

Iratzé glanced at me, then she turned and left.

Zoriaa sighed. "We may need to move things along a little faster."

I finished swallowing a bite of some kind of melon as I thought about that. "What was that banesy thing she was asking about?"

"*Baensiari*," she corrected me. "It's... sort of like a high priest- ess. It's a title we use for things like the custodian we were talking about."

"And she wants to know one way or the other if that's me. What's the rush?"

"Well," she paused. "It's a combination of things. First, it is said that the sword only shows up when it is going to be needed. So, the fact that it is suddenly brought to light after so long is alarming in itself. But *you* have brought the sword to us. If you are *baensiari*, then the sword must be left with you until you grant it to a champion. If you are not *baensiari*, then it must be taken from you and held until a *baensiari* or champion appears."

"So, take it." I shrugged. "I don't want it."

"It's not that simple. If you are indeed *baensiari*, then we must ensure that you keep the sword and are protected."

I nodded. Then something occurred to me. "Protected from what?"

"From any who would seek to take the sword for their own purposes." She looked at me. "Only the *Baensiari* of the Sword can bestow the sword to a champion that they may wield it with all of its power, but even without *all* of its power, the sword can accomplish great destruction."

I sat back from the table, no longer hungry. Letting someone rummage around in my mind sounded pretty invasive.

"You are worried about what this will entail," she observed.

"Can I just do this myself?" I asked her. "Can you tell me how?"

"If you were to attempt it on your own, it could be dangerous. But with a gentle guide, it is very simple."

"I don't get it. Why would it be dangerous?"

"Throughout our many lives, we have had many traumatic experiences. If you wander into one of these, the sudden shock of contact with the emotional charge could damage you, even damage your current identity. An old identity could even rise to ascendency. Every life gives us, to some degree, a clean slate. A fresh start. Old identities, resurfacing, with no tether or connection… that way lies insanity."

"Yeah, that sounds pretty scary."

"But as I say, with a gentle guide, someone to act as a tether, it is quite simple. There is no risk at all."

It sounded like trying it on my own would be a really bad idea. I walked back to the sword and picked it up. My anxiety seemed to fall away, and I felt more calm.

"Fine," I told her. "What do you need to do to set it up?"

"Oh, that is simple," she smiled. "So long as you are fed and rested, we could proceed now."

"Now?" I turned to face her. My stomach started to tense again, but then relaxed. Now. *Why wait?* I took a breath. "What do I do?"

"Come sit back in the chair," she told me. "Bring the sword."

At her direction, I sat in the chair with the sword across my lap and my hands holding it. She sat across from me in another chair.

"You're going to do it now?" Emma asked. I nodded. "I wish I could understand what you guys are saying."

"Ready?" Zoriaa asked me.

"Ready enough," I answered. "Go ahead."

"Close your eyes. Focus on the sword. Without opening your

eyes, *see* the sword. Picture it. Feel it. Feel your connection."

I could feel the weight of it on my lap and in my hands, felt the texture of the scabbard against my skin. I could feel its energy, its light.

"Now," she went on. "Return to another time with the sword. Go back to another time you felt this connection, an earlier time when you saw the sword."

The image in my mind went dark with shadows, then they were shifting and there were flickerings of color.

*I was in a forest, moving fast through the trees. Sunlight dappled through the leaves. There was water... a shore... crossing blue water... the cries of seagulls. A verdant island, green and luscious with life... a beautiful city of towers and stone... People were going about their business in the city... I passed through them, but they didn't see me... A young man was smiling at a woman. He said something, and she laughed... I smelled spices and cooking food amid the odors of spring blooms... children played in a park, chasing each other around a fountain... a breeze tickled the silver-green leaves of a tree...*

*I was in a room. There was a man. We were talking.*

*"I tell you this is not a good idea," I was saying. "It is not well-suited for human hands."*

*"There is no one else." He lifted his empty palms. "Besides, this is a problem of Earth. Who better to champion Earth than a human? It is their world, after all."*

*"That is for me to judge, not you. The mantle of judgment is mine, passed from my mother."*

*"Even she," he argued. "Even Aradi bestowed favors to humans, at the behest of her mother, Duanna."*

*"I have no cause to trust them."*

*"Then trust me."*

*"Oh, Merlain. You don't know what you ask." I sighed. "But I will do this. For you. For what could have been. But when it is over, the sword must be returned to me. Make Artur swear it, by blood and by soul. Without the oath, he will not draw the Sword of Light. I will make sure of it."*

*"Do you require an oath ceremony?"*

*"He need but speak it. I will hear. He will be bound."*

*"Agreed." He looked at me. "Nimué, I wish—"*

*"Do not speak to me of wishes," I told him.*

*"Then I will speak of hope."*

*"Some things, once lost, can never be recovered."*

*"And the girl?" His eyes were on the floor.*

*"She is safe."*

*"This time will pass." He sighed. "Perhaps after Seighdlacht—"*

*Seighdlacht! I felt terror threaten to engulf me as the scene went dark. Merlain was gone. The room was gone. Someone was coming, I had to run! Who was coming? Where was he? He must be close. Faster!*

*There! Light! I was in the forest, and I was running. I could hear something behind me, coming fast. There was a structure ahead, I could see it as I approached. Two broad stone pillars stood amongst the trees, an arched stone connecting them at the top.*

*Was that where I needed to go? I ran toward them; I was so close. The darkness followed me, relentless. Across the arch I could see depictions of the moon in all her phases. I could feel the hot breath of my pursuer on my neck... he was reaching...*

*Something launched from the arch, from the moons. Birds! A swarm of birds. They emerged as stone but soon shifted to feather and flesh. They flew toward me... past me... the darkness was gone. The cries of seagulls.*

"Nora! Come back!" It was Zoriaa. She had her hands on my arms and she was shaking me. "Nora!"

"Yeah." I blinked. "I'm here."

"I am so sorry! I don't know what happened! That should not have happened!"

"No, it's not your fault." I shook my head, trying to slow my breath. "I knew that name. Seighdlacht. I've had nightmares of Seighdlacht before. Pretty much all of my life. It just... never happened when I was awake before."

# CHAPTER THIRTEEN

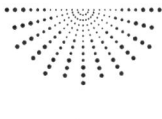

## MIRA

*I* looked at Katya's wound. The ice shard was melting, but slowly. Her eyes were closed. It didn't take long for the guard to come back with a healer; it was Shigara. She knelt quickly next to Katya, and I could see her extending her senses with the *Ralahin*.

Shigara looked up at me. "I am sorry. She is gone."

"No!" Grace snapped. She couldn't understand the words Shigara had spoken, but she understood the tone. Katya lay on her side with her head in Grace's lap. "She's— she's—" Something seemed to break inside her and a keening sound cut through the air. She pulled Katya closer, rocking her body. "My sweet Katya… why must you leave me so soon?"

"I'm so sorry, Grace," I told her. "This is my fault. I shouldn't have gotten you involved."

Grace froze and then turned her face to me and met my eyes with a fury and an intensity that made me draw back.

"No." Her voice was low and as unforgiving as the sea. "*You* did not do this. *You* are not responsible. The one who *is* responsible will pay. Blood for blood. There will be a retribution."

I nodded. I knew what she felt. I had been there and had

barely survived the journey. All I could do would be to be there for her the best that I could.

Shigara put her hand on Grace's shoulder. "Let her go. We will take her." She motioned to two assistants who had brought a stretcher.

The assistants gently moved Katya's body to the stretcher and lifted it from the floor. They exited the room with Shigara following behind.

"I am sorry for your loss." It was Neelu, speaking to Grace. She was speaking English, so she must have started carrying around something with a translator spell, like my pendant. I hadn't seen her come in. She turned to me and put a hand on my arm. "Mira." She pulled me in for a hug. Then she stepped back and looked at the others. "All of you, welcome to Su Lariano. I am Neelu Ulané Pulakasado. Please call me Neelu."

"These are my parents," I told her. "Jill and Tony. And this is Grace, a friend of mine."

Neelu nodded to them. "It saddens me that we should meet under these circumstances. Jill, Tony, I have heard much about you from Mira. I'm glad to be able to put faces to the names."

"We've heard some stories about you, too," Jill told her. "I'm so glad Mira found you. I don't want to think about what might have happened to her otherwise."

Neelu looked at me sideways with a smile. "Mira proved to be surprisingly resourceful; don't give me too much credit." Then her face turned serious again. "First. Mira, you have clearly fled here. Will you be pursued? Should we prepare?"

I shook my head. "I seriously doubt they'd be able to follow me here."

"Who were those people, *mija*?" Tony asked me. "What did they want?"

"I don't know. Grace called me and then I heard something happening over the phone. But that had to be a second group at the house."

"It's a good thing Grace called you for help," Jill said.

"I didn't." We all looked at Grace when she spoke. "I didn't call Mira for help. I called because of something else."

"The sword!" I remembered. "You said someone took the sword!"

She nodded. "I was seated at my desk in the office. Suddenly there was— it looked like a puddle, but in the air. A glowing woman stepped through, and the sword started glowing, too. It was a young woman, maybe just a girl. Red hair. I didn't recognize her. She picked up the sword and immediately disappeared. That's when I called you."

"What's going on?" Rispan asked.

I shifted position to include him. "Sorry... Mom, dad, Grace, this is Rispan and Shéna." I turned back to him. "These are my parents, Jill and Tony. And this is Grace."

Rispan took Neelu's hand; the contact would include him in the translation spell.

"That sword you mentioned. What's so special about it?" Neelu asked,

"I don't know anything about it. It was another thing that was in my mother's chest. Like the daggers and the pendant."

"You were saying that Alex Stone found you because of the daggers," Grace said. "Maybe these people were looking for the sword."

"This is all my fault!" Jill looked stricken. "That box! If I hadn't given it to you, none of this would have happened! Ms. Leon said to wait until you were eighteen, but— you've always been so mature for your age... I thought it would be okay."

I was shaking my head before she finished talking. "There was no way for you to know, for any of us to know. Waiting until I was eighteen would only have delayed things, not changed them. None of this is your fault."

"It seems things were set in motion long ago," Grace mused. "We need answers about the beginning, about how this all started." She thought for a moment. "Jill, it does not seem to me that it's normal for a box like this to pass through the foster system to be held for a child."

"Oh." Jill glanced at Tony. "I don't know. Ms. Leon, the woman from child services, she brought it over a couple of years ago. But… No, you're right. Why would she keep it for so long?"

I pulled out my cell phone. No signal. Of course not.

"I need to go back and talk to her," I said. "And to Alex Stone. I need to get more answers. But," I looked at Grace and my parents, "I don't know how safe it is. They attacked the house and the store. Until we know more…"

"Yes." Grace nodded. "Your parents should stay here until we know it is safe for them. We should get a good night's sleep and go back in the morning after a good breakfast."

"You should stay, too," I told her.

"You will not go back without me," she was indomitable. "I will have my answers as well. You will not leave me here. Promise!"

"Alright. I promise. But," I hesitated, "what about Katya?"

She took a breath and slowly let it out, her eyes unfocused. "We must bring her back." She looked at me. "There will be questions we cannot answer. But she cannot simply disappear. Her family won't have closure otherwise. They can never know the truth of what happened, but they must have something."

I nodded, thinking. "If we portal directly to the store, we can call the police and say we got there in the morning and saw there had been a break-in. We can just say we found her there."

"It will have to do," she agreed. "And it is true; there *was* a break-in."

"What if whoever attacked you is still there?" Rispan asked. "I'm coming with you."

Neelu smiled at him and ruffled his hair. "I'm coming too," she said.

"I appreciate the back-up, guys," I told them. "But you'd kind of stand out."

"If your attackers are gone," Neelu cocked her eyebrow at

me, "you can send us right back. But if they *are* there, we can teach them some manners."

"I have a better idea," Bar Rizina cut in.

In the end, a full squad of guards went through with us, two of them carrying Katya on a stretcher.

"Don't worry," I'd told Jill and Tony. "You'll be fine here, and I'll send for you as soon as it's safe."

"Don't forget to call-in to work for me," Tony said. "Just tell them it's a family emergency. I have plenty of vacation hours stocked up."

All the extra protection turned out to be unnecessary. The shop was deserted. After we laid Katya gently on the floor, I opened another portal back to my rooms in Su Lariano.

"Come get us if you need us," Neelu said. "You know we will always have your back." She gave me a hug and stepped through the portal.

"Don't have too much fun without me." Rispan smirked over his shoulder as he followed Neelu.

Grace crouched on her knees beside Katya's body, running her fingers through her hair to straighten it.

"I'm sorry," I told her. "I know you two were close."

"She was my apprentice," she answered. "So full of promise and life. I do not take apprentices." She turned her gaze to me. "But Katya was different. She convinced me to take her on."

I went to the front of the store, leaving Grace to have a private moment with Katya. One of the display racks was knocked over and the front door was ajar. The shop didn't usually open until ten, so it was still too early for people to be walking in. I felt the urge to pick up the fallen rack, but I left it where it was for the police to see.

"I'll call," Grace said, coming out of the back.

While she was calling the cops, I had some calls of my own to make and I pulled out my cell. First, I called Tony's work and told them he had a family emergency and would probably be out all week. Then I called Luciana Leon.

"Yes?"

"This is Mira," I told her. "We need to talk. And not just two minutes like last time."

"Something has happened," she said. "Alright. When and where?"

"At the store. As soon as you can." I disconnected the call before she could say anything else and keyed in another number.

"Stone," he answered on the third ring.

"You're supposed to be protecting people from magic and supernatural stuff, right?"

"Mira?"

"Grace and Katya were attacked at the shop," I told him. "Katya is dead. My house was attacked. Do you know anything about it?"

"This is the first I'm hearing of it," he answered.

"The attackers wore black robes and used magic. I need you to stop screwing around and tell me everything you know."

"I'm— Yes. I'll come to you. As soon as I can. I'll find you. Don't trust anyone."

"I don't trust you," I pointed out.

He was silent for a moment before answering. "Understood. I'll see you soon."

I waited with Grace for the police to arrive. A uniformed officer took our statements separately in the parking lot; first with Grace, then with me. I was Carmen Cansino. I was visiting my friend, Grace Ndané, from out of town. We'd come in to open the shop and found it that way. We hadn't spoken to Katya since the night before. No, there were no security cameras. My knives?

*Oh, no!*

"They aren't real," I told him. "They're part of a costume I'm working on for a ren-faire."

"A what?"

"Renaissance faire," I'd heard of these things, but never been to one. "It's where people dress up like old times. And there's swords and stuff, but it's not real. Here, try it." As I pulled one of the daggers with the scabbard from my belt, I reached out to the *Ralahin* and wove a binding to prevent the knife from coming out of the sheath.

The officer took it and tried to draw the knife. It didn't budge.

"See? It's not real."

"Seems pretty heavy for being a fake."

"Oh, it has to be realistic," I said. "But not real. Otherwise, people could get hurt."

"Right," he said, handing it back. "You can wait with your friend. Since there's a death involved, they sent a couple of detectives from homicide. They're inside now. You're probably going to have to go over all of this again with them. It's just procedure."

I glanced up the sidewalk and saw Luci Leon coming. She was still a block away. I hadn't thought she'd be coming so soon. I pulled out my cell and sent her a quick text.

*I am Carmen Cansino visiting Grace from out of town.*

I saw her pause her step to read her message. Then she looked up and met my eyes. She slipped her phone back into her pocket and continued toward us.

A couple of men in street clothes stepped out of the front door of the store, talking to each other in low voices. One of them, the younger of the two, a slender man with sandy hair, spotted me and Grace leaning on her car and nudged the other one. The second man was stocky and as dark as Grace. His expression wasn't friendly as he looked us over, like he'd just bitten into something that tasted bad. They spoke briefly with the officer who'd taken our statements and looked over their notes.

I glanced around and saw that Luci was staying back in the crowd that had gathered. There weren't a lot of people, but it didn't take much to make people curious, so several onlookers had gathered. I thought I noticed another familiar face, but the two men were walking toward us.

"I'm Detective James Doyle," the sandy-haired one was saying as he approached with the other man. "Most people just call me Jimmy." He grinned. "This is Detective Sarpong Udu. Nobody calls him Jimmy."

I guessed he used humor to get people to relax. He also seemed smooth enough that it was probably an effective technique most of the time. Something about the other one got my hackles up, though; I just couldn't figure out what or why. Other than the looks he was shooting at Grace.

"Nobody's nobody," I answered.

Udu turned his eyes on me.

"Interesting time to be making a joke," he said.

"Tell that to your partner." I shrugged. "I just didn't want him to feel awkward about it. You know, empathy and all that."

Dunn's grin faltered as he looked at me. I was starting to act more Like Nora, and that probably wasn't a good idea in this situation. The last thing I wanted to do was make them suspicious.

"I'm sorry," I said, trying to back-pedal in my approach. "I guess I'm not dealing with this very well. It's not even my store and I feel… violated. I can't imagine how it is for Grace. Especially with Katya… I think we just need to go someplace and take some time to process all of this."

"We have a few questions first," Doyle said in a sympathetic tone. "Just to make sure we have all the details."

I nodded. "I wish we had more we could tell you. We already told that nice officer everything we knew. We came in early to open the shop. The only car in the parking lot was Katya's. We found the door ajar and went inside. We found Katya. We called the police."

"It looks like she'd been dead since last night," Doyle looked at both of us, "and from the way— and I don't mean to be harsh, but the way her blood had pooled in her body, she had been moved since she died."

"We may have moved her a little when we found her." I pretended to think back. "I think so. We thought she might just have been hurt. I hope we didn't mess up any clues or whatever."

"Is there any reason she would have been in the store so late after closing?" he asked.

"She would sometimes meditate in the back," Grace told him. "Or just catch up on paperwork. She would generally tell me, but then again, she would often get caught up and forget."

"What kind of business do you do here exactly," Udu cut in.

"We sell antiques," Grace answered. "As well as herbs, incense, and other curiosities."

"I saw some books in there and things with different symbols," Doyle commented.

"*Bayibaa*," Udu said, looking at Grace. "*Bronsam*."

Grace glared back at him. "I would think a police detective would be less ignorant." She turned to Doyle. "Is this police procedure now? To call citizens witches? Evil?"

Dunn glanced at his partner uncomfortably. "Sorry, I don't understand the language. I only speak English."

"Of course." Grace looked away from him in disgust. "Most people in the world speak at least two or three languages so they can better understand each other. But white Americans don't wish to understand anyone but themselves."

"Sorry, detectives," I cut in. "This has all been very upsetting and tempers are running a little high. It's been quite a shock. I really don't think we can tell you anything else, but if you give us your card, we can call you if we think of something."

Dunn fished out a business card while Udu looked at us silently. We started to walk away, and Udu spoke.

"We will talk again *bayibaa*."

"Be sure to lock the store when you leave," Grace answered without looking at him.

We started to get into the car and I looked over to where I'd seen Luci Leon, but she wasn't there. I checked my cell as we started to exit the parking lot and there was a message to go to a nearby diner. We went in and I saw Luci sitting at a booth in the back corner.

A waitress walked over as we sat down across from Luci, and we ordered coffee. Grace and I had eaten breakfast before leaving Su Lariano, and I for one wasn't ready for an early lunch.

I looked at Luci and waited. She indicated Grace with her eyes.

"She's earned it," I told her.

"Alright." She met my gaze. "There are a few things I haven't told you yet. And I don't have all the pieces to the puzzle."

"Let's start with the pieces you *do* have," I prompted her.

"There's more to why I put Nora with you," she said. "She went into the foster system before you did. I was still in a more junior role at the time and wasn't able to control where she went. But when it was your turn, I was in a better position. Your parents, yours and hers, knew each other. Your mother Sofia met Deirdre at college. This was before either of them had met Jorge or Martin. Jorge was Daruidai, and Sofia joined as well, she had family history in the organization; it wasn't long before they were married."

I knew practically nothing about my parents except their names, so I expected to find out new things. But the fact that they were connected to Nora's parents caught me totally off guard.

"Deirdre…" she paused. "Your mother lost touch with her for a while. But then out of the blue, Deirdre reached out to her. She said she knew Sofia was Daruidai and she needed her help. Someone was after her; after something that she had."

"She didn't tell you what it was?" I asked.

"No, but your mother was worried that someone might try to find Nora. She did say something about a birthright. She wouldn't give me all the details, but I did as she asked. About that time, your mother became pregnant with you. She was afraid that whoever was behind what happened with Deirdre and Martin was also in the Daruidai. So, Sofia and Jorge broke ties with the Daruidai and changed their names."

"What difference would that make?" I asked.

"They went into hiding with new names, and you were all safe for nearly ten years."

"And then my parents died."

"Yes." She nodded.

"A car accident."

"It was no accident," she said. "Natural flame doesn't burn that hot."

"You think whoever killed Nora's parents killed my parents, too?"

"I think it's likely. And since I was connected with Sofia, I needed separation. I was still Daruidai, and I was transitioning from agent to inquisitor, and I wanted to be able to investigate both incidents without risking putting you in danger. I thought hiding you would only make whoever was behind this suspicious, so your parents' deaths were listed under their real names, and I put you into the foster system using your real name."

"I don't understand. Why would I have been in danger from your investigation?"

She opened her mouth to speak but suddenly looked away. She was struggling with something, and I couldn't imagine what it could be. I just waited. Finally, when she looked back at me I could see that her eyes were starting to tear.

"Your mother's maiden name was Sofia Leon," she said. "She was my sister."

# CHAPTER FOURTEEN

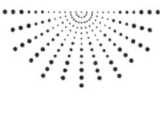

## NORA

"Who or what is Seighdlacht?" Zoriaa asked me.

"I don't know exactly," I told her. "I get the idea it's a he. And he's… dangerous. But it's just a bad dream."

Zoriaa shook her head. "It is not simply a dream; it is a vision. But whether it is of the past, or a warning for the present or future we cannot say for certain. However, we do know he *is* connected to your past if Nimué and Merlain were discussing him."

"You're telling me Seighdlacht is real?"

"From what I saw in your vision, he is." She nodded. "And unless I am mistaken, he is seeking you. Merlain just saying the name triggered the second part of the vision."

I shrugged. I'd been having the nightmares for so long; I was bored with them. When I was awake, anyway. When I was asleep, they were still pretty terrifying.

"Is it over already?" Emma asked. "I thought it was going to be more exciting."

"It was exciting enough for me," I told her. "I'll tell you about it later. Who were those people?" I asked Zoriaa. "It sounds like you recognized them."

"Nimué and Merlain are well-known. Nimué was the third

*baensiari*. She is the daughter of Aradi, who taught witchcraft to humans. Aradi is daughter to the Great Mother."

"You mentioned this Great Mother before." I looked at her. "But I assumed she was some mythical person."

"The Great Mother is known by many names; Arduanna, Arduinna, Dunna, Dana, Danu, Diana. She was very real."

"Was?"

"She left this world with the *Uthadé*, those you would call *Tuatha de Danann*, to Tir Nya Nog, but she is still revered and honored. Those who migrated here also honor her; the *Dannu Fé*, the *Ande Dannu*, and the *Wyl-Dunn*. The realm itself is called Danu."

"Migrated? So, none of you are originally from here?"

"Not originally." She shook her head. "Originally, we were mostly *Loiala Fé* from Daoine. But that was many centuries ago."

"How many different worlds are there?"

She laughed. "Who knows? But that conversation can wait for another time. We have learned of at least one connection you have to the Sword of Light; you were once Nimué. It is likely that you are indeed *baensiari*. Especially if you have a blood connection as well. In all probability, you do. Spirits often stay near to family or close friends after a body is shed. It is not uncommon for them to be born into another generation."

"And that's why I did what I did last night?" I asked her. "And why I've been able to use magic?"

"You have used magic before last night?"

"A little. Just recently."

She nodded. "Yes, given those connections, that wouldn't surprise me at all."

"And if I am this *baensiari* thing, what does that mean? What am I supposed to do?"

"You will need to learn how to defend the sword, and how to bestow its full properties to a champion."

"And how am I supposed to learn that?"

# ADAM K. WATTS

"You were actually where you needed to be." She smiled. "The Great Library of Tir Nya Lu on the island of Avalon."

"There's a problem with that."

She looked at me questioningly.

"That place where the library was? There's no food or water there," I pointed out. "That's why Jack took that food."

"That is simply a matter of logistics."

"I need to check on Jack," I told her. Bringing him up had reminded me of my new duties. "Iratzé said he was my responsibility. I don't know what all that means, but I'm guessing if he screws up it will be bad for both of us. And he seems to be good at screwing up."

"I'll take you to the healer's tent." She stood up. "While you are looking in on him, I can set things in motion." She indicated the sword. "Carry that with you at all times until you can find a place to keep it hidden."

"Let's go see Jack," I said to Emma.

"That sounds boring. Can I look around the camp instead?" she asked me.

"I don't think it's safe," I told her. *Did I just sound like an overprotective mom?* "Actually, there's no reason you shouldn't be okay. You don't speak the language; so just be respectful. And don't go inside anyone's tent."

Emma grinned as she rushed toward the exit. "I promise!"

"And be back here in an hour!" I called after her. I held back a facepalm as I heard myself. If Mira had heard me, she'd be rolling on the floor.

Zoriaa and I found Jack seated on a stool in the healer's tent, staring into space and cradling what was left of his right forearm with his other arm.

"Jack? How are you doing?"

He moved his eyes momentarily to glance at me and returned to his unfocused stare.

"Right. Stupid question. Um—"

"What do you want of me?"

130

"Want? Nothing, I just wanted to check on you and see how you were recovering. They told me you're my responsibility, to make sure you don't get into trouble."

"The mighty Jakarael Abalaan, shepherded by a human." I could only describe his tone as self-loathing. "Gaze upon the fallen. Even one such as you is now greater than I."

That just annoyed me, and I tried to temper my response.

"I was always greater than you, Jack." His eyes snapped to me in anger. "In some ways," I went on. "And not in others. That's just normal, Jack. And it hasn't changed."

He considered that silently. "It does not matter," he said finally. "I am less than nothing now. I have no power. I am not even whole."

"You think that's the most important thing about a person? How much power they have?"

"I have heard it said people are defined by their actions. With no power I can do nothing!"

"What about your mind, Jack?"

"What about it?"

"I think you know things. Maybe you're not so great at understanding people, but you know a lot of other things. Yes?" He didn't answer, so I went on. "Something happened last night. I mean after what happened to you. I did something. Now they're saying I'm a *baensiari*. I still don't know what that is. I'm supposed to learn some stuff. Magic stuff. I bet you could help with that."

He blinked at me a few times. "Why do they think this? What did you do?"

I held up the sword. "I got this from somewhere. I don't know how."

That seemed to get his attention. He looked at the sword, his eyes studying every line and curve.

"Those are two extremely powerful artifacts," he said. "I don't know that I have ever seen anything so powerful."

"Two?" I looked at it. "It's just one sword."

"The sword and the scabbard have completely different attributes." He continued to stare at it as if he could see something I couldn't. Then his eyes got big, and he sat back a little.

"What is it?" I asked him.

"Will you do something for me? It is… of significance."

"What?"

"Draw the sword from the scabbard and extend the scabbard toward me."

Sounded a bit weird, but alright. I did as he asked. With his good hand, he took hold of the scabbard.

"Now," he said. "Feel the sword in your other hand. Envision light coming from the sword, through your body, through the scabbard, and to me. Can you do this?"

The healer from the night before was in the tent and she stepped closer to see what was going on and I glanced at her.

"Close your eyes if it helps," Jack told me.

I closed my eyes and did as he said. I felt the sword. I imagined it was glowing, like it had the previous night. But brighter. Then I imagined that I was some sort of a conductor and that the light was coming through me and the scabbard to Jack. I heard Jack gasp, and I opened my eyes. He was glowing and his body was arching.

"Don't stop," he commanded. "Focus!"

I didn't understand what was happening, but I didn't stop. Jack's body started jerking like he was having some kind of seizure. Then the light flashed brighter, and he fell to the ground. The light went out.

"Jack?" I knelt by his side. "What happened? Are you alright?"

"Yes," came the answer. "Give me a moment." He rolled over and got to his knees, then climbed to his feet. He held up his hands and looked at them.

*Hands?*

"The sword has the power to destroy," he said. "The sheath

has the power to heal. I wasn't sure if it would work. But thank you."

"You're healed?"

I was only barely aware that the healer who had been standing nearby had rushed out of the tent.

"My body is healed, yes. I may not have my power, but at least I am whole. And yes, I will help you to learn what you need to learn."

"How is this possible?" I asked, looking at his re-grown hand. It looked the same as his other hand, except that it had a silvery sheen to it.

"The atomic structure of my body makes it fairly simple to repair," he answered. "At least, compared to other structures. However, it was mostly because of the power of the sheath. How did you acquire it?"

I shrugged. "Evidently, I'm kind of a... hereditary protector for it. It's pretty ironic, really. Since I don't have a real family." Saying that made me feel guilty, so I amended it. "Not a biological one, anyway." Mira was definitely family. And if I let myself admit it, Jill and Tony were up there, too.

"Yes," he answered. "You mentioned that you had a substitute family. Correct?"

"Yeah, we don't call it that," I told him. "Foster family."

"Foster. To assist in or promote the development of something. I see. And the members of this foster family assist each other in their development?"

"I guess you could say that."

"And is that not what we will be doing? I will assist you in developing your knowledge of magic and you are to assist me in developing my knowledge of this society?"

"I suppose so."

"Does that make us a foster family?"

"Um, maybe."

"Would that make you my foster mother?"

"No!" I shook my head. "Definitely not mother. Sister, maybe. Not mother." *I'm too young for that.*

"Ah! So, you are my sister like Mira is your sister?"

"Big sister." I scowled at him. "And good brothers listen to their big sisters."

"I have never had a sibling," he mused. "And now I have a sister. This could be interesting."

It didn't sound quite so interesting to me.

"What about Emma?"

I shook my head. "She has her own family."

"Not on this world," he pointed out. "She is a child, yes? She would need someone in the parent role. Will that be you?"

"Anyway." I changed the subject. "It looks like we're going to go back to that library in Tir Nya Lu."

"Good!" He nodded. "I like the library."

I heard a sound behind me and glanced over my shoulder to see that the healer had returned with Zoriaa.

"It's true then." Zoriaa was looking at Jack's hand. "You have healed him with the power of the sheath. How did you do this?"

"Um." I glanced at Jack. "Something to do with his atomic structure?"

"You learn quickly." Jack grinned at me. Then he turned to Zoriaa. "Nora is my sister."

Zoriaa blinked at him and then looked at me.

"Don't ask," I told her. "Just roll with it."

She nodded. "I have spoken with Iratzé. We are to leave tomorrow morning for Tir Nya Lu."

"And that logistics thing we were talking about?" I asked.

"Kerbas is being tasked with keeping us supplied and keeping us safe."

"He must be thrilled," I said wryly. "I don't think he likes us very much."

"Don't mind him." She laughed. "He's pretty much like that with anyone besides his brother."

I had dinner that night with Zoriaa in her tent, along with

Emma and Jack. We had chicken in a spiced sauce that reminded me of curry, but not quite. I liked it, but the spice also had a bit of a kick to it, so I swallowed a good deal of the chilled juice from the pitchers on the table to cool my tongue. I was halfway through my third refill before I realized that the drink was alcoholic.

"Thish ish quite good!" Jack commented. I noted that his speech was slightly slurred.

"Careful, Jack," I told him. "There's alcohol in that drink."

"I've had alcohol before," he assured me with a serious look. "It should be... should NOT be a problem."

"I hadn't thought of it," Zoriaa said to him. "Your body may not deal with alcohol in the same manner as when you had your powers."

"Kartahn Zeg!" Jack scowled. "He shtole my powers!"

Yup. Jack was drunk. I glanced over at Emma and was rewarded with a sleepy grin. Great. I was supposed to be watching out for these two, not letting them get drunk. Emma was just a kid and Jack wasn't much better.

Not for the first time, I wished Mira was here. She was much better at dealing with other people than I was. Mira might be my little sister, but she was also a guide. Mira always knew what was right and never hesitated. I wouldn't say I needed her as a moral compass, but she did help as a reminder and her example motivated me to try to be that way, too. She would never have let Jack and Emma drink too much.

"I think we need to switch to water," I told them.

"Nonshensh!" Jack shook his head. "We are fine. Everything'sh fine!" He reached for the pitcher and almost knocked it over.

"Have you tasted the water here?" I asked him. "It's amazing. Practically magical. But maybe its properties are too much for you."

"Too mush?" He drew his brows together. "Nothing ish too mush for me! I'll try shum of that water!"

I couldn't believe he'd fallen for that, but I'd take my victories wherever I could. That had definitely been a Mira move. I stood up to reach for the water and had to catch myself as I almost lost my balance.

"I'll get it," Zoriaa said.

As she poured the water for Jack, I looked over at Emma again. She'd pushed her plate out of the way and had dozed off with her head on her arms.

"I guess I'm not very good at taking care of others," I said. "I don't do that. It's not my thing. I'm just not a people person."

Zoriaa gave me a silent smirk.

"What?" Was she laughing at me? Was I really that bad at being responsible? I felt myself getting hot from the invalidation.

"You sell yourself short." She smiled.

*Huh?*

"Did someone force you to watch over Emma?" she asked.

"No." I frowned at her. "But who else is going to do it?"

"And I seem to remember that you volunteered to keep Jack in line."

"What was I supposed to do?" I demanded. "Let them cut off the other hand, too? Or let them leave him in the Waste to die?"

"Some would have done that." She nodded. "Why not you?"

"Because…" I struggled for an answer.

"Because you care about Jack too much to let that happen to him?"

"No." I shook my head. "I don't know him that well. Sorry, Jack, but it's true." I needn't have worried; Jack was too busy examining his water for special properties to pay attention to the conversation.

"Then why?"

"I don't know!" I glowered. "You seem to have all the answers."

"Maybe you care more about people than you think."

"People can't be trusted!" I snapped. "They're mean and they only care about themselves!"

She nodded. "Sometimes. So, you don't let anyone close, and yet you care for them anyway."

"I don't need anyone," I told her. I was saying too much... revealing too much. I knew it was the alcohol, but I couldn't hold back. "Mira's the only one I trust. She's different. She cares about everyone else. She cares about me. That's why—" I stopped as the thought solidified.

"Yes?" Zoriaa prompted gently.

"That's why," I told her. "Emma and Jack. Because it's what Mira would do. If I didn't help them and Mira found out..."

"She would be angry?"

"No." I shook my head. "And Mira would never say anything. But I know she'd be disappointed."

"Is Mira here?" Emma raised her head and peered around.

"No," I said to her softly. "We were just talking about her. You can go back to sleep."

"Okay." She put her head back down, then looked up. "Promise you'll wake me if she comes?"

"I promise."

"I miss Mira," she said as she settled her head down again.

"Me too."

"You're lucky," she mumbled. "I wish I had a sister like Mira."

"Mira is your sister?" Zoriaa asked. I nodded. "I think your sister would be proud of you."

I shrugged, turning my face away from her to hide that tears were welling in my eyes. I'd definitely had too much to drink if I was wearing my emotions on my sleeve like this.

"I should probably get some sleep," was all I said. Jack had already passed out.

By the time the sun came up the next morning, we had mounted a half-dozen griffins and were on our way back to the ruined city. Jack, Emma, Zoriaa and I were each assigned a different person to ride along with. The other three riders brought supplies.

As we neared the dry seabed, it was too big for me to really think of it as a lake, I got a better look at what they called the Scourge. It was as though there was a sharp line between the life of the surrounding area and the complete lack of life within the Scourge.

I couldn't imagine what would have caused this, but then if magic was involved, I had no idea what was possible. As we crossed over into the Scourge itself, I studied the ground, looking for any clue as to what might have happened. There wasn't debris like I'd expect to see from an explosion. Instead, the ground was smooth, almost like everything but the island had been scooped up.

The island itself, what had been the island, was mostly the ruined city. On the western end of the city along the south, I could see parts of a wharf and the desiccated remains of ships.

The more I looked, the more I got the feeling that there was something I wasn't quite seeing. Like when you were trying to think of a word and it was on the tip of your tongue, but when you tried to say it out loud it just wasn't there.

"What caused all this?" I asked Kerbas, who rode in front of me on his griffin.

"The cause is unknown," he answered over his shoulder. "Tir Nya Lu was neutral in the war between the *Uthadé* and the *Fu-Mo Ri*. Both sides tried to capture it. Then one morning, the sun rose, and it was as you see it." His expression took on a wry look. "Do you know why the *Uthadé* called the *Fu-Mo Ri* monsters?" he asked. "They had red hair. And freckled skin."

Yeah. Kerbas could be a real jerk.

# CHAPTER FIFTEEN

## MIRA

"My mother was your sister? You're my aunt? And all this time you didn't say anything?"

"Mira," she started. "You need to understand—"

"*I* need to understand? I'm sorry! What is it exactly that I don't understand that I need to understand? Like why an *actual* relative who knew where I was just abandoned me?"

"The only way to protect you from this life that killed both of your parents, that killed my sister, was to keep you away from it!" She matched my intensity. "Do you think that was easy? Do you think—" She stopped and took a breath to get hold of herself. "Whoever was responsible was *in* the Daruidai. It wouldn't be the first time the Daruidai had been led astray. Ponce de Leon used the Daruidai to do terrible things. He saw anything that didn't align with his vision of Christianity as something to be crushed. Miguel de Cervantes did a course correction after de Leon died. For me… there was no one I could trust. At the beginning," she shook her head, "it was just too dangerous. I made sure you were fostered to good parents, and I tried to find out who was behind everything. I was going to take you back as soon as I could. And then they tried to adopt you."

"You're the one!" The realization hit me. "You kept blocking the adoption! Dragging it out!"

She nodded.

"But then you finally let it happen? Why?"

"It had been more than six years." She shook her head. "Six years, and I was no closer to finding out who was behind it. I had stopped officially working for the Daruidai while I continued my investigation. And I was always looking in on you. I saw how much they loved you. And how much you loved them. So, I brought Jill the box of your mother's things and told her to give them to you when you turned eighteen, and the next time the adoption came up for approval, I let it go through. I thought that once you were eighteen, I could go to you… talk to you…"

I tried to understand, but my emotions were conflicted. I heard what she was saying, but it was hard to be completely rational; to not feel in some way that she had rejected me. Would I have made a different choice if I'd been in her position? Maybe. I don't know, maybe not.

My cell buzzed and I looked at the message. It was from Stone.

"*Where are you?*"

I fired off a response and put the phone back in my pocket.

"Alright." I nodded, pushing aside my doubts and insecurities. Worrying about that wasn't getting any onions chopped. "You're my aunt. Do I have any other family out there I don't know about?"

She shook her head. "Not that I'm aware of. But I never really knew anything about your father's family. I only know he wasn't from this country. But he was Daruidai, like your mother."

I tried to get my head around that. It was possible I had grandparents out there. Aunts? Uncles? Cousins? I shook my head; no point in wondering about that right now.

"Do you know anything about a sword?" Grace asked. "Or a red-headed woman?"

*Aunt* Luci furrowed her brows. "Sword?"

"That box has a false bottom," I told her. "There were some things hidden underneath. Things that should not have been able to fit. That's where I got the daggers." I put my hand on the hilts. "There was also a sword, but we just found it yesterday." I related what Grace had told me about the woman showing up and taking the sword.

"I don't know anything about that." Luci frowned. She was lost in thought for a moment, then shook her head. "Have you read any of the letters yet?"

"No, I haven't had a chance."

"Maybe they'll hold some answers," she suggested. She looked over my shoulder and then lowered her voice. "Let's keep this sword business just between us for now. Until we know more."

A shadow stepped up to the table and I looked up to see Stone. He opened his mouth to say something, but I didn't give him a chance.

"Sit," I told him, pointing to the bench next to Luci. I wanted both of them where I could see their expressions.

Stone looked uncertainly at Luci but sat down as she shifted over to make room.

"So," I said to him. "You and your people have clearly been keeping an eye on me recently, right? At the shop? At my house?"

He glanced at Luci and Grace and then back to me. "Should we be talking about this right now?"

"You let me worry about them. Answer the question. Surveillance?"

"Well, yes," he admitted.

"Then how is it that two groups of magic users attacked both the store and my house last night and you and the Daruidai don't know anything about it?"

"I don't know." I had his attention now. "This is bigger than we thought. You seem to have powerful enemies. We can take you into protective custody; keep you safe."

"That's not going to happen." I shook my head. "I have no reason to trust any of you. The attackers were wearing black robes. The first time I saw you, you were wearing some kind of robe, too."

"There'd just been a special meeting, I needed a team to establish the first portal, I was in traditional attire. But black robes?" He shrugged. "That's not what we wear."

"That's not completely true," Luci cut in.

Stone turned to look at her suspiciously. "I'm sorry, we haven't been introduced. I'm Alex Stone."

"Luciana Leon," she replied. "Grand Inquisitor." Stone's face paled at her words. "Retired," she added.

"Retired?" He cocked his head. "But—"

"Technically, I took a leave of absence and didn't come back." She shrugged. "Enforcers sometimes wear black robes for anonymity. Were they wearing masks?" she asked me. I nodded. She turned to Stone. "You were saying?"

"That doesn't make any sense," he objected. "Why would enforcers go after her?"

"That is exactly what we would like to know." Luci studied him with an intensity that practically had him squirming in his seat.

"Why don't you tell us what you do know," I told him. "And no BS."

He scowled but nodded. "I was just assigned to monitor certain detection spells. They are designed to watch for specific things to show up. Those daggers of yours set off all kinds of alarms. I reported it and I was given some basic information about your parents—"

"I thought you said you knew them?"

"I was told to say that." He almost looked apologetic. "It helps to build a rapport. But that was later. First, I was ordered to retrieve the knives, which I was told were stolen, and whoever possessed them. I could tell they were connected to you somehow, even if you looked young for a thief. I thought it would be a simple assignment. Clearly, I was mistaken. That's really everything I know. Basically, nothing."

"What did they tell you about the daggers?" I asked.

"Nothing."

"Did they tell you what else they were watching for?"

He shook his head. "I don't know anything more than I've told you."

"Who gave you the orders?" Luci asked him.

"It came down the lines through my boss," he answered. "But I don't know where the orders originated."

"What are your current orders?"

He hesitated before answering her. "To take Mira into protective custody."

"Here's the problem with that," I told him. "I don't trust you or any of the Daruidai. I'm not going to *let* you take me anywhere until I know I *can* trust you. You want me to trust you? Get Nora back. If you do that, you'll have taken a big step forward."

He frowned. "They may not wait for you to come willingly."

I narrowed my eyes at him. "Trying to force me into something could be very costly. You have absolutely no idea what I am capable of. Take the safe route; find Nora. Bring her back."

"I will… relay your request."

"Good," I told him. "Then that should be all for now."

He bristled at my dismissal, but he got to his feet and nodded to us before leaving. "Ladies."

"I don't trust him," I said after he was gone.

She shook her head. "He's just a foot soldier. He'll report anything he finds out and he'll follow orders."

"As for you." I frowned at her. "I'm still pissed at you. And not pissed." I took a deep breath. "One of the easiest things in the world for people to do is to second-guess other people's decisions after the fact and tell them what they should or shouldn't have done. I wasn't in your position, faced with the decisions you had to make. I can't say what I would have done."

"Just—" There was an almost desperate intensity in her voice as she put her hands on one of mine across the table. "Don't think I abandoned you! I would never—" She looked away. "Our mother was Daruidai, but our father didn't know anything about it, or magic, or anything from that part of the world. When he found out what our mother was involved with... he couldn't deal with it. He just left. He abandoned us all." She met my eyes, "I would never do that to you."

I nodded. "I believe you."

We sat in a companionable silence for a few minutes and sipped our coffees.

"Where do we go from here?" I asked her.

"The last time we talked, you said you'd been on another world. Two years?"

I nodded.

"I've heard of people creating little pocket universes where time moved differently, but to change a whole world?" She shook her head. "Can you tell me about it?" She looked embarrassed. "I've had to keep my distance from you, but I really want to know more about you, all the little details of your life that people who aren't *in* it can't see. Maybe this is a good place to start?"

She listened as I repeated the story to her. Something about Luci told me that she'd been through some struggles of her own, that there were things she would understand that others wouldn't, I didn't hold back on the parts I'd glossed over with my parents and with Grace. Like when I was on Dimétrian's estate, fighting his soldiers. Hating them and killing them when I could get away with it. I gave her the details of how I'd almost died of dreams and illusions on that island; of how I'd wanted to surrender. Though Grace had heard the story before, she was hearing some of those details for the first time.

I also related what had happened the previous night with the attacks, how I'd taken Jill and Tony to Daoine for safety.

"Your mother would be so proud of you," she said when I'd finished. "*I'm* proud of you. I'm sorry that you lost so many years."

I shifted in my seat uncomfortably. "I'm not so sure I'm proud of myself," I admitted. "Some of the things I did… I didn't always make the best choices."

"Mira, that's what makes you human, like the rest of us." Then she gave a low chuckle. "I guess it's not just humans. The other races are in the same position. We're imperfect. We have free will. We have limited power and limited knowledge. We make mistakes. Don't regret your mistakes; learn from them."

That made me feel better; I'd given her the unvarnished truth and she'd accepted me.

"Now," she went on. "We need to figure out the next thing and do it." I laughed at that. "What's so funny?" she asked.

"That's what I always say," I explained. "Do the next thing. You do, too?"

She nodded with a smile. "I learned it from your mother."

"We still don't know who attacked us," Grace pointed out. "You think it was Daruidai enforcers?"

"It may have been," Luci answered. "It sounds like it was, but I don't want to jump to conclusions." Luci looked at me for a moment. "You used the name Carmen Cansino with the police. That was smart. No one will believe you are sixteen, and you need an alias. I can arrange proper documents. Are you satisfied with that name?"

"It works for me!" I grinned.

"Meanwhile," Luci went on, "we need to take a look at both places you were attacked. Maybe we can find some clues as to who was involved."

"I don't think the cops are going to clear out of the shop anytime soon," I said. "Maybe we should try the house first."

"Good idea." Luci nodded.

"Let's do it then." I scooted out of the booth.

Luci left some cash on the table to cover our coffees plus a tip and we headed out.

On the way out of the restaurant, I saw Shelby, the girl from school, sitting in a booth by herself with a half-eaten plate of French fries in front of her. She wasn't looking at me, but I turned my face away just in case. Had that been her I'd seen in the crowd by the store?

When we got to the house, nothing seemed out of the ordinary. We walked up to the front door and noticed it wasn't quite closed. In fact, the frame was cracked and broken.

I shook my head. "Tony just fixed this, too."

# CHAPTER SIXTEEN

## MIRA

*T*he inside of the house was a stark contrast to the calm exterior. We'd been throwing magical attacks up and down the hallway, and a lot of the furniture in the front room was knocked over or even destroyed.

Neither Grace nor Luci had magical vision, like I did with the *Ralahin*, but they had other things they could sense for.

"Some of what I see here looks similar to what Daruidai enforcers are taught," Luci said.

We went down the hall to my bedroom. The door was blown to splinters and the frame was blackened. I glanced down the hall at the door to the fourth bedroom that Jill used as her art studio. No damage there. We stepped into my room to look around. It was a disaster nearly as bad as the front room.

"Mira!" Grace was staring at a family photo that had somehow remained upright on my desk. "That's her!" She pointed. "That's the woman who took the sword."

"Nora?" That was crazy. "How could Nora have done that?"

Luci was shaking her head. "Everything is starting back up again," she said. "Like with her parents." She looked at me. "I think finding Nora is even more important than we thought. I think the attacks… I think maybe they were looking for that sword. And now Nora has it."

"And Alex Stone and the Daruidai will find out about it if they find Nora." I shook my head. "I still don't want to tell them about the sword. But I don't see how we can find Nora without the help of the Daruidai. We need them."

"Maybe not." Luci had our attention.

"It sounded like that whole world is locked down." I frowned. "Is there another way in without going through their controlled gateways? And even if we got there, how could we find Nora without help?"

"Of course, it would be easier with the help of the locals," Luci agreed. "But a locator spell should point us in the right direction."

"We tried that," Grace told her. "We didn't get anything."

"Right." Luci nodded. "A locator spell wouldn't work for someone on a different world, or even the same world if they were too far away. But it should work once you're on the same world and not too distant."

"Okay," I agreed. "So, we get there and then use a locator spell. Or Grace does, since she knows how. But that still leaves us with the problem of getting there."

"That's not as much of a problem since you're so good with portals," Luci smiled.

I shook my head. "I can only go someplace I've seen before and know well."

"There's a way to trace the path of a previous portal; I've seen it described. Why don't you and Grace go back to your house and I'll meet you there later? I need to get hold of that manuscript. It shouldn't take me more than an hour or two to find it."

"Where is it?" I asked her.

"It's in the library at the local Daruidai headquarters."

"That's not a problem?"

"Technically, I'm still a member." She gave me a half-smile. "I can still come and go as I please. I'll still want to keep it low-key, though. If they see my face too much, they'll try to pull me into different things. But I can make use of some of their resources."

"Alright." I nodded. "The sooner we can find Nora, the better. You find your manuscript and we'll wait here."

We went back to the front room and Luci left. I looked around at the destruction and felt guilty about bringing trouble to Jill and Tony. What would they say when they saw all this?

"Why don't we start cleaning this up while we wait?" Grace suggested.

"You don't mind?"

"You can help me at the store later." She looked around. "Some of this can't be fixed."

"I know. We can drag it out back for now."

By the time Luci arrived, we had a good-sized pile of broken furniture going in the backyard and had swept up the front room. It was still going to need some paint, and the front door needed to be repaired. Again. Otherwise, it was looking much better.

"Any trouble finding what you were looking for?" I asked her when she walked in.

"No, I just had to remember where I saw it." She glanced around. The front room was absent of anything to sit on besides Tony's recliner, which had somehow managed to come through the ordeal unscathed.

"Let's talk in here," I suggested and led them to the kitchen table. "Actually." I turned to them. "I'm starting to get hungry. Why don't we order some pizza?"

"I could go for that," Luci said, sitting at the table.

I looked at Grace, who nodded her agreement.

I grabbed the phone. "Any toppings to avoid?"

"I'm not a fan of pork," Grace told me.

"I don't care for bell peppers," Luci answered.

"Perfect!" I pressed the speed dial for the local shop. They should be open for lunch.

Grace looked at me in surprise when she heard me order: thick crust, white sauce, shrimp, mushrooms, pineapple, artichokes, and jalapenos. My favorite. I should talk to Mouse about adding pizza to the menu at Raven's Nest next time I was in Su Lariano. Did they have shrimp on Daoine? If not, it was almost as good with chicken.

"It should be here in about a half an hour," I told them as I hung up. I plopped down in the seat across from Luci. "Tell us about the manuscript you were after."

"I came across it years ago when I was doing some research on pocket universes," Luci told us. "It was in Italian. I translated enough to find out it wasn't what I was looking for at the time. It was talking about portals. It was over my head, but I remember it was talking about tracking someone through a closed portal. Or reopening a closed portal. I'm fuzzy on the details."

"Okay." I nodded. "Let's take a look."

She brought out a folder from her bag and opened it on the table. It held several pieces of paper.

"Like I said, it's in Italian. I can translate, but not very well."

"That shouldn't be a problem." I smiled, my hand going to my pendant. "I have a universal translator."

Her eyes went to the opal. "That?"

I nodded.

She furrowed her brow. "May I see it?"

I took it off and handed it to her. She looked at the stone and the woven wire setting holding it in place.

"This was in your mother's things?" she asked.

"Yup. It was pretty much the first thing I found."

"I had no idea she had such powerful artifacts." She shook her head.

"What's so special about it?" I asked. "I've run across other amulets and such that had translation spells."

"Yes," Luci agreed. "Those are fairly common. But if I am not mistaken, this is much more." At my look, she continued. "Legends talk about the Four Treasures of the Tuatha de Danann.

King Nuada's sword, the Sword of Light, is the first. Then there was Lugh's spear, Dagda's Cauldron, and the Stone of Destiny. But there were other artifacts that were just as important, just not as well known, because they were less obvious. One of them was Ogma's Pendant; the Stone of Tongues."

"I have heard of this." Grace nodded. "It doesn't only translate, but also grants eloquence and the right choice of words to bring others to your point of view. Yes?"

"That's my understanding as well," Luci told her. "I just wonder how it ended up with Sofia. These treasures are all considered lost." Her eyes fell to the knives at my waist. "Those were in the box as well?"

"They were under the false bottom, like the sword." I looked down at them. "I know they have strong magic worked into them."

"Do you know what they do?" Luci asked me.

"They can cut through spells," I told her. "That's one thing they can do. And— Veron told me something else about them. If I can remember." I thought back. "He said they were linked to each other, and to whoever owned them, and he called them light and shadow. No! I remember now. He said they were the strike and the glide; the *Grève* and the *Glissé*. Not that I know what that means. I kind of think of them as yin-yang."

I drew one of the daggers and placed it on the table.

"I have a sort of dampening spell on them right now," I said. "To keep them hidden."

"I believe this is another lost artifact," Luci said after she had studied the dagger for a moment. "I think these are the Scian of Goibhniu."

"The Scian? Of what?"

"Scian just means knife," she explained. "Goibhniu was said to be the son of Danu and Dian, brother of Nuada. He was a smith. A master craftsman. Not much is known of the daggers, but your yin-yang concept does seem apt. I just can't imagine how Sofia ended up with two such powerful treasures."

"I wonder if there's more to the shadow and light concepts that I could be using with them," I mused.

"And I am wondering what else your mother may have had," Grace commented. "Do you think this sword may have been another such treasure?"

"I don't think so." Luci shook her head. "The only treasure that was a sword was—" Her eyes widened. "Nuada's Sword! The Sword of Light! What if Nora has the Sword of Light?"

"Would that be good or bad?" I asked.

"Both?" She shrugged. "It's one of the most powerful known artifacts."

"I've never heard of it," I joked.

"I bet you have." Luci smirked. "You could probably find a dozen completely different stories about a sword of light or a shining sword. Stories from different cultures, or even different stories in the same culture. All the stories have different names for it. But there's at least one I'm sure you've heard of."

"Like?" I prompted her.

"Excalibur."

That sat me back in my chair. "You're serious?"

"That's just one of the names from one of the stories." She nodded.

"That's all very interesting." I took a breath. I had all kinds of questions coming to mind now, but I couldn't let myself get distracted. "But as my friend Mouse would say, that's not getting any onions chopped. Let's focus on finding Nora."

I pulled the small stack of papers around so that I could read them. The pendant worked its magic, and the Italian was completely understandable for me.

"Hmmm," I said, reading through the top sheet. "This one tells how to create an anchor without having to memorize the location. Handy." I read through it. "You still have to go there first to create the anchor, though."

I went on to the next page.

"Okay, this one talks about detecting a portal." I flipped to the next sheet and looked it over. "Creating a portal from a visual image; that's what I do already. I could have used this a few months ago." I went on to the next page. "This one talks about creating a stable, two-way portal. It looks like it usually takes two people, one on each side."

"That's probably what was used to create the access stations for Danu," Luci commented.

I skimmed through it. "It looks like this one takes several pages to explain how that works. Nothing so far on what we're looking for." I flipped to the final page and stopped. "Here we go." It was just a few short paragraphs. "I think I can do this." I looked up at them. "It says I have to be able to see magic flows, which I can. Apparently, if I study the location where a portal has been, I should be able to see a residual trail. If I follow that to its end point, I can recreate the exit." I frowned as I read the last notes. "The trail fades over time as the magic dissipates and returns to its natural state."

"We should see if the trail is still there," Luci said. "But we should prepare before we actually follow it."

I nodded and we went down the hall to my bedroom, which was still a disaster since Grace and I hadn't started cleaning it up yet. Fortunately, there wasn't much damage aside from the door.

Stone had created his portal just inside near the door. I made my connection to the *Ralahin* and looked at the room.

"There." I pointed. "I can see the trail from the portal I created to get everyone to Daoine."

I looked to where Stone's portal had been. It was a tangle of fading flows.

"This," I tried to sort through the confusion. "It's like there are a dozen trails."

"You and Nora ended up on different worlds," Grace pointed out. "The spell must have fractured somehow and created multiple paths."

"But which is the right one?" This was going to be harder than I thought. I studied the trails. "I think I might be able to figure out which ones were actually used. At least for some of them. This is going to take a while."

Luci nodded. "While you do that, I need to get these papers back before they're missed. Oh." She reached into her bag and pulled out something else. "I got an ID for you under Carmen Cansino."

I glanced at the image of the driver's license. It was me, alright. Me as I looked now. I didn't know how she'd done it, but it looked real. I slipped it into the back pocket of my jeans.

"Alright." She stood to go.

"Wait." I got out my cell and took pictures of every page, then sent it to my printer.

"Good thinking." Luci smiled. "I'll return these and come straight back."

There was a knock on the door.

"Have some pizza first," I told her. "I need to eat something before I try this."

The girl delivering the pizza looked uncomfortably at the broken door frame as I gave her the cash for the pizza, along with a healthy tip. I could tell she wanted to say something.

I grinned at her. "Boys, parties, alcohol, and wrestling are a bad mix. They are *so* going to regret this once they're over their hangovers."

"Good luck with that." She chuckled. "Enjoy your pizza."

Grace eyed my choice of toppings suspiciously, but her expression changed to pleasant surprise after her first bite.

"You like?" I asked her.

She nodded, smiling around a mouthful of heaven.

"It's an unusual combination of ingredients," Luci said, washing down a bite with a swallow of ginger-ale. "But tasty."

I'd added red-pepper flakes to mine, and I was too busy digging-in to reply. After we'd eaten, Luci left to return the papers.

"I'd like to go see if the police have finished at the store,"

Grace told me. "I need to pick up a few things if I need to do a location spell. I shouldn't be gone very long."

"Would you mind grabbing my backpack from the office while you're there?" I asked her. "Oh! And my staff? We don't know what we'll be walking into, I'd like to have it with me just in case."

Back in my room, I sat down on the floor and leaned against my bed. I made my *Ralahin* connection and used my Sight to start tracking the trails of Stone's fractured portal. Several I could discount immediately as being too faint to have been used. That left seven possibilities. I started tracing them, one by one; following them to their end and expanding my senses past that point to learn something about what was on the other end.

The first one I followed took me to a hillside surrounded by a forest. Daoine. It made sense that I would be drawn first to the path I'd taken. The next one I followed ended someplace very cold and dark. I got the impression of an underground cavern. That didn't match with Stone's story of ending up in a forest, so I went on to the next one.

I followed the trail through twists and turns and the feeling I got of the exit was hot and dry and unpleasant.

The next trail felt more solid somehow. The end felt like a forest. I tried to extend my senses further and definitely picked up the impression of a lot of trees. And the trail felt like it had been traveled. This must be it. I marked the trail with a magic flow of my own, like a little ribbon, and I sent a surge through the trail to make it stronger. Would I be able to create a portal to the end of that trail? I tested my connection to it to be sure. Yes.

I released my connection to the *Ralahin* and stood up. I was surprised to see that the light coming in the window had shifted quite a bit. Grace was sitting in a chair nearby and she was dozing off. She started awake at my movement.

"That must have taken longer than I realized," I said, stretching.

Grace rubbed her face with her hands. "Yes. Luci came back and left again," she said. "Did you find the trail?"

"I think so." My stomach rumbled. "I don't know about you, but I'm hungry again. I'm going to have a snack."

I was finishing another slice of the pizza when Luci got back. I looked up as she walked in.

"That's going to take some getting used to," I told her.

"What?"

"Aunt Luci."

She smiled at that. "I think I could get used to it very quickly."

I noticed she had changed clothes. Earlier, she had been wearing clothes for the office. Now she had on sturdy jeans and hiking boots. I glanced at Grace and saw that she was dressed for hiking as well. I had the jeans I'd put on the previous night before rushing to the store, so I was good.

"So." I looked at them. "Are we ready to see if I can get this portal opened?"

# CHAPTER SEVENTEEN

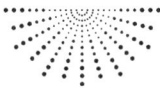

## NORA

*I* spent the next two days with Jack and Zoriaa scouring the library for anything having to do with the sword or with *baensiari*. I was still wrapping my head around the fact that I was speaking and understanding a different language. I can't say *new* language, since this was supposed to be recovered knowledge from some past lifetime, but for the only life I remembered, I had only spoken English.

My recovered ability wasn't as strong for the written form, though. I could figure out what it was saying, but it was slow going. This would probably get easier over time, with some practice.

Emma hadn't been very happy with the language situation.

"It's not fair." She pouted. "You guys are all talking and I can't understand what you're saying, and then you don't tell me anything."

"I'm sorry." I understood her frustration. "I already checked; Kerbas has the only translation ring."

"But you speak their language now, right? He doesn't need it."

She had a good point, and when I brought it up to Kerbas, he shrugged and tossed her the magic ring. Emma grinned as she slipped it on her hand. She had to put it on her thumb because it was too big for her fingers.

"Thank you!" She beamed at him, speaking the common tongue.

Kerbas and the other guards stayed mainly outside, taking care of the griffins, or sparring or gambling with some strange-looking dice. I imagined this was terribly boring for them.

I was amazed at how well preserved the inside of the building was. It was as if it was a pocket outside of time that had escaped the ravages of whatever had caused the Scourge. Every book seemed pristine, every page cool and crisp.

Somehow, the whole city felt different than it did before. Something wasn't quite right. I couldn't put my finger on it, but it was just a little off. The lack of life and moisture was a separate thing. By itself, that had a sort of draining effect that robbed me of my motivation and gave me an urge to leave. It made it very difficult to focus. I pushed those feelings aside; there was information here, somewhere, that I needed. That Zoriaa thought I needed. And maybe, I'd find a way home while I was at it.

They hadn't had much luck finding material, but a small stack of books was growing at the corner of the table. Using the ring with the translation spell, Emma was able to read as well and had managed to find a romance story from the many books in the library. I didn't want to hear about it, but at least it kept her entertained. There was a glass door at the back of the room that opened into what looked like had once been a garden. Emma had taken to sitting on a bench there to do her reading.

We also spent some time with Jack talking me through some basics about magic. Of course, without his power, he couldn't demonstrate anything for me.

"My ability to manipulate magic may be blocked after Zeg stole my powers," he said, "but I still can See power and the flows of magic. This is a basic foundation for magic use. Using magic doesn't require this Sight, but it makes it much easier to manipulate raw power."

"I know," I tried not to sound frustrated. "You've told me this. But I'm still having trouble seeing it."

"There is another way to quickly draw power," he told me. "You can use life force. It can be your own life force or that of another."

"Isn't that dangerous? I mean, if you use your life force…"

"Certainly, if you drain all the life force from someone, or you use all of your own, it can be fatal. Otherwise, it replenishes naturally over time."

"So," I pondered this, "as long as I only use a little, there's no harm done?"

"Well," he admitted. "It has been noted that the more you draw, the source tends to behave more emotionally. Reactionary rather than rationally. But after a few days they return to normal. Whatever normal was for them."

"But using life force… isn't that sort of like what Kartahn Zeg does?"

"Correct." He nodded. "Necromancy is one form of this type of magic use. It is also the way some species feed. You consume organic matter to provide fuel for your biological construct. Some races, such as *Daijheen* and *Qélosan* survive by draining the life force of others, or even simply from their emotions."

"*Qélosan*? I don't think I've heard of them."

"Be glad for that. They are creatures of light. They can beguile and hypnotize. Similar to how some carnivorous plants attract their prey with beautiful and fragrant blossoms. *Qélosan* are usually more like scavengers though, preying upon those whose physical constructs have recently failed."

My jaw dropped as that sank in. "So, when I die, don't go to the light?"

"That would be a sound approach," he agreed. "But let's not rush to that situation any time soon."

"Well, I don't like the idea of stealing someone's life force."

"As I said, you can use your own. But keep in mind, using the life force of another can also be done with permission. It doesn't have to be stealing. In fact, an interchange of life force in some species is an act of extreme intimacy."

"You mean like tantric…" I felt my face heat up as I realized where my thoughts were going. I did *not* want to have a conversation with Jack about sex. Or with anyone else for that matter. I had other matters to worry about without cluttering things up with that. "Never mind. You also told me about other magic systems? Other ways that people on different worlds used magic?"

"Yes." He launched again into explaining to me how different worlds could have completely different systems for using magic, or even more than one. It was interesting and I wanted to understand, but my mind kept wandering and eventually he'd gone silent.

"What do you keep staring at?" Jack asked me.

"What do you mean?" I looked at him.

"Every few minutes, your eyes look over in the same direction," he told me. "Perhaps if we address whatever is distracting you, you will be able to focus on what I'm saying."

I frowned. He was right. More and more, my attention had been drawn to a narrow bookcase on the back wall of the room. It was like a sore tooth that you just couldn't leave alone. Looking at it from where I sat, there was nothing remarkable about the bookcase. I shrugged and looked back at Jack. Almost immediately, I found myself looking at the shelf again.

"Do you find my instruction that boring?" Jack pulled my attention back to him.

Jack had seemed to be getting better at understanding people and emotions. Maybe it was a side-effect of losing his powers and being at the same level as the rest of us.

"No." I shook my head. "It's not boring, I just—" My eyes were back on the shelf. "Sorry, Jack." I looked back at him.

Jack sighed. "Go ahead. Whatever it is, go look at it and get this out of your system."

"Fine."

I got up from the table and walked over to the shelf. Most of the bookcases were in sections that were about six feet wide. Every so often, at a regular spacing, there was a three-foot wide section separated on both sides by about a foot of paneling. I glanced at the other smaller units, but none of them pulled my attention. Just this one.

Now that I was standing in front of it, there was one book I was focusing on. It didn't really look any different from the others. It was fifth from the end on a shelf that was about shoulder height. I tried to pull the book from the shelf, but it didn't budge. I put my hand on the top edge of the binding and pulled. There was a click and the book pivoted outward. Then suddenly the entire shelf swung away from me into an opening that appeared behind it in the wall.

"Jack? Zoriaa? What's this?"

They joined me and we looked into the dark passageway. We could see steps leading down.

"There's only one way to find out." Zoriaa shrugged.

"You learned how to create a floating flame," Jack said to me. "Let's see if you can light the way."

I scowled at him. I'd learned it all right. That didn't mean it was so easy. He'd actually shown me a few ways to do it, more talking about the theory of multiple magic systems, but the way that worked best for me was to find the fire within myself, the spark, and draw it out. Jack had said that this spark was a point of internal conflict that would eventually resolve itself and not to rely on it too much. But as long as it worked for now, that was good enough for me.

It was easier to make a flame when there was something physical to burn. This was a lot harder. I concentrated and slowly a small blue flame grew in the air about five feet in front of me. I turned to him with a grin.

"I did it!"

"Very good." He nodded.

I took a couple of steps toward the flame when Jack stopped me.

"You need to direct the flame to move with you or you will have to keep creating new ones as you go."

Right. Duh. I hadn't thought of that.

"I know that!" I told him. "I'm just getting ready."

Jack didn't reply and I wasn't sure whether he'd believed me. I just hated making stupid mistakes like that. But how could I make it move? I thought about how the light would move if I was carrying a torch; how it would align with me and move with me as I walked. I reached out with my mind and imagined the flame was at the end of a stick. I took a step forward and the flame retreated. I'd done it!

"Nicely done," Zoriaa complimented me.

We followed the steps down. They only went one level and opened into another room. It was a cozy little space with bookshelves along one wall, some kind of workbench on another, and a desk and some chairs. There was an open book on the desk.

There was some sort of cantilevered crystal decoration hanging from the ceiling. I reached up and rotated one of the crystal slats and light began to shine from the whole thing. The further I rotated the slat, the brighter the light got. After adjusting the light to a comfortable level, I released the blue flame. The chair behind the desk looked very attractive and I went around the desk and sat down.

"This is comfy." I smiled.

Zoriaa was already looking at the books on the shelves. Jack was studying the crystal lighting fixture.

"This is promising," Zoriaa said. She reached up to touch a book and as her hand got close electricity shot from the shelf to her fingers. "Ouch!" She pulled her hand back. "Maybe not so promising!"

"What about this one?" I asked, indicating the open book in front of me.

Zoriaa walked over and looked at it. There was a loose paper set on top of the book with writing on it. She looked at the paper and at the book underneath.

"I don't recognize the language," she said, shaking her head.

I glanced at the page. "It looks like it's talking about some kind of spell."

"How do you know that?" she asked me.

"Because it says—" I looked up at her. "Wait, how come I can read this, and you can't?"

Zoriaa picked up the paper again and examined it, then she turned the book so she could get a better look at that as well.

"These were penned by the same hand," she said, comparing them side by side. "And it looks like they are in the same language."

I took the book and letter and studied the words.

"I think these are in different languages," I told them. "But also, some kind of code. Or maybe different characters." In the loose page, I could see how it was phonetically representing words that I clearly recognized from what we had been speaking. The common tongue, Jack had called it Valikari. The book seemed to be written in Italian.

Zoriaa flipped through the book. There were a few more pages of writing after the place it was opened to, and then the pages were blank. She thumbed through the earlier pages.

"I think you're right," she said. "I may not be able to read it, but I think this is a grimoire, a book of spells. Mages and such document the things they discover or develop. It wouldn't be unusual for such a book to be in some sort of code to keep the knowledge secure."

I looked at the loose paper again. "This is a note. Or maybe a letter."

"What does it say?" Jack asked me.

I skimmed through it. "It's talking about *Uthadé* and *Fu-Mo Ri*. About them trying to take control of Tir Nya Lu... This part..." I started reading it out loud.

*I cannot allow either faction to take control of Tir Nya Lu. This city of light holds too much power to entrust to either side. I have sent all of my people to Daoine. There, they should be safe until the conflict has passed.*

*I have devised a spell to remove Tir Nya Lu itself from the realm, and a way to bring it back. The Eye of the Goddess will be closed in slumber, as it were, to one day be reopened. This spell will act as a scourge should either side seek to remain in the area. I must enact the spells at the same time, I fear the effort may be too much for me. The key to return Tir Nya Lu will be simple; the spell will be ready and only waiting to be activated.*

*If I do not survive this spell, I know at least that my people will be safe and that Tir Nya Lu will be kept out of the hands of these foolish clans, bickering back and forth. Even without me, someone may use the key if they can cipher the words.*

*Tir Nya Lu has always had a spell of protection against attacks, yet these are not powerful enough to resist both the Uthadé and the Fu-Mo Ri at the same time. The restoration process is in two stages. The first stage will begin to reestablish the protection spell. The second will fully restore Tir Nya Lu and bring the protection to full strength.*

*Heed me: if you seek to restore Tir Nya Lu, you will be bound to it upon its return. You will become its master. Its protector. This is also part of the spell. Surely as I am baensiari to the sword, you will be baensiari to Tir Nya Lu. May the Great Mother bless you if you are both, and may she have mercy upon you if you are not. Dulcinea was to take this burden. With her loss, it will fall to Merlain's line.*

*The spell mechanism itself is not without its defenses. If you do not approach from a lighted path, you will be cast far.*

*The moon is about to rise. It is time.*

*Nimué Rinn, Daughter of Aradi*
*Baensiari of Tir Nya Lu of Avalon*

I looked up at them. "Nimué Rinn? Is this the same Nimué that— that I was?"

"That would explain why you can read it," Zoriaa commented. "After all, you *were* Nimué. You may be the only person who *could* read it." She thought for a moment. "You said Nimué *Rinn*? Daughter of Aradi?"

"That's what it says, why?"

"It seems to support one of the old legends," she answered. "When so much time has passed, it is hard to know what is truth and what is speculation. Even with this information, we can't say how much of the story is accurate. But if she used the family name of Rinn, there may indeed be truth to the tale."

"Would you like to share with the rest of us?" I asked her.

"If the story is of interest to you," she said. "It has to do with Nimué and her parents and grandparents."

"Sure," I told her. "I'd like to hear it. I guess it's my history, too."

"The history of a past you," she corrected. "Remember, you are not Nimué; you are Nora."

"Yeah, I get that. But I'm still interested."

"Alright." She nodded. "The letter confirms she is the daughter of Aradi, whom we know to be the child of the Great Mother, Arduanna, and Lugh. It is important to note that Lugh was born of a union between *Uthadé* and *Fu-Mo Ri*."

"So, he was a half-breed?"

"Yes." She nodded. "The name of Rinn would come from her father's side. Aodhan Rinn was a simple hunter on Earth who followed a wounded bear through a gateway and ended up on Daoine."

"That's the place that Nimué said she sent her people, right?" I asked.

"Correct. Aodhan had been badly injured in his fight with the bear. He was discovered in the hills by a beautiful *Loiala Fé* maiden named Cerise. She nursed him back to health."

"I think I know where this is going." I gave her a look.

"During his recovery," Zoriaa continued with a smile, "she told him stories of the Tuatha de Danann. They read

165

the poetry of the great Oisin. And yes, by the time he had recovered, they had fallen in love. They had a son, Oisin Rinn, named for the poet whose works they had spent so much time reading together. Oisin took after his father and became an exceptional hunter. He was renowned in all three realms, Earth, Danu and Daoine, though he never sought fame. Arduanna had heard of him and sent her daughter, Aradi, to test him to see whether he was truly a worthy hunter."

"And why would she care about that?"

"Arduanna was known as the goddess of the hunt," Zoriaa explained. "So, she saw it as her purview. Aradi was already on Earth, Arduanna had sent her to teach humans how to perform witchcraft. If Aradi found Oisin to be worthy, Aradi was to seduce him into swearing allegiance to Arduanna."

"What?" I was shocked. "That's not cool."

"However," Zoriaa went on, "Oisin became aware that someone was spying on him, and he laid a trap for her. When he discovered who he had captured, he was angry that the gods were interfering. He threatened to proclaim to all that the gods were no better than men if they could be caught by men. Fearing her mother's reaction, Aradi begged him not to do this. He agreed on the condition that for three years she would stay with him. She would clean the skins from his hunts, and she would prepare dinner for him every night. She agreed."

"Was that kind of thing normal?"

"I couldn't say." She shrugged. "But before the time had passed, their feelings for each other had changed and she bore him a daughter; Nimué."

"Hang on." I held up my hand. "Then Nimué was *Uthadé*, *Fu-Mo Ri*, human, and… What was the other one?"

"*Loiala Fé*. Yes."

"How is it that all of these races are genetically compatible?" I asked her.

"I don't know that term."

"I mean." I searched for words. "They can have offspring, but they're different species."

"Ah." She nodded. "Humans seem to be the key to this for some reason. They can breed with most other species. So as long as someone has human blood in their ancestry, they should be able to have children with a number of other races. Otherwise, a mix would not be possible."

"Like a universal donor." I nodded. "What about Lugh? You said he was a half-breed."

"Of *Uthadé* and *Fu-Mo Ri*, yes. But those are really the same species. They just had different coloring. The *Uthadé* had pale blonde or even white hair and blue eyes and pale skin. The *Fu-Mo Ri* had red hair. Their eyes were blue or green."

"And they had freckles." I rolled my eyes. "Kerbas said something about that. Okay, sorry. Go on."

"Well, Arduanna eventually learned what had happened and was furious. She left Danu, coming to Earth, and she swore to take vengeance on Oisin. Oisin fled east with Nimué to avoid her wrath. Arduanna followed, but Oisin was wily and according to the story, she was never able to catch them."

"But then how did Nimué end up here?"

"Much of Aradi's work was done in Italia," she explained. "In that region, Arduanna became known as Diana. I don't know the details, but I understand that Nimué assisted Aradi in her task, so Arduanna forgave her of her... parentage, and accepted her into the royalty of the *Uthadé*."

"Forgave her of her *parentage*?"

Zoriaa shrugged. "Evidently, Arduanna liked humans, but didn't want to be related to them. Or perhaps she objected to the mix with *Loiala Fé*. I don't know. Clearly, whatever the original disagreement, it was resolved and Nimué ended up here in Tir Nya Lu in a very important position."

"It would seem that whatever this Nimué attempted here resulted in the destruction of the entire region," Jack mused. "I cannot imagine this is what she intended."

Zoriaa nodded. "I believe you're correct. If, as she feared, she did not survive the attempt, there are any number of ways the spell could have gone wrong."

"Even if it went wrong," I asked, "would this 'restore' spell she talked about fix it?"

"Possibly," Jack answered. "It could also make things worse. Without understanding how the spell went wrong, there is no way to know for certain. And don't forget she said the restoration mechanism was defended."

I reread the letter. "What if it didn't go wrong? What if the spell went exactly like she planned?"

"If it had," Zoriaa replied, "surely she would have restored Tir Nya Lu as well, once the war was over."

"Sure." I nodded. "If she survived it. And if nothing else happened after that to stop her."

"True enough," Jack agreed. "But we have insufficient data from which to conjecture."

"Speaking of information," Zoriaa cut in. "It looks like everything we've been looking for is on these shelves. But we can't access them."

"Unless," Jack looked at me, "maybe you can touch them, since it was apparently your previous self that owned them."

I stood up from the desk and walked to the bookshelf. I glanced at the titles. These were written in the common tongue, but I had no idea which ones would be important. I shrugged and reached for one at random. *Zzap!!!*

"*Mother f—*" I shook my hand. That hurt! "We're not trying that again!"

"Unfortunate." Jack shrugged.

"Maybe you should try, Jack" I scowled at him, my hand still smarting. "Maybe it won't hurt a *Daijheen*."

"Ah." He shook his head. "I would prefer not. I just got my hand back. I'd rather not risk it again so soon."

"Jack, did you just make a joke?"

"Did I?" He looked at me, surprised. "Should I not?"

"No, that's fine," I told him, sitting back down at the desk. "Don't quit your day job, though."

"My what?"

"Never mind. What about this grim thing?" I asked, flipping through the pages of the open book. "Will this help?"

"Perhaps it will tell of the spell protecting the other books," Zoriaa answered. "But since you are the only one who can read it, you are the only one who can find out."

"So... Do you think I should read this? Or the books upstairs?"

"What we found upstairs really only had hints," she told me. "I think your time would better be spent with this. Meanwhile, Jack and I can continue to look for something more substantive upstairs. And we can help you with any questions you have about Nimué's grimoire."

# CHAPTER EIGHTEEN

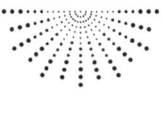

## MIRA

"First," Luci said, "let me tell you about the people on Danu. There are three groups. The first two are the *Dannu Fé* and the *Ande Dannu*. The *Dannu Fé* are also known as the Unseelie Court or the Winter Court. They tend to be very mistrustful of outsiders. They will take advantage when they can. The *Andé Dannu* are the Seelie Court or Summer Court. They aren't friendly, per se, but they are easier to get along with than the Dannu Fé. Either group can be a problem if we aren't careful. We want to avoid trouble with them as much as possible."

"Okay." I nodded. "And the third group?"

"That's the *Wyl-Dunn*," she answered. "They are nomadic. They're hunters and they live in tents. They are very strict if you break their rules, but otherwise they aren't so bad. But just like with the others; if we run into them, be respectful and try to avoid trouble."

Luci reached into her bag and pulled out a double shoulder-holster and strapped it into place.

"What's that?" I gaped at her.

"This?" She looked at me. "A pair of Springfield Hellcats. Nice, compact 9mm semi-automatics."

"I thought you said we were supposed to avoid trouble?"

"We are." She nodded. "With the pinky extenders they hold thirteen rounds plus one in the chamber. That can avoid a lot of unnecessary trouble. If trouble finds us, I like to be ready for it."

Grace tried to stifle a laugh. I looked at her and she just gave me an innocent shrug.

"I suppose you're *packing*, too?" I asked her.

"Not guns." She smiled. "But I have my own precautions. So do you," she added. "Isn't that why you asked me to bring your staff from the shop? Isn't that why you always carry those knives?"

"Touché." I smirked. "Point taken." I looked back at Luci. "If you were Daruidai, I'd think you would use magic, too."

"Sure. But spells can take time. And there's an old saying about powerful wizards being susceptible to a knife in the ribs. These are faster than knives." She patted one of her pistols.

We gathered in a semi-circle in the bedroom facing the door and made ourselves ready. I connected to the *Ralahin* and looked toward where the portal had been.

"Wait!" I had something I wanted to try.

I looked quickly around the room for some object I could use, remembering the night that Laruna had bound me and tied off the spell on a teacup. I grabbed a two-inch piece of the broken door frame from the floor. I pulled a flow of the magic and tied it around the shard of wood. When I was satisfied, I shoved it into my pocket.

I saw my backpack leaning against the wall where Grace had evidently deposited it when she got back, and I put it on. I probably wouldn't need it, but it wouldn't hurt. I grabbed my stuff and then resumed my position with Grace and Luci. I looked at the mess of flows where Stone's portal had been and located the trail I had marked earlier.

"Are you ready for the locator spell?" I asked Grace.

"Everything is prepared." She nodded. "I can activate it once we are through and get a direction and maybe even a distance."

"Alright, get ready. And remember; this is a one-way portal. I'll have to open a new one for us to get back, but that one will be much easier."

I concentrated on the thread; the trail of magic that started here and went through the in-between space and ended on another world. Once I was solidly connected to both ends, I opened the entry and exit portals. It was a little unstable at first. Once it was in place I used the words of power Tesia had taught me to strengthen it.

"*Shrolin chalé.*" It looked good. "Let's go," I told them.

We went through the portal, and I closed it behind us. We stood in a forest I didn't recognize. Grace immediately drew some marks in the dirt. In the center, she put the hairbrush I had given to her previously to try the spell. It had been Nora's. She moved her hands in a circular motion to draw magic in and then sent it through the brush and into the markings on the ground.

"This way!" I heard a voice speaking the common tongue come through the trees.

I could hear the sound of many feet approaching quickly. What looked like two dozen *Loiala Fé* soldiers burst through the trees and surrounded us with weapons drawn. I hadn't expected such a fast reaction. I pulled the shard of wood from my pocket and threw it northward, using magic to propel it further; it would land a couple miles away with the assistance.

"Archers!" one of the soldiers called out. "Release!"

I quickly erected a barrier around us and opened a portal back to my bedroom. Crossbow bolts were bouncing off my barrier.

"Go now!" I yelled as soon as the portal was in place.

Luci and Grace went through the portal, and I was close behind, closing it as soon as my feet were on the carpet.

"That was a very fast and harsh reaction," Luci said. "I'd expect that more from the *Dannu Fé* than the *Ande Dannu*. Something must have happened."

"Stone said something about them thinking that Nora

escaped and murdered a bunch of guards," I told her. "I know she wouldn't do that. The murder part, I mean. But if there was some kind of incident…"

"Yes." She nodded. "They might react violently to the next strangers that showed up through an illegal portal."

"Were you able to get anything from your locator spell?" I asked Grace.

"Yes," she answered. "Nothing precise, but she is definitely there and far to the west of where we were."

"How far?"

Grace shrugged. "I'd say hundreds of miles. Two hundred? A thousand? I don't know. I'm sorry I can't be more exact."

"No, that helps," I told her. "That's a long way to hike, though. I'd suggest driving a car through a portal, but we'd have a problem with fuel. And I doubt there'd be good enough roads."

"Dirt bikes?" Grace asked.

"Still the fuel problem." I shook my head. "We don't know how much we'd need and we can only carry so much."

"We might be able to get horses," Luci suggested. "But that would still take a lot of time to travel hundreds of miles."

I remembered how fast Farukan could travel when he didn't have to wait for slower horses. If only he was with me now.

"I might have another option," I told them. "Maybe we could get some *Rorujhen* to help."

"Who are they?" Luci asked.

"They're like horses," I explained. "Big ones; like a Friesian or bigger. But they're sentient, like you and me. Remember, I told you about Farukan? *Rorujhen* are also really, really fast. They can easily cover in a day what would take a week for a regular horse."

"That's impressive!" Grace nodded. "But would they help us?"

"We can only ask," I said.

"I think I'm going to need to use some of my vacation time at the office." Luci grinned. "I take it we're going back to Daoine? That's where the *Rorujhen* are, right?"

"Do you need to make some phone calls?" I grinned back at her.

"Yes. But mostly I need to send some emails. Which I can also do from my phone." She pulled out her cell and went down the hall.

"What about you, Grace?" I looked at her. "If we're going to be gone for a few days, is there anything you need to take care of?"

"If we're gone for more than a few days," she answered. "I'll need to come back and see to Katya's burial. But I don't know when her body will be released."

"Of course. I can get you back whenever you need." I thought about that. "I guess technically, I could portal us back every night to our beds and just open a portal to our last location in the morning to come back. But I don't think we need to bother with that. Plus, if the *Rorujhen* do help us, I wouldn't want to leave them without any protection."

I assumed we would be going directly to Danu from Su Lariano, so I made doubly sure I had everything I would need in my pack. We would be able to get supplies for the journey to track down Nora once we got to Daoine.

"Alright," Luci came back in. "Everything is taken care of. It does sound like this might take at least a couple of days. We'll probably need to bring a change of clothes or two. And maybe some toiletries."

I nodded, looking at them. "So, you guys wanna meet back here in an hour?"

An hour later, they had their travel items in small packs and were ready to go.

"Should we have dinner before we leave?" Grace asked. "I'm starting to get hungry again."

"No!" I smiled when I thought of it. "I own a restaurant! Half-owner, anyway," I amended. "Tonight, you'll be in for a special treat. Oh! I want to bring what's left of the pizza for the chef to see. I think it might make a good addition to the menu."

I retrieved the box of pizza from the kitchen. After verifying that we were all ready and had our backpacks, I opened a portal to my suite in Su Lariano and we stepped through.

Jill and Tony were sitting around the table with Tesia and Ree. They had evidently stopped their conversation when the portal formed.

"Guess who can speak a new language!" Jill grinned at me. She'd said the words in the common tongue.

"How—" I looked and saw that both she and Tony were wearing bracelets I didn't recognize. These must have translation spells imbued. "The bracelets?"

"What?" Jill teased. "You don't think we're smart enough to learn that fast on our own?"

"And I created a few more, just in case you brought any more friends," Tesia said. She opened a small box that was sitting on the table and pulled two more bracelets out.

I went to the table and put down the pizza box.

"Thanks!" I took the bracelets and handed them to Grace and Luci. "These will let you understand and speak the local language."

"You brought pizza, *mija*?" Tony asked me. "Is that for dinner?"

"No," I told him. "Tonight, we're having dinner at the Raven's Nest. You guys, too!" I said to Tesia and Ree. "I need to talk with Neelu first. Maybe she can join us. Do you know where she might be right now?"

Tesia smiled. "Don't you have your comm-dev?"

"Yes!" I took off my backpack and started digging through it to find the magical communication device.

"Don't worry," Ree said. "I already spoke with her. She'll meet us at the Raven's Nest."

"By the way," Tesia added. "These comm-devs have become very popular. It's still a secret, but pretty much everyone in a

175

senior role has demanded one, for themselves and for other key personnel." She looked over at Jill and Tony. "Mira's ideas have had quite an impact here. She's done a lot to make this world a better place."

"And here's my next contribution." I grabbed the pizza box with a grin. "I want to show this to the chef!"

On the walk to the Raven's Nest, Jill and Tony talked about everything they'd seen that day. Tesia and Ree had shown up for breakfast and then given them the grand tour.

We crossed Market Square and went into the restaurant. Mouse was behind the bar, wiping it down with a cloth. As soon as he saw me, he dropped the cloth and rushed around to us.

"Mira!"

Mouse was a lot bigger than most *Ulané Jhinura*, in height and bulk, though he was still a few inches shorter than I was. But when he wrapped his arms around me it felt like he was a huge bear.

"I was afraid I'd never see you again!"

I returned his hug as best as I could with the pizza box in one hand. He stepped back and there were tears in his eyes.

"I'm sorry I left without saying goodbye," I told him. "I—"

"Rispan told me everything," he said. "It's okay. I understand." His eyes turned to the rest of the group, and I introduced him around.

"I'm sure you are all interested in some dinner," Mouse said. "Let me show you to a table. Neelu is already waiting for you."

"Can you bring Jakeda out?" I asked Mouse as we took our seats. "I have something to show her as a possible addition to the menu."

He nodded and stepped toward the kitchen to find the chef.

"That was a fast return," Neelu said. "Did you get things figured out?"

"Some," I told her. "Right now, we're trying to focus on finding my sister. But we need fast mounts. After dinner, I'd like to talk with the *Rorujhen* and see if I can get some volunteers. I'm hoping we can leave again first thing in the morning."

Mouse returned to the table with Jakeda.

"Good to see you again, Raven," Jakeda nodded to me. "What do you have for me?"

I opened the flat box I'd set on the table.

"This is called pizza," I told her. "It's normally served hot."

She pulled off a piece and examined it, looking at the toppings and the crust.

"Interesting." She nodded. "I think we can try some variations. This bread underneath is meant to be crisp or soft?"

"There's actually a lot of ways to do that. Some like a thin, harder crust. I prefer a thick crust that is slightly hard on the bottom but still doughy. There's other options, too. Besides cheese, the sauce is one of the most important ingredients. This one uses a white sauce, but it's more traditional to use a red sauce made from tomatoes and herbs. There's also a huge variety of topping combinations. Do you have shrimp here on Daoine?"

"We do." She nodded. "But it's tricky to get seafood here from the coast and keep it fresh. It requires a mage to preserve the shipment, and that makes it more expensive since preservation spells are usually proprietary."

"Hmmm." I thought that over. "What if we had a permanent, two-way portal from the coast to speed up transportation?"

"That would ensure fresh deliveries, certainly," she answered.

"Two-way portals?" Tesia asked. "Permanent?"

"Yeah, I just got some information on that." I gave her a smile. "You already know a bit about portals, right?"

"Yes, that's how we got here so quickly from Shifara."

"Great! What would you say about a partnership in a business that provides portal service to get goods and produce to market? I think we should pull in Réni and split three ways. She knows trade and can manage contracts and fees, and we'd need someone to keep an eye on the business aspect, and you to do the heavy lifting of creating these things when I'm away."

"Wow, *mija*," Tony said. "I never knew you were such an entrepreneur!"

"This will just be the beginning." I grinned at him as more ideas came to mind. "Wait until we start transporting things to and from Earth!"

# CHAPTER NINETEEN

## MIRA

*A*fter dinner, Tesia took Jill and Tony back to the suite and Neelu led the three of us to the paddock where the *Rorujhen* congregated when they were in the area. Some had taken to their newfound freedom with a will and spent all of their time running out on the plains, but many others liked to have more of a home base to orient around. The *Ulané Jhinura* of Su Lariano had provided them with that.

"I didn't even ask you two if you knew how to ride." I looked at Grace and Luci.

"I've ridden since I was a child," Luci answered. "I'll be fine."

Grace shrugged. "I've ridden camels and even elephants. But that was many years ago. I was to learn horse riding, but it never happened."

We reached the paddock area and I could see maybe thirty or so of the *Rorujhen*, some in small groups and others standing solitary. Of course, being telepathic, they didn't have to be right next to each other to be talking.

It always amazed me how much the coloring could vary with the *Rorujhen*, and every possibility I had ever seen on any breed of horse, and then some, could be found among them. I just stood there for a moment, admiring their beauty. But I was there for a reason.

"Hello everyone," I called out. "I know I haven't met most of you. My name is Mira." As I spoke, I also projected the words with my thoughts. Since I had previously bonded with a *Rorujhen*, I was already attuned to them. Plus, once the restrictions of the Riders had been removed, they'd been able to communicate more easily with strangers as if the mandate and fear of reprisal had somehow stunted their abilities. "I've come to ask for your help."

*"You are Farukan's Mira?"* a male voice in my mind questioned.

I had managed to avoid thinking of him until that moment, but hearing his name sent a knife of loss through me and I winced from the pain. I tried to gather myself for a response but didn't get the chance.

*"We know you, Farukan's Mira,"* the voice told me. *"All* Rorujhen *west of the Great Mountains know you. And we thank you for working for our freedom with Farukan. What do you require of us?"*

"Um." I took a breath. "I don't *require* anything. I ask. We are trying to find my sister, Nora. She's on another world: Danu. We have a starting point and a direction, but it could be very far to where she is. And I think she's in danger. No one can travel as far and as fast as the *Rorujhen*. I'm looking for volunteers to act as mounts. This is Grace and Luci." I motioned the two of them forward. "Would any of you consent to come with us and act as their mounts?"

One of the largest *Rorujhen* I had ever seen stepped forward. His body was a beautiful chestnut color, and he had a blonde mane and tail. He walked around the two women, looking them over and smelling them. They were both dwarfed by his immense size. Neither of them looked very comfortable under his inspection.

*"This one may do,"* he said, shoving Luci with his nose. Luci reached up a hand to touch him but he drew back. Then he

raised his head to gaze out to the other *Rorujhen*. *"Who will stand for the other?"*

A buckskin mare with a black mane and tail came over and looked Grace up and down. She was average size for a *Rorujhen*, but still much larger than a regular riding horse.

*"She seems nervous."* Her voice was soft and playful. *"I can see why you would prefer the other. You are far too impatient for this one."* He flipped his ear at her without responding. *"I will be her mount,"* she said. *"Her heart is strong."*

*"You must tell them how to initiate the bond,"* the male spoke again.

I nodded and spoke to Luci and Grace. "If you put your hands on them, you'll be able to hear their thoughts after that."

Luci immediately raised her hand again and looked questioningly at the male. I could hear his chuckle as he took a step toward her, allowing the contact this time.

Grace's glance at the mare was uncertain, but the mare stepped close and nuzzled her gently and Grace's hand went naturally to the mare's neck.

*"I am Mehrzad,"* the male voice boomed in our minds and Luci and Grace both jumped. *"I consent to be your mount, Luciana Leon."*

*"I am Laleya. I consent to be your mount, Grace Ndané."*

"You honor us," Grace found her voice. "And we thank you."

*"Mira."* Mehrzad looked at me. *"Any of the* Rorujhen *would stand for you. You must choose."*

"I—" Of course. I would need a mount, too. I hadn't wanted to think about that part. "I haven't ridden since—"

*"I understand. It is a hard thing to lose a bond-mate. Harder still to find another."*

I shook my head, completely at a loss for moving forward, for even *wanting* to move forward. "How could I replace Farukan?"

*"You cannot,"* Laleya said. *"You are not replacing him. Only*

*Farukan is Farukan or will ever be Farukan. But you* can *ride and bond with another."*

*"Take your time,"* Mehrzad said. *"We will get acquainted with our new riders."*

I walked around the paddock area, observing all of the *Rorujhen*. They continued doing whatever they'd been doing before we arrived, but I could tell they were aware I was there. They were all magnificent. I went to one side and sat down on a rock to watch them.

Two colts were chasing and nipping at each other, one was a blue roan, and the other was as white as snow. I had to chuckle at their antics. A warm feeling came over me. We had accomplished this. Farukan and I and all those who had helped. We had made a bargain, he and I, and we had both kept it. He had kept us safe, and his people, the *Rorujhen*, were no longer slaves to the White Riders.

On one end of the paddock was a three-sided structure with hay and grain, with a roof above to keep it dry in case of rain. Several of the *Rorujhen* were eating or standing under the overhang. There was a shadow just on the other side of the far wall. At least, I thought it was just a shadow, but it shifted position. Curious, I got up and walked toward the structure.

As I neared, I could see that there was a dark colored *Rorujhen* standing in the shade of the building. It was a mare. Her head was low and turned away.

"Hello there." I smiled. "You're not hiding back there, are you? Why don't you come out where I can see you?"

The mare seemed to freeze for a moment, then she took a few hesitant steps out of the shadow of the building. When she stepped into the evening sun, I was able to see her coat. It looked like someone had thrown water balloons with black and brown and white paint all over her and then sprayed her lightly with water to give the whole thing a murky, splotchy, speckled look. I'd never seen anything like it.

*"I know,"* a soft voice whispered in my mind, and she stepped back into the shadows. *"I am ugly. Now you have seen."*

"What?" Her words had taken me as much by surprise as her coloring. "No! Just different, that's all. You don't need to hide."

She didn't respond or even look at me.

"Maybe you can help me," I said to her. "You know everyone here, right?"

Her only response was to shift her ear, listening to what I was saying.

"My name is Mira, by the way. I need to choose someone to come with us, to be my mount." I looked out over the field. "I can't. I don't know any of them. Mehrzad said that all of them would be willing. Is that really true?"

*"You are known to us,"* the soft voice answered. *"Mehrzad speaks true. Any here would be honored to serve as mount for Farukan's Mira."*

I was still at a loss. "Can you help me choose?"

She stepped out from the shadows again and I glanced at her. There were scars on her neck and hindquarters. I looked back out over the field.

*"What do you seek?"*

"What do you mean?"

*"The best choice for you depends on what you seek. Strength? Speed? Beauty? Bravery? Loyalty?"*

"All that's good, I suppose. Farukan was all of those things. But more than anything else, he was my friend."

She was silent at that. Finally, she answered. *"I know what it is to lose a friend. I do not know who can be that for you."*

She turned and started back toward the shadows. I felt a kinship for her through our shared loss.

"Wait," I called to her. "What's your name?"

*"I was called Mud,"* she answered.

"No, not that. I mean your true name."

As slaves, *Rorujhen* had been forbidden many things. They weren't allowed to communicate to anyone but their rider, thereby revealing they were intelligent, and they weren't allowed to use their own names; they had to use whatever name their owner dictated.

*"I am Anazhari."*

"That's a beautiful name," I told her. "Thank you for talking with me."

I looked back over the field at the *Rorujhen*, but I couldn't make myself choose one.

"Anazhari." I turned to her. "Would you do it? Of course, you don't have to if you don't want to. But…"

*"Do you joke? I would not be the best choice,"* she answered. *"Any here could serve you better. I am ugly and broken. You cannot depend on me. Choose another."*

"I—" I looked at the other *Rorujhen* again. "Please, it was hard enough to ask you. I don't know if I could do it again…" I stopped myself. "I'm sorry. I didn't mean to pressure you. Of course you are free to say no."

How selfish of me! She was obviously going through her own pain and there I was trying to push her into being my mount. I needed to honor her wishes. I promised myself that whenever I was in Su Lariano in the future I would check in on her and see how she was doing. That was something I could do at least.

I walked back to where Luci and Grace were getting to know Mehrzad and Laleya.

"Did you find someone?" Luci asked.

"Not yet," I told her. "I need more time. I'll pick someone in the morning when we're getting ready to go."

When we got back to my suite in the royal wing, Arané-Li, the chamberlain, was there getting everyone sorted out. Rispan was getting his own suite, which I expected now that it was known he was the lost prince, Karis Ulané Panalira. Mouse had gotten quarters for himself closer to the restaurant.

"Hello, Mira." Arané-Li smiled and gave me a hug. "It's good to see you again." She drew back. "I can set your parents up in the second bedroom or get them their own rooms. And I see you have two additional guests…"

"Oh, we don't want you to go to any trouble," Jill said. "Or," she looked at me, "how long do you think we'll need to stay here? Is it safe to go home yet?"

"I don't know," I told her, thinking it over. "I didn't see anything to worry about. Let me see if I can arrange some security for you first." I pulled out my cell phone. No signal. Right. "Be right back!"

I formed a portal to my bedroom back home and stepped through. As soon as my cell had reconnected to the network, I punched in a number. I rang twice before there was an answer.

"Stone."

"Yeah, this is Mira."

"Mira, I'm still working on getting the approval to go find your sister—"

"That's not what I'm calling about right now," I cut him off. "I need to know if it's safe for my parents to come back home."

There was a pause before he answered. "I can have a security detail there in thirty minutes. Since there was a magical attack, that's easy to arrange. They'll stay outside and monitor from there. Will that work?"

"Yes," I told him. "If anything happens to them…"

"Don't worry, I'll see to it."

"Good. They'll be waiting."

I cut the connection and started to make another portal back to my suite when I heard a sound from the front of the house, followed by a voice.

"Mira? Nora?" The female voice was familiar.

I walked down the hall toward the sound of the voice. Shelby was standing in the front doorway.

"It *is* you," she said as soon as she saw me. "I knew it!"

I started to come up with something to say, but she cut me off.

"Don't even try it," she snapped. "I know it's you, Mira.

185

Older somehow, but it's you. Did using magic age you? I've heard it can do that if you're not careful."

"Sorry," I said, "I'm not Mira. I'm her cousin, I—"

"Don't lie to me!" There was an anger in her eyes that I didn't understand. "I'm not a child!"

"That's not what I said." I tried to calm her down. "Of course you're not a—"

"I don't need you to patronize me, either!" She glared at me. "I was going to give you a chance. I was going to let you join me. But I see I was wasting my time. You always thought you were better than everybody else."

"I never thought that—"

"You went to some pocket universe didn't you? Different time? That's why you look older. I did that too! And I trained. I'm powerful now. You're not so special! Maybe I'll let you live if you tell me where my sister is."

"Your sister? Emma?"

"Whatever," she sneered. "Don't tell me, then. Play ignorant all you want, I don't really care, anyway. Our parents are always so high they haven't even noticed she's gone."

She flicked her wrist and an ice shard shot at me from nowhere. She was using magic! I barely had time to dodge the first one before several more were flying my way.

"Shelby! What are you doing?" I tried to connect to the *Ralahin*, but one of the ice shards slashed across my left bicep and broke my concentration.

I had just reestablished my connection when another figure appeared in the room. I saw him whip a strand of magic around Shelby, holding her in place with her arms pinned to her sides and her jaw clamped tightly shut.

"Who are you?" I demanded, standing ready for anything.

"You must be Mira." He grinned. "I'm Charlie. What are you doing here? I thought you were trying to find Nora?"

Shelby struggled to get free, and Charlie tightened the magical bindings.

"Did Stone send you?" I asked him.

"Stone doesn't send me." He laughed. "He's a useless twit!"

"He's supposed to be sending protection for my family!"

"Oh, he can do that." Charlie nodded. "I suppose he isn't totally useless."

"But you aren't one of them? The bodyguards?"

"I'm sure they'll be along shortly." He glanced at Shelby. "I'll have this one out of here before they arrive."

"What are you going to do with her?"

"I'll just keep her out of your way while you take care of things." He cocked an eyebrow at me. "You were on your way to take care of things, yes?"

I scowled at him. How could this stranger just show up knowing so much about what was going on?

"Who are you?" I asked him again. "What are you doing here?"

"There'll be time enough for that later," he said, "when we don't have unwanted ears listening in. I'm a relative of Nora's. Not close, and we've never met, but I do care what happens to her. So you do what you need to do, and I'll clean up here."

"Charlie, huh?" I wasn't happy not knowing more, but he was right about unwanted ears. I didn't know why Shelby had attacked me, but she already knew more than I wanted her to. And how did she learn magic? He did seem to be helping me. "Alright. We'll talk more another time."

"I'm counting on it." He smiled. He walked across the room to me and extended a business card. "Call me when you have a few minutes."

I slipped the card into my pocket and looked back at Shelby. She'd stopped fighting and was glaring daggers at me.

"Stone's bodyguards should be here any moment," Charlie said. "I'd prefer to be gone before they arrive. I'd like to keep my participation a secret from other *Daruidai* for now."

That jived with what Luci had told me about different factions.

I nodded to him and headed back down the hall to my bedroom. I pulled his card out of my pocket and looked at it. Just a number. No name or anything else. Charlie who? I walked back to the front of the house, intending to ask a few more questions, but when I got there he and Shelby were both gone. He certainly hadn't wasted any time clearing out.

I grabbed some gauze from the first aid kit in the bathroom and wrapped up the cut on my arm. It wasn't deep, but I didn't want blood getting on everything. I changed my shirt and then whipped up a portal to take me back to my suite in Su Lariano.

"You guys can go back any time," I said to Jill as the portal closed behind me. "I arranged some protection for you, just in case."

"That's amazing how you can just go back and forth between worlds like that!" Jill marveled. "How did you get used to all this magic stuff?"

"I'm still getting used to it." I grinned. "It does come faster when you have to use magic just to turn on the lights. But I wouldn't talk about it back home. People will think you're crazy."

"Don't worry." Tony smirked. "Everybody already knows she's crazy."

# CHAPTER TWENTY

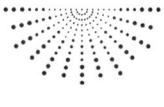

## NORA

"*J* still don't know how to restore Tir Nya Lu or how I'm supposed to be a *Baensiari*," I grumbled over dinner with the others. I'd spent two frustrating days reading and rereading Nimué's grimoire. "All I have been able to find out is that this location, not just Tir Nya Lu, but the whole area, the Sulosh Sea?"

"Suloshné." Zoriaa nodded. "The Sulosh Sea. Sea of the Sun."

"And it's also called the Eye of the Goddess?"

"That's more of a nickname," she explained.

"Okay. Well, it seems it's some kind of a major nexus for magic. That just gives me more questions."

"Perhaps the answers lie in the other books in the study," Zoriaa suggested.

"Maybe." I shrugged. "But I'm not crazy about getting zapped every time I try to reach for them."

"Maybe you need a key for that, too," Emma said around a mouthful of chicken in a mushroom sauce. "Maybe it's the same key."

"A key implies a lock of sorts," Jack commented. "We have yet to locate such a mechanism, magical or otherwise."

"Oh!" Emma looked up from her plate. "That reminds me. I think maybe I found the lock. Or *a* lock, anyway."

Just then, Kerbas entered the library, a serious expression on his face.

"We are going to have to leave this place," he said. "It is no longer safe."

"Why?" I asked him. "What's going on?"

"One of the tasks allocated to the Wyl-Dunn is watching the borders," Kerbas told me. "We patrol from the air on griffin-back. A scout just came through. The ruined city of Murias in the west has been occupied and a large army is marching east, apparently toward Solaian. But a group has split off from the main body and is heading this way. We can only assume they mean to take control of Tir Nya Lu as they have Murias."

"Why?" Emma asked. "It's just a bunch of ruins."

"Maybe because of that magical nexus thing," I mused. "Maybe they want to take control of it."

"You said an army?" Zoriaa asked. "Whose army?"

Kerbas frowned. "They are *Bahréth*. And it seems the party coming here is led by Kartahn Zeg."

Jack's head swung around at the mention of the necromancer, the expression on his face made me glad he wasn't looking at me that way. Then Jack's eyes fell to the floor.

"Without my powers," he said. "I cannot beat him."

"We need to leave while we can." Kerbas nodded.

"What's a *Bahréth*?" Emma asked.

"They are a reptilian race from the far south," Kerbas told her. "From beyond the Great Desert. A massive fleet lies at anchor near Murias. We assume this is how they arrived."

"Reptiles?" Emma scrunched her nose. "Like lizards?"

"If by lizard," Kerbas looked at her, "you mean creatures which stand ten feet tall on their hind legs, bear a spiked tail of another six feet, have razor-sharp claws, a venomous bite, chameleon abilities, emit a call that pains the ears and sends shivers down your spine, *and* are extremely cunning then, yes; Bahréth are like lizards."

"We must not leave the tomes in Nimué's study for Kartahn Zeg to steal," Jack interjected. "He grows too powerful already."

"But they're protected by magic," I answered. "If we can't get to them, how will he?"

"Do not forget he has my powers." Jack looked at me. "We do not know what other powers he may have accumulated. We cannot assume he will be balked by the spells protecting the books. You must find a way to access them."

"Me?" I flustered.

"And we have little time," Kerbas told us. "There is also a smaller, second group approaching from the east. Three of them on horseback. They appear to be humans, but we don't know anything about them. They will be here within the hour. Kartahn Zeg's group has reached the edge of the seabed and they are coming toward us rapidly. How quickly can you retrieve the books?"

"I don't know how!" I objected.

"Maybe it's about this whole *Baensiari* thing," Emma suggested. "Didn't you guys say the *baensiari* of the city was also supposed to be the *baensiari* of the sword?"

"That is my understanding," Zoriaa answered.

"Have you tried reaching for the books while you were holding the sword?" Emma looked back and forth between us. "Or touching that protection spell with the sword?"

"No," I said flatly. She raised her eyebrows at me in response. "Fine," I grumbled. "But if I get zapped again I'm going to be—" I bit off the rest. I guess she wasn't too young to hear it. I'd never spoken with her parents though, so I didn't know what they thought was acceptable language for their thirteen-year-old daughter to hear.

I picked up the sword and they followed me downstairs into Nimué's secret study. I paused in front of the bookshelf and looked at the others, but they just watched silently. I lifted my hand and moved it toward the books, remembering the last time I'd tried this. I braced myself as my hand got closer. Then my hand was on a book and there'd been no zap. I let out a breath.

"Okay," I said. "I'll move all these out and we can pack them up."

After moving the two dozen or so books, I picked up Nimué's grimoire and went upstairs. Kerbas passed some saddlebags to Zoriaa and she went back to load the books.

Emma watched as we prepared to leave. I could tell she had something on her mind.

"What?" I asked her.

"Don't you want to take a look at that lock I found?"

"What lock?"

"I told you earlier." She pouted. "You never listen to me."

"We don't have a lot of time," I told her, trying not to sound exasperated. "If you have something to show me, we have to be quick."

"Okay!" She grinned. "Over here!"

Her mercurial mood swings never ceased to amaze me. I followed her as she skipped to the garden where she'd been reading.

"There!"

She pointed at an elaborate sundial set on top of an ornate pedestal. The sundial itself was made of two tones of metal, but from the age and disuse, I couldn't tell what metals. There were gems inset as markings around the edge. The pedestal was an artistically formed column that was probably a foot and a half around.

"It's a sundial," I told her.

"I know *that*," she rolled her eyes, "but check this out."

Emma walked up to the sundial and grabbed the plenum on top that would cast the shadow to point to the time. She gave a twist, and it flipped up, revealing a slot almost a half-inch wide and about a couple of inches long.

"That looks like a keyhole to me," she said smugly.

I stepped closer to take a look at it. I couldn't see how deep the slot was.

"I don't know," I told her. "If that's a keyhole, it would take a pretty big key. I've never seen a key that big."

"Oh, really?" At my look, she rolled her eyes. "What about the key you used to get those books?"

"You mean the sword?" I looked back at the slot. It actually did look like the sword would slide right in.

"Zoriaa! Jack!" I called them. "Come take a look!"

They joined us in the dead garden, and I pointed at the sundial.

"If the sword is the key," I said, "then that might be the lock or whatever it is we've been looking for to activate those spells."

They both stepped up to examine the sundial. I retrieved the sword from where I'd left it inside while they studied the slot.

"Maybe with Kartahn Zeg and his guys on the way," I went on, "we could activate the protection spells Nimué was talking about."

I pulled the sword from the sheath.

"Wait!" Jack stopped me. "Too much is not known. This is a very dangerous course of action."

"Since when did you worry so much?" I asked him. "If you're afraid, stand back."

He frowned at me. "I do not fear for myself." He seemed to struggle with conflicting emotions before he went on. "Nora, you intervened for me. You protected me when I would have been abandoned in the Scourge to die. You took me as your responsibility. You healed me. And… you have taught me. I owe you much, and it is for *you* that I fear. If you would accept me, I would be bound to you, to serve as your advisor, as your protector, in whatever way I can." His eyes dropped to the floor. "I know it is a weak offer, since I don't have my powers—"

"No, it's not weak," I told him. I was shocked at the emotion in his voice; and somehow moved. I touched his shoulder. "Jack, you can be my protector if you want. But in the end, I still make my own decisions. You can protect me, but you can't take that away from me."

He nodded once.

"The letter said it was a two-stage process," I mused, looking back at the sundial. "Maybe we should just try to do the first part. From some of the other notes, I think that gives us partial protection but doesn't restore anything."

Slowly, I slid the sword into the slot. It went in perfectly. The keyhole was centered above the pedestal, and the sword sunk into it to the hilt. As soon as it was fully in place, some markings on the dial began to glow. One marking was straight up, away from me along one edge of the sword. The second angled slightly on the right, halfway to the third which was at about a forty-five-degree angle from the first.

At the same moment, I felt a sensation inside that was similar to what I had felt the night Zoriaa had sung that song at the wedding reception. Then I noticed that I was glowing, too.

"So far, so good." I took a deep breath.

Placing my hands on the hilt of the sword, I twisted clock-wise. At first, it resisted, refusing to move, but then the sword started to glow and the brown leather on the grip turned white. Finally, the sword turned and clicked into alignment with the second marking. I felt a wave of something ripple out in all directions.

I withdrew my hands from the hilt of Fragarach, the Sword of Light. I realized that was its name. Fragarach. But it had other names that came to me as well. Claíomh Solais. Caladbolg. Gram. Excalibur. Guardianship had been passed to me by my mother, Aradi. No, not my mother. Nimué's mother. I saw images in my mind of a beautiful woman with pale hair and skin. Aradi. I knew her.

A wave of distant memories washed over me. Aradi and Oisin, my parents. Arduanna. Avalon. Tir Nya Lu. It was only bits and pieces. Somehow, activating that spell with Fragarach had brought these memories back. But they weren't mine; they weren't my life. They were Nimué's memories. Nimué was dead.

"I'm not Nimué," I muttered to myself, trying to shake off the images. "I'm Nora."

"What?" Emma scrunched her nose at me.

"Did we do it?" I looked at Jack and Zoriaa.

"You did *something*!" Emma beamed. "I *knew* that was the lock!"

Kerbas rushed in the front door of the library, and we went inside from the garden to find out what was happening.

"Some kind of barrier has been erected around the island!" he said.

We followed him outside and could see what he meant. The setting sun reflected off a translucent dome above us. With the buildings around us, I couldn't see how far it extended.

"I think I did that," I told Kerbas. "We found the mechanism to activate the protection spells. I wasn't sure whether it worked."

Kerbas breathed a sigh of relief. "I feared it was something from Kartahn Zeg to trap us here." He looked at me. "Even so, we cannot stay. There is no certainty that he cannot breach this barrier. We should be gone before he arrives."

"We are almost ready," Zoriaa told him.

"Very good." He nodded. "We'll get a fresh look from above to best choose our course."

Kerbas and the other scouts took to the air on their griffins while we went inside to finish packing up. I grabbed Nimué's spell book. I wanted to keep that with me.

"We just need to turn that sword one more notch," Emma was saying. "Then we'll have the full protection thingy."

"I don't know if that's a good idea," I told her. "The second part includes the restoration spell. Jack thinks that would be dangerous. We do need to get the sword though."

I went with Emma to the garden and tried to pull the sword back out of the sundial, but it wouldn't budge. This wasn't good. I called to Jack and Zoriaa and they looked it over.

"It seems that it is locked in place by the spell," Jack said. "I believe it can only be removed if it is either returned to the original position or advanced to the third position."

"And switching it back will turn off whatever protection we have?" I asked.

"I would assume so."

"Maybe there's something in here," I said, thumbing through the spell book.

Kerbas and several of his scouts had come in and they were half carrying, half dragging some figures. They brought them to us in the garden.

"The humans," Kerbas said. "They must have reached the shore of the island just as the barrier went up."

"Are they dead?" I asked him.

"Unconscious," he answered. "As were their mounts."

"I didn't know you had humans here." I looked at the three figures. They were the first humans we'd seen since we'd left Earth.

"We don't have many," Kerbas said. "But these are not from Danu. They are dressed strangely."

All three were wearing jeans.

"I think they're from Earth," I told him.

I looked closer. Three women. One was black and the other two looked like they were probably Latina. One of the Latinas had shoulder holsters with guns in them. The other Latina… she looked a lot like Mira, but older.

"I wonder…" I got to my knees and put the spell book down as I checked their pockets. The one that looked like Mira had a driver's license in her back pocket. I read the name. *Carmen Cansino?* I knew that name from somewhere, but couldn't place it. The one with the guns had a small wallet with an ID that said Luciana Leon.

That name I did recognize. I looked at her face. It had been a while since I'd seen her. How could my social worker be here? I retrieved the spell book and got back to my feet, shaking my head. More questions.

"The barrier goes around the entire island," Kerbas said. "We were also able to see Kartahn Zeg and his people. They are preparing to assault the barrier."

"I think we're ready to go." I looked at Zoriaa for confirmation and she nodded.

"What should we do about these three?" I asked. "I don't think we should just leave them here."

"Nora," Emma interrupted, "we just need to turn it up to full power and we'll be fine."

I shook my head and turned back to Kerbas. "Can we carry them on the griffins?"

"I believe we can manage," he answered.

"Nora?" The one with the Carmen Cansino ID was starting to wake up. "Nora? Is that you?"

"You never listen to me!" Emma stomped to the sundial and grabbed the sword.

"No!" I shouted. I grabbed her arm just as the sword clicked into the final alignment.

I felt power building in the pedestal. I shoved Emma away from it and she stumbled backwards. There was a blinding flash and I felt a blurred sensation of traveling, of moving. Then darkness swallowed everything.

# CHAPTER TWENTY-ONE

## MIRA

*T*esia came by with Réni and we worked out the details of our transportation business using portals. Once I'd gone over the notes on the permanent portals with Tesia, she'd immediately gotten the idea. Réni knew all the contacts and we planned to get started with seafood from the coast.

"You have a good head for business, *mija*," Tony said as my meeting with Tesia and Réni drew to a close. He and Jill had been listening from the side.

I shrugged. "Once I started thinking about commerce, about how it was all about exchanging things to get people what they need or what they want, I just started seeing all the possible connections."

"Well, it looks like you're going to do very well for yourself here." Jill smiled.

"I think it is probably easier here than on Earth," I mused. "On Earth, there's so much paperwork for permits for everything. I mean, I think there needs to be regulation there, because there have been so many abuses, but it's easier here."

Jill glanced at Tony. "It's really lovely here, and we'd like to spend more time," she told me, "but I think we'd like to go home if that's okay. I know the house is trashed right now, but we'd like to sleep in our own bed."

"No problem." I stood up and opened a portal back to my bedroom. Creating the portals had gotten much easier the more I did it; I just needed to have a clear idea of where I was putting the exit.

Jill was shaking her head. "That's just amazing!"

"I can't call," I told them. "We don't have a way to talk between worlds."

"Yet." Jill grinned. "I'm sure you'll solve that problem, too."

I started to object, but then I thought maybe there could be a way to magically link the cell phones to connect directly. If I could connect the two ends of a portal between worlds, there should be a way to link two objects.

"I see the wheels turning already." Tony laughed.

"Well." I gave him a mock scowl, "for now we won't have a way to talk unless we're on the same world."

"That's so *crazy*!" Jill shook her head. "Talking about being on different worlds like it's no big deal."

She was right; the idea was pretty awesome. I supposed that aspect had been overshadowed by some of the experiences I'd had. While some of those experiences were painful and had left scars I would always carry with me, there had also been wonderful experiences. Those would always be with me, too. It would be up to me which experiences I focused on.

I guess that was why a lot of times when someone died their friends and family hold a celebration of life for them. That way they had their attention on all of the gifts the departed had brought to their lives rather than dwelling on the loss of not seeing them again. I needed to take that approach with Mooren and Farukan and the others I had lost along the way. My connection and experiences with them were the gems I should treasure. Wanting more was just being greedy. I smirked at the thought.

Jill looked at me quizzically; a silent question about my moment of introversion.

"Let's get you two home," I said, bringing my attention back to the topic at hand. "I'm not going to hold this portal open forever. I'll let you know what's happening when I can."

After a brief round of hugs, they went through the portal and I closed it behind them.

Grace and Luci had been chatting quietly on the couch and they paused to look at me. I glanced around the room; the central hub to my suite in the royal wing of Su Lariano. I realized that even with all the time I'd spent in Pokorah-Vo and up north in Shifara and Shianri, this had come to feel like a home for me.

"That's the spare bedroom." I pointed to the door. "It only has one bed, but it's pretty big if you don't mind sharing. Otherwise, you can always draw straws for the couch."

"We'll figure it out." Luci smiled.

"It's been a wild few days," I said to them. "I know what sounds good to me. Check this out."

I led them to the room with the bath and showed them the controls for temperature and humidity for the bath, shower, and room.

"It's like you have your own private health spa!" Grace shook her head.

"The only thing missing is the masseuse!" Luci grinned.

I laughed at that. "I could probably arrange it. But I was thinking how good a soak and some steam sounded after everything we've been through."

"I'm in!" Luci said. "It sounds heavenly!"

"Me too." Grace smiled.

The room was designed to accommodate several people, and I even managed to make some magical air bubbles in the huge tub to make it more like a jacuzzi. I don't know about the others, but I slept very well that night.

We rose early the next morning. Neelu came by as I was finishing breakfast with Luci and Grace. I was so glad they had coffee on Daoine. And soon there would be pizza. I wondered what other things would start to pop up once travel got going to and from Earth.

When we arrived at the paddock area with Neelu, we could only see Mehrzad and Laleya. There were also some grooms on hand to load up the saddles. We had our backpacks — daypacks, really — and I could see there were saddlebags loaded with supplies.

"Where's everyone else?" I asked the *Rorujhen*.

"*Their presence was unnecessary,*" came Mehrzad's answer.

"*Mehrzad!*" Laleya scolded him.

"*Am I wrong?*"

Her response in my mind felt like a sigh.

"What am I missing?" I asked.

"*Three selections were made,*" Laleya told me. "*Three are here.*"

"What selections?"

"*I chose Luciana,*" Mehrzad answered. "*That was the first selection.*"

"*And I chose Grace,*" Laleya added. "*And Mira chose Anazhari.*"

Anazhari stepped forward hesitantly from the barn, her head low.

"No." I shook my head. "That's not what happened. We spoke, but she wasn't interested. You aren't slaves anymore; you have free choice. That's what I fought for. That's what Farukan— That's what Farukan fought for. We can't force her. I couldn't live with myself if we did that."

"*You reject Anazhari?*" Mehrzad asked.

"No! Of course not!" I looked at where she stood, listening to our conversation. "Anazhari, I'm sorry for putting you in this position. You already said you didn't want to be my mount."

Anazhari looked at me. I heard no words in my mind but felt her embarrassment. And shame. *Why shame?*

"*Anazhari.*" Mehrzad's voice was stern. "*Did you say you did not wish this?*"

"*I said I would be a poor choice.*"

*"Do you refuse Farukan's Mira?"* he persisted. *"Be clear. Is this something you wish or do not wish?"*

*"I wish it,"* she admitted. *"But any would be better suited. I do not wish to fail her."*

*"If you do not wish to fail her, do not start your bond with self-recriminations. Stand tall Anazhari! Are you not* Rorujhen? *Have you not been offered a great honor?"*

She stood silently for a few moments before saying anything.

*"Mira."* I felt her attention fully on me now. *"If you truly wish for me to be your mount, I would indeed be honored. But you also have free choice and are not obligated to choose me because of a casual comment made last night. The others are not far if you wish another."*

"It wasn't casual," I told her. "I just—"

*"Enough!"* Mehrzad cut in. *"It is decided. I suggest we get into these saddles and get going."*

I thought I felt a brief chuckle from Laleya and Mehrzad's head swung around to look at her. Laleya somehow exuded complete innocence.

"Now that everything's settled," Neelu smirked, "I'll leave you all to your travels."

"Thanks for everything." I gave her a hug. "Hey." I pulled back. "What was that Rispan was saying about a wedding?"

"We'll talk about that when you get back." She laughed. Then she nodded to Grace and Luci. "Good luck!"

The *Rorujhen* were saddled, and our daypacks were tied behind the saddles with our bedrolls. We mounted up and I looked at Luci and Grace.

"It's a long way to the ground from up here," Grace said nervously.

*"You only think that because you have such short legs,"* Mehrzad chuckled in our minds.

"That's going to take some getting used to," Luci remarked.

"Hearing voices in your head?" I asked her. "Yeah. It took me a while, too."

I connected to the magic, the *Ralahin*, and followed the thread of magic I had attached to the piece of wood I had left on Danu until I located the end. I expanded my awareness to the area around it. It wouldn't be good to step through and find we were on the edge of a cliff or in the middle of a lake. Fortunately, the ground was fairly level and forested.

"*Are you ready?*" I sent the thought to only Anazhari.

"*I am with you,*" came her answer.

"Alright," I said out loud. "I've got it. Here we go."

I opened the portal, placing the exit near the end of the thread.

"Go slowly," I told them. "It's forested and you don't want to walk into a branch or something."

I led them through the shimmering air of the portal, and we stepped forward until all of us were through, then I closed it behind us. I gave a small tug on the thread I had followed, and the piece of wood snapped into my hand. I stuffed it into my pack.

"Grace." I turned to her. "You said the locator spell indicated Nora was several hundred miles to the west?"

"Yes." She nodded. "It was too far to be more precise."

"Let's just start heading in that direction and clear out of here. We can do another location spell later. I don't want to stick around here and risk a confrontation with the *Ande Dannu*."

We let the *Rorujhen* have their head, choosing our path and speed for us. We traveled swiftly. Despite their great size, the *Rorujhen* were extremely agile and had no trouble navigating through the trees. If any *Ande Dannu* showed up to investigate the unauthorized portal, we'd be long gone.

We maintained a companionable silence as we rode. There was no path, and we didn't ride in single file. The *Rorujhen* were able to instinctively keep from getting too spread-out.

Around midday we paused to rest and sample the food supplies stuffed into the large saddlebags. My stomach had been complaining for more than an hour and I hoped whatever had been packed for us would satisfy it. One thing I had appreciated on my travels as Raven the trader on Daoine was the simple preservation spells they had for food items.

I say simple, but you had to have a decent mage handy to do the spells. I remember reading stories from Earth where they had to use dried meats and such on the trail because otherwise the food would spoil. We didn't have to worry about that with these preservation spells; they kept each item in a sort of stasis. I wasn't sure how it worked, the bites you take would somehow be separated from the spell, and when the item was completely eaten the spell would dissipate. If I could figure a way to mass produce the spells for the general population— I shook my head when I realized my thoughts had once again turned to commerce.

*"It comes naturally to you,"* Anazhari commented from nearby.

*"Maybe so,"* I sent back. *"Really, I just see things that would help people who don't have it, and then I try to think how they could get it. The commerce aspect isn't what drives it."*

*"I know this,"* she said. *"This is what stands out about you. You do not seek first for yourself."*

*"I don't know that it's unusual. I think most people have some desire to help others."*

*"This is true as well,"* she agreed. *"But they too often become sidetracked by their own interests, and this eclipses the original purpose."*

*"Yeah, the whole 'what do I get out of it' thing."*

*"What about giving these things away?"*

*"Not practical."* I shook my head. *"And not equitable. I under-stand that part of it, too. It takes time, effort, and skill to produce things. That has value. If there's no exchange, then it equates that time, effort, and skill to having zero value. Who wants to work when your contribution is just expected but not appreciated? And those who benefit, if they give nothing for it, they would take it for granted. Like air. It's readily available and free; we all feel we are entitled to it. So, while getting something in return isn't the motivation, it is definitely an important factor for the relationship between consumer and*

*supplier."* I realized I'd been rambling and stopped, embarrassed.

*"As I said."* Anazhari chuckled, *"it comes naturally to you."*

I was glad that Anazhari was feeling comfortable enough to open up and have a conversation. I'm sure the bond had something to do with it. The bond between a *Rorujhen* and their rider was difficult to understand, let alone explain. At the same time, we were distinct individuals, yet we were one. I couldn't imagine how it had been for them when they'd been slaves of the White Riders; but I was glad we had put an end to that tyranny. The *Rorujhen* were now known to be fully sentient beings and were free to choose their own riders or to not have riders. In the end, that war had taken Farukan. Though I know it was a price he'd paid freely, I did miss him.

Before we got going again, Grace did another locator spell.

"I would say close to four-hundred miles," she told us. "North-west, or just a hair south of that."

I could see the beginnings of a mountain range on our right. Hopefully, our path wouldn't take us into the mountains. That would slow us down considerably.

"How about we skirt the southern edge of those mountains?" I suggested. "That should take us in the right direction."

The first night was uneventful. We made camp in the foothills more than a hundred miles from where we'd stopped for lunch. We removed the saddles and gear from our mounts, and, after a quick meal, all three humans fell into an exhausted sleep. My last thoughts before darkness claimed me was that maybe there was a way to use magic to make our bed rolls as soft and comfortable as a regular bed.

We woke with the sun the next morning. After a quick breakfast, we discovered that putting the saddles back on the *Rorujhen* was harder than taking them off had been the previous night. The saddles were heavy and the *Rorujhen* were tall. In the end, I lifted the saddles into place with magic and the *Rorujhen* guided us through the rest of the procedure. They were cooperative, but not beyond a little teasing. Especially Mehrzad. I was getting the idea he was a bit of a prankster.

As the sun was nearing the horizon, we reached a dry seabed. In the distance, we could see the shadow of a mountain rising up through the haze and heat waves.

"That must have been an island at one time," Luci commented.

Grace did another location spell before nodding to us. "I think that's where she is."

"Alright," I told them. "We're close now. We should be there in a couple of hours at most."

The *Rorujhen* went down the slope to the dry ground, making for the mountain. As we got closer, I noticed a cloud of dust to the west. It seemed there was another party heading for the same place.

"I wonder who they are?" I said aloud.

The others noted the dust cloud with no comment. I kept an eye on it and it looked like we would reach our destination at about the same time. We had farther to go but were moving a lot faster than they were.

The sun was down as our *Rorujhen* started to scramble up the slope from the seabed to the shore of the once-was island. At that moment, a silvery bubble sprang up around the island. As the barrier struck us, I tried to erect a shield but I didn't have time. A powerful blow struck us and I felt myself falling.

Voices.

My head was groggy and I was hearing voices. The barrier must have knocked me out. I felt someone going through my pockets. I struggled to open my eyes. *Wait— Is that Nora's voice?* I tried to make out the conversation.

"Nora?" I struggled to get the words out. "Nora? Is that you?"

I cracked my eyes open, but my vision was blurred. Then there was a blinding flash, and I felt the waves of some powerful magic washing over me. I sat up, shaking off the effects of unconsciousness as best as I could.

I looked around the room at the faces of strangers, all of them looking very alarmed about something and none of them looking at me. I didn't see Nora, but I was sure I had heard her voice and someone saying her name.

"Who are you people," I asked. "And where's Nora?"

# CHAPTER TWENTY-TWO

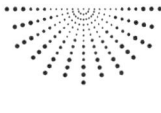

## MIRA

"You look like Mira," one of the men said to me. He was the only one of them who didn't appear to be *Loiala Fé*. He was about six feet tall and had dark hair and eyes. His right hand and forearm had a silvery sheen to it. "But not like Mira. I know this from images I have seen in Nora's mind. You are not the same, yet I feel that you are she."

His comments raised a number of questions, but none of them were as important as the ones I'd already asked.

"Speculate later," I told him. "Where's Nora?"

He shared a look with a woman who appeared flustered about something.

"We don't know!" the woman answered. She looked like she might be *Loiala Fé*. "She— The spell—" She pointed to a sundial on a pedestal. I could see what appeared to be the hilt of our missing sword embedded in its center. Then she gasped. "The garden!"

I glanced around but didn't see anything unusual. It was a garden area in the middle of the building, with an open roof, the sky visible above. The others were also looking around in surprise. Emma was there; how was that possible? She was standing up, as though she'd tripped or fallen.

"What am I missing?" I asked.

"Mira?" Emma was looking at me strangely. "You can't be Mira. You look so… old."

"It's me." I frowned. "What are you doing here?"

"I don't know," she answered. "I went to your house to talk to you. You know, to your window? I've been stuck here with Nora forever."

I nodded. She did have a habit of showing up at my window at night sometimes. It was kind of weird, but she was just lonely, and her home life wasn't that great. I didn't have the heart to tell her to stop.

"Where's Nora?" I asked, looking around. "She was just here."

"It's my fault," she mumbled.

Before I could ask her what she meant, the woman's face changed from consternation to surprise.

"The restoration spell must have worked!" Then she looked at the man who had spoken before. "What about the rest of the city?"

They all turned and rushed through the building to what looked like doors to the outside, leaving me alone with Grace and Luci, who were still unconscious, and Emma with her hang-dog expression. Where were our *Rorujhen*? I followed in the wake of the small group to the front exit.

"*MIRA!*" The voice in my head was more like a scream. Then I heard roaring and neighing through the doors and rushed out to see what was going on.

Anazhari had charged, plowing into men and griffins, knocking them from their feet just as I stepped through the door.

*Griffins?*

Anazhari's eyes blazed with a terrible rage; hatred and malice radiated from her in waves. Mehrzad and Laleya were coming from down the street, Mehrzad was staggering and seemed dazed.

The largest of the griffins launched itself at Anazhari. She dodged its claws and beak, spun in a full circle clockwise, then reversed direction and spun again, hooves flashing out all the while. The griffin was struck and before it could move, Anazhari had it pinned to the ground with her teeth gripping its throat tightly.

*"WHAT HAVE YOU DONE WITH MIRA?"* she demanded.

From the reactions of the people around me, it seemed that *Rorujhen* could indeed manage some sort of communication to strangers without needing a bond between them. Maybe it was just emotion. My curiosity would have to wait, though. The soldiers, who also looked to be *Loiala Fé,* were reaching for their weapons.

"Stop!" I called out. The soldiers snapped their heads in my direction. "Stand down!" I ordered them. "Anazhari, I am here! I am safe!"

Her eyes found me, and she paused. Her breath was coming in ragged gasps, her teeth still clenched on the throat of the griffin.

"I'm alright," I told her again. I approached and laid my hand on her shoulder.

She seemed confused for a moment. I felt the tension still gripping her as she released the griffin and stepped back. Her eyes darted around to the faces that stared at her. I could feel a jumble of emotions from her — rage and hatred were being replaced with dismay and shame. And grief. She reared with a great cry and then rushed off, dodging between buildings and out of sight.

"Anazhari!" I called after her.

*"Give her some time,"* it was Laleya. *"She will return once the Rage is fully spent. And once she feels she can face us."*

"The Rage?"

*"A rare affliction. She has suffered the condition for many years,"* she explained.

I had more questions about that, but it wasn't the time or the place. I sent that thought to Laleya and turned back to the strangers.

"*Loiala Fé*?" I asked them.

The woman gave a quick shake of her head. "Our people have not gone by that name for centuries. We are *Wyl-Dun*."

"I thought *Loiala Fé* were from Daoine?"

"Yes." She nodded. "But when a faction of the *Uthadé* left here and became the *Ashae* on Daoine, many *Loiala Fé* came here to Danu and eventually became *Ande Dannu*, *Dannu Fé*, and *Wyl-Dun*."

"Traded places, huh?"

"Some *Loiala Fé* did not care to be ruled by outlanders and these lands were available." She shrugged. "I am Zoriaa of the *Wyl-Dun*."

"I'm Mira. Nora's my sister. I think you were telling me where she is?"

She shook her head again, slower this time. "The young one, Emma, interfered with the spell. The defenses were activated."

That must be why she was looking so guilty. Shelby had said Emma was missing, but how did she get here?

"Nora tried to stop her," Zoriaa went on. "But— The spell— Nora disappeared."

"What spell?"

She raised her eyes and looked around us. "Do you see this city?"

I glanced around. It was a nice-looking city. There were trellises of flowers and tall trees along the streets. I wondered why I hadn't noticed all the tall, white, spiral towers and the high bridges connecting them as we were approaching across the dry seabed. The city was full of curves and arches. The greens of the plants and bright colors of flowers in balcony gardens and window boxes contrasted with the pristine white of the buildings. There were no other people to be seen, but otherwise the city was quite beautiful, an architectural work of art.

"Yes. What about it?"

"This city has lain in ruins since before my people came to this world," she told me. "The sea around the island dry and dead, the island itself bare of any life." She turned to one of the others. "Kerbas! Look from above! What is our situation?"

He nodded and leapt to the back of a griffin. A moment later, he was in the air and rising into the deepening twilight.

"What happened to us?" I asked Zoriaa.

"It seems you reached the island just as a protection barrier was erected," she explained. "It would have felt as though a mountain had fallen on you. Perhaps we should go inside and check on your companions."

"I'm concerned about *all* of my companions," I told her. I turned to Laleya and Mehrzad. "Are you two alright?"

"*It was nothing.*" Mehrzad shrugged it off. "*It simply caught us by surprise. See to the humans; they tend to be frail. Not strong like a* Rorujhen."

I kept myself from rolling my eyes and turned back to Zoriaa.

"It seems they will be fine."

She cocked her head at me and looked at Mehrzad and Laleya. "They are not horses? They are something more? You are communicating with them, yes?"

It was easy to forget that most people weren't hearing the thoughts of the *Rorujhen*. Some could, but the *Rorujhen* had been forbidden to let anyone discover their intelligence while they'd been slaves of the White Riders. Even so, I was surprised she hadn't heard Anazhari.

"Yes," I said. "They are much more."

I followed Zoriaa back inside. Grace and Luci were sitting up and looking around. Emma sat nearby looking dejected.

"What happened?" Luci asked when she saw us coming toward her.

"We hit some kind of magical barrier," I told her. "Nora's gone. We missed her."

"Gone where? Back to Earth?"

I shrugged. "I doubt it would be that easy."

"Give me a few minutes," Grace said. "I'll do another locator spell."

"Speaking of spells." I turned to Zoriaa. "Tell me more about this spell that sent Nora… Wherever."

Zoriaa swept her hand up to point to the sundial again.

"It was an ancient spell," she explained. "It was put in place by Nimué many centuries ago to hide and protect the city of Tir Nya Lu. It seems the inside of this library is the only thing that has been real on the island."

"You said the city was in ruins. Was it a glamour?" I asked her. "An illusion?"

"I do not believe so. It is as if Tir Nya Lu was somehow replaced with a different version."

"Mira?" Emma was looking at me strangely. "Is that really you?"

"Yes, Em. It's me."

Emma ran to me and wrapped her arms around me, holding me close.

"Nora's gone and it's my fault," she sobbed. "I'm sorry! I was just trying to help."

"Don't worry," I told her. "We'll find her."

Just then, the one she had called Kerbas came in the front door wearing an expression of disbelief. Perhaps even awe.

"Suloshné has returned," he announced.

"Suloshné?" I asked. I unwrapped Emma's arms and sat her in a nearby chair.

"The Sulosh Sea," Zoriaa answered.

I looked at Kerbas. "Are you saying the seabed isn't dry anymore? There's water?"

"Aye." He nodded. "Beautiful, blue water now laps at the shores of Avalon. Kartahn Zeg survived and is regrouping on the western shore."

"Avalon? Like in King Arthur?"

"Avalon is the island on which Tir Nya Lu stands," Zoriaa told us. "Nimué once selected an Artur as champion to bear the Sword of Light. He was a king. Is this who you mean?"

"Um… I think so." I looked at the sword hilt standing at attention in the middle of the sundial. "I take it that's the Sword of Light? Excalibur?"

"Yes, that is one of its names. The sword was the key to activating the spell. Nora was able to use her memories of being Nimué to unearth the secret of how Tir Nya Lu had been—"

"Wait, what?" My attention snapped from looking at the sword to what she was saying. "Memories of being Nimué?"

She blinked a few times before speaking. "Perhaps I should start at the beginning. Let us take a seat inside."

Grace and Luci seemed to be mostly recovered and we all stepped into the library from the garden and sat around a table. Zoriaa started her story with an interrupted wedding feast and Jack, the man who wasn't *Loiala Fé*, showing up and taking a bunch of food and how Kerbas and some others had followed him to the library where Nora and Emma were waiting.

"Hang on," I stopped her. "Do you know what happened before that? How did they get here? This isn't where they came through to this world."

Zoriaa nodded to Jack expectantly.

"I brought them here," he said. "I discovered Nora and Emma in the city of Solaian. They were enclosed in a room which they were unable to exit. I assisted them in leaving and brought them here."

I nodded, putting the pieces together. "In other words, you broke them out of jail and killed a bunch of guards in the process, which is why the *Ande Dannu* are hunting them and want to execute them for murder. And then you stole food from a wedding?"

"I am not aware of what the *Ande Dannu* may have done after we left Solaian," he replied.

"Uh huh." I frowned at him. His attitude was strange, and I

didn't know what to make of him. "You seem completely unaware that there was anything wrong with what you did."

His brows knit together. "Nora said something about this as well. And the *Wyl-Dunn* determined I must suffer punishment for my method of acquiring food. However, I am still trying to understand the rationale behind these things."

"You don't understand that people have a right to their lives? To their property?"

He shook his head. "This concept of rights is something else that confuses me. In my world, Sheobal, you have only the right to what you can hold of your own power."

"No *Universal Declaration of Human Rights* on Sheobal?" I asked wryly.

"We are not human. We are *Daijheen*."

"Semantics." I shrugged. "Overall, I have found that people are people, regardless of species. Not to say that cultures can't go wrong." I looked between him and Zoriaa. "So, you guys ended up here, you stole food, and then Zoriaa's people came after you and you've been here ever since?"

"No. After Kartahn Zeg took my power, the *Wyl-Dunn* arrived and took us to their encampment."

"That's the second time I've heard that name," I said. I had Jack back up and go through everything until his story had overlapped with Zoriaa's and then she took over.

"I don't get it," I said after she had finished. "If Nora is this *baensiari*, why was the sword in my mother's things?"

"No, it makes sense," Luci said. "Nora's parents were on the run. They were hiding from someone. And remember, Deirdre knew your mother and asked her for help. After Nora's parents died, your mother must have taken possession and hid the sword."

"Then the sword isn't mine, it's Nora's."

"Technically," Zoriaa interjected, "Nora is not the owner of the sword. She is its custodian. Nora would not even wield the sword; she would select a champion."

I shrugged. "In practical terms, the one who is responsible for something has a kind of ownership of it. Though not necessarily exclusive ownership. But whatever." I looked through the window at the sword in the sundial. "To sum up the situation, that's some kind of magical mechanism. The sword activated whatever spell was woven into the mechanism. And then Emma did something that caused the spell to send Nora someplace else. And you don't have any idea where it would have sent her. Yes?"

Zoriaa nodded.

"Alright, let me take a look at this."

I went back into the garden and approached the sundial. I reached for the *Ralahin,* and it came rushing to me.

"Whoa!" I looked around and the flows of magic seemed stronger and brighter than what I was used to. I pulled in power and it filled me instantly, ready for whatever use I had for it.

"Why does the magic flow so easily here?" I asked.

"Every world has its own current," Jack answered. "Magic flows with a different imperative from one place to the next."

That must be why magic had felt so sluggish on Earth; it must have a slower flow.

"And even within the same world," he continued, "there are areas where magic flows even more strongly, such as nexus points or along ley lines. This city is placed over a major nexus point. However, the nexus was hidden and unreachable before Tir Nya Lu was restored. I have only become aware of it since the restoration spell was invoked."

"This must be why the *Uthadé* and *Fu-Mo Ri* sought to take control of Tir Nya Lu," Zoriaa suggested.

"Perhaps," Jack acknowledged. "But the sword seems to be the key to that as well. I suspect it is part of the spell we have just activated. Without the sword, the nexus is unreachable."

Tesia had taught me a little about ley lines. If magic was in the world like blood was in the body, ley lines would be the major arteries. But I was more interested in what happened to Nora than in their conjectures about the place.

I studied the bright flows. A huge knot of them wound around the sundial. Somehow, the threads from the sword and the sundial completed an overall pattern. The complexity of it was way over my head. Maybe Tesia could make sense of it, but it was just a big tangle to me.

I looked for a thread that might help me find Nora the way I'd been able to track her through the closed portal spell, but there were no traces that a portal had ever been here. It hadn't even been an hour. If a portal had opened here, I'd have been able to see it.

I shook my head. "No clue. However, it sent her wherever it sent her, it didn't use a portal."

"Let me try a locator spell," Grace said, standing up. "I'll get my pack."

I looked back at the sword. The spell was no longer active. I took hold of the hilt and tried to draw it out of the sundial, but it wouldn't budge. Then I noticed that some of the threads coming from the sword appeared to have a different purpose than the connection to the sundial. They seemed to be a more fundamental aspect of the sword itself. I followed the threads and they led directly to Jack.

"Why is the sword linked to Jack?" I asked.

Zoriaa frowned at me. "The sword is not linked to Jack. It would only be linked to Nora as *baensiari*."

"Uh huh." I gave her a look. "So how *could* it be linked to Jack?"

"You are certain it is linked to me in some way?" Jack asked.

"Can you see the flows?" I asked him.

Jack put his attention on the sword, and I could see his eyes narrow with concentration.

"I see what you mean," he said finally. "But I cannot explain it."

"The sword can only be linked to the *baensiari* or to her appointed champion," Zoriaa objected. "No other."

This time I turned a questioning expression to Jack, but he just looked confused.

One of the guards rushed in and spoke in low tones with Kerbas. Kerbas turned to us as the man rushed back out.

"Kartahn Zeg and his group have breached the shores of Avalon," Kerbas told us. "They are approaching Tir Nya Lu as we speak."

"We do not have a strong enough force to stand against Kartahn Zeg," Zoriaa said. "He will have his most powerful *Bahréth* mages with him."

"*Bahréth*?" I asked.

She nodded. "We were preparing to evacuate. The last thing to collect before leaving was the sword. All else is ready."

"Alright." I stood up. "Then let's get out of here."

I walked to the sword and tried to pull it out of the sundial, but it wouldn't budge.

"Bit of a problem here," I said. I connected to the *Ralahin* again and looked at the threads of magic. "It looks like it's being held in place by the linking spell." I turned to Jack. "Try it."

Jack approached and put his hand on the hilt. He pulled and the sword came free easily.

"How can this be?" Zoriaa wondered out loud. Then I saw realization on her face. "Jack, earlier you swore a promise to Nora to protect her. You offered to be bound to her as her protector, to serve her, and she accepted."

Jack nodded.

"I believe this somehow made you the champion," she told him. "The Sword of Light is now yours to wield in all its power."

# CHAPTER TWENTY-THREE

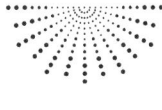

## MIRA

*I* had a lot of questions regarding the significance of what Zoriaa had said, but if we were in a hurry to leave, those questions would have to wait. Grace came back in with her pack. It would only take a moment for her to do the location spell, and we needed a direction to travel.

Grace didn't waste any time pulling out what she needed and performing the spell.

"It's too indistinct," she said after a moment. "I can tell she's on this world somewhere, but she's too far away to get a clear read on a direction. And I think there's a large body of water in between us; like an ocean. A lot of water like that can interfere with the spell."

I frowned at that, then turned to Zoriaa. "I think we should all stick together for now. We have more talking to do."

"I agree." She nodded. "Your mounts can swim? I don't know whether there will be any boats, but since the sea has returned…"

The thought hadn't occurred to me. "I can always open a portal. Let's move."

We exited the library and I could see that Kerbas and his guards were ready to leave. I noted that Jack had sheathed the sword and hung it from a strap over his shoulder. Mehrzad and Laleya stepped toward us. Anazhari stood not far away, head down but attentive.

Laleya seemed hesitant. Mehrzad moved toward Grace but then staggered and took a couple of steps to the side.

"Mehrzad, are you alright?" I asked him.

"*Of course!*" he replied gruffly. "*I just lost my footing for a moment.*"

"Laleya." I turned to her. "What's going on?"

"*We... We are still recovering from the blow that rendered us unconscious,*" she answered. "*Perhaps we need a little more time?*"

I nodded to her and turned to Zoriaa. "They're still getting over being slammed by that barrier. We can't leave yet." I waved Anazhari over and retrieved the chunk of wood from my pack.

"Hang onto this," I said, handing it to Zoriaa. "If we get separated, I can find you and make a portal."

"We can't just leave you here for Kartahn Zeg," she told me.

"What's the deal with this guy?" I asked her. "Is he looking for a fight?"

"He seeks power," Zoriaa answered. "We have removed the grimoires from the library. We must prevent him from gaining that knowledge. We can leave the city to him."

"Then if we just step aside and let him have the city, he'd leave us alone?"

"Eventually, he might." Jack frowned. "But he would first look to see if you have anything of value to him. Including power."

"Okay, so not a friendly guy. That just leaves the problem of getting off the island."

"You can create a portal to leave?" Zoriaa asked.

"Yes, but I need a connection or anchor for the exit," I explained. "I have a thread of magic tethered to that piece of wood."

She handed it to Kerbas. "Have one of your guards fly this to the shore and place it upon the ground. They must take the books, too. Zeg must not know we have them. We will follow when we can." Then she turned back to me. "Perhaps we should go to the western gate and observe Zeg's approach."

The library stood on a small rise. Along with Kerbas and the remainder of his guards, we followed the street down the gentle slope to the west. The *Rorujhen* and griffins walked along with us. After a few minutes we entered a large open plaza about a hundred yards across that gave us a view of the sea to the south and west. I could hardly believe that only hours ago it had been a dry wasteland. Now, I could see and hear seabirds. There was salty moisture in the air, and short waves lapped at the shore of the island. The light from the setting sun reflected off the water; the waves winked at me as though we shared a secret.

We'd walked halfway across the plaza when we saw a large group of figures coming toward us from the other side. They were at the head of a column that disappeared around the corner of the road that wound through the buildings behind them. Those at the front rode on huge creatures with some sort of shaded structure on their backs to sit in. I think they're called houdah. The mounts looked almost like elephants, but their tusks were longer with a different curve than I'd seen before, and their heads were shaped differently. They had to be at least fifteen feet tall, and their tusks were nearly as long as their bodies. Plus, their rear hips were significantly lower than their front shoulders.

"What the heck are those?" I asked out loud.

"Some kind of mammoth, maybe," Grace supplied.

"I thought mammoths were hairy."

"That's the wooly-mammoth," she answered. "The rest didn't have that. But the ears on these are bigger than a mammoth. More like elephants."

They drew up as they saw us, and I got a better look at the riders. These were evidently the *Bahréth* Zoriaa had mentioned earlier. They were great, big lizards. Or maybe snakes with arms and legs.

Several *Bahréth* slid from their mammoth mounts to the ground and fanned out in an arc ahead of their party. I heard an odd scuttling sound and several large, yellowish scorpions with heavy pincers appeared from behind them; their tails raised above them with their stingers hovering almost level with my head. Their enormous claws looked powerful enough to snip a person in two.

Something else was different about these things besides their size. They took up a ready position I'd seen in pictures and videos with their pincers open and raised and their tails up behind them. One thing that had always bothered me was how completely still they could be. That was the difference; these scorpions were breathing, and I could see the bodies expand and contract with each breath. In the silent moment as our two groups regarded each other, I could actually hear the air going in and out. Somehow, this only made them even more disturbing.

A figure on the central mammoth pulled aside the gauze curtain and looked intently in our direction. He appeared human, but there was something strange about it. Using the *Ralahin* I looked again and saw that he was using a glamour. Zeg was a *Bahréth*.

"Kartahn Zeg," Jack called out. "I know you. What is your purpose here?"

"Ah, the *Daijheen*." The figure chuckled in reply. "Still here, are you?"

"I ask again." Jack ignored the question. "What is your purpose here?"

"Our purpose? Zolat, tell the *Daijheen* our purpose."

One of the *Bahréth* stepped forward. "We shall spread the word of the *Jhyeh* throughout the world and beyond."

"I have met your *Jhyeh*. And your *An-Jhyeh*," Jack commented blandly. "I did this when I first came to your world. They seemed focused only on the *Bahréth*."

"We do not need you to tell us of the *Jhyeh*!" Zolat snapped. "We have the Envoy of the Transcendent among us."

"Your Transcendent are imposters," Jack scoffed, "preventing you from reaching the *Jhyeh*."

"Blasphemer! You speak against the *Jhyeh*!"

"No, I speak against the Transcendent."

"If you speak against the Transcendent you speak against the *Jhyeh*. The Transcendent serve the *Jhyeh*. This was revealed by the Prophet Olsahg."

"I've read your Tolkeda, including the Book of Olsahg. Have you not noticed that the only ones to tell you about your Transcendent were the Transcendent themselves? Your *Jhyeh* and your *An-Jhyeh* have never mentioned them. As I said, they are imposters."

"Heretic!" Zolat drew a weapon and started toward Jack. "I will silence your deceiving tongue!"

Jack stepped forward to meet the angry *Bahréth*. Zolat was huge, probably ten feet tall, and towered above Jack. As soon as he was within range, the *Bahréth* raised his sword and started a downward strike at Jack.

Jack had dropped his sheath from his shoulder to his left hand near his waist. He drew the sword and in the same motion swung it up and across diagonally at Zolat. The blade glowed brightly and cut through Zolat's torso like it was paper; his body falling to the ground in two pieces. The sword glowed so brightly it was hard to look at. The hilt had been a brown color, but it showed white now. I could feel the immense power radiating from it.

"What do you have?" Kartahn Zeg demanded. He slid to the ground and stepped forward. "You have found the Sword of Light! Give it to me and I will spare your lives. I may even return your powers to you."

"The only way I will give you this sword is in your gut!" Jack snarled at him.

"You swore oath you would not oppose me!" Zeg objected.

"My oath is intact." Jack smiled at him as he sheathed the

sword. "I swore I would not oppose you on that day. That day is gone. This is another."

Zeg glared at him, then he seemed to relax and looked away casually. "It is not important what you do. Your companions will join me when they meet the Envoy of the Transcendent. Behold, Chenosh!"

There was movement from behind the front line of mammoths and something was launched into the air. Warm, yellow light emanated from the most beautiful creature I had ever seen. It was a man, but it had huge, white wings. The feeling of raw power was almost overwhelming.

A sense of love and complete acceptance of who I was radiated from him. I realized that he must be an angel. I saw Zoriaa drop to her knees at my side as I did the same.

"I am Chenosh," he said as he landed in front of us with a beatific smile. "I am here to show you the path to eternal happiness. Be at peace. Lay down your worries and your burdens."

I felt so relieved I almost wept. Everything would be alright. Chenosh had come to show us the way; there was no need to struggle or fight.

There was a scream and suddenly Jack had leapt on Chenosh. Jack had one hand on a wing and the other on Chenosh's throat. Chenosh beat at Jack with hands and wings, trying to free himself but unable to take flight while Jack gripped his wing.

What was Jack doing? How could he fight against such a being? What perverse nature must he have to do that?

Something was happening to the features of both combatants; Chenosh's face blurred, and the skin on Jack's face kept shifting to red. There was another scream and Jack had sunk his suddenly longer teeth into Chenosh's neck where it met his shoulder. The light emanating from Chenosh flickered off and on as he struggled.

Finally, the light faded completely and Chenosh no longer struggled. Jack's bite had ripped flesh from Chenosh's throat and his head was nearly separated from his body. Jack got to his feet and I could see blood dripping down his chin.

What had just happened? I looked at the body at Jack's feet, but what I saw wasn't Chenosh, the Transcendent — Chenosh the Angel. What lay at Jack's feet had wings, but its huge, bulbous body was covered in colorless skin and looked more like a giant maggot than anything angelic.

"You were a fool to let your *Qélosan* collaborator so close to me." Jack was looking at Zeg. "You know *Daijheen* are immune to their illusions."

"What have you done?" Zeg's glare was full of hatred and fury. "You shall pay for this!"

Jack stretched and somehow appeared taller. "And I have regained some measure of power. I wager you are still adjusting to what you stole from me. Try me, Zeg. You have no hostage this time. No leverage. Let us see if you are as great as you think."

"You are the fool!" Zeg spat at him. "You do not face me alone! You also face mages of the Exalted and warriors of the Anointed." Zeg laughed. "Not to mention a few of our pets. Now, it is time for all of you to die!"

I heard a sharp report and a spot of red appeared on the right side of Zeg's chest. His eyes grew wide and he clutched at the wound. Several of the *Bahréth* rushed to his side as he collapsed to his knees. I turned to look at Luci who stood with her pistol still extended.

"When it's time to fight," she shrugged at my expression, "I'd rather get things going than wait around."

The *Bahréth* were withdrawing, carrying Zeg with them, but the huge scorpions were scuttling quickly in our direction. They ran with their tails extended straight out behind them with astonishing speed. Just as they neared, I regained my composure enough to throw up a magical barrier to keep them from reaching us. The magic rushed to me. I still wasn't used to how easily magic flowed on this world but reveled in the sensation of power filling me.

The scorpions slammed into the invisible wall and fell back. They only paused for a moment before they came forward again more slowly. The scorpions lifted their pincers and identified the location of the barrier, then they crouched low and pushed slowly forward. Little by little, the barrier gave way. Instantly, I thickened it, but the scorpions pressed toward us inexorably.

"I can't keep them out!" I shouted.

I heard movement behind me and turned to see the griffin mounts of my new friends coming forward. One let out a loud *scree* sound and the scorpions stopped moving for a moment before resuming their push toward us.

Actually, from their direction and how they were bunched up, it didn't seem like we were all on the menu.

"Jack!" I warned. "They're heading for you! Get ready!"

Then the scorpions were through the barrier and swarming toward Jack. He drew the sword again and it shone brightly, causing another momentary hesitation from the scorpions. There had to be at least a dozen of them and they were making a beeline for Jack.

I threw a ball of magical energy at the lead scorpions, but it had no effect.

"They are resistant to magic!" Kerbas called out; his heavy sword in his hand as he moved to stand with Jack.

The griffins leapt toward the onrushing scorpions. Jack's sword flashed as the scorpions came at him, severing a huge pincer from one of the scorpions. Then he was blocking pincers and stings. He was actually pretty good with the blade, but he was outnumbered. Scorpions swarmed to Jack, but several others charged in among us and the soldiers tried to drive them off.

The griffins came at the scorpions, striking with their beaks and slashing with their talons. I saw at least two of the griffins take direct stings to their bodies, but they showed no ill effects. They were ripping the scorpions apart, but not fast enough.

Jack was overrun and had taken several stings before the last of the scorpions attacking him was turned into a broken, gooey mess. The *Rorujhen* had come joined in the fight, their heavy hooves smashing down to crush the scorpions. Several other scorpions were retreating back to across the plaza.

The sword slipped from Jack's hands, and he dropped to his knees. I rushed to him and eased him to the ground just as he had started to collapse.

"Easy there, Jack," I told him. I could see the skin swelling and turning purple where he'd been stung. I looked at Kerbas, but his stony expression told me nothing. "Zoriaa?" I asked, shifting my gaze to her.

She gave her head a small shake.

"Way to go, Jack," I said. "I guess you really pissed them off when you killed their angel."

"The *Qélosan*. You must steel your mind to their influences, *Daijheen* are their natural enemies, and we are immune." A shudder ran through his body. "Their magic beguiles; they cast an illusion of love and acceptance and whatever you find most beautiful. The most… admirable."

"You sure talk a lot for a man in your condition." I gave him a wry look.

"You must be wary. They feed off of your emotion and life energy. In turn, *Daijheen* are capable of doing something similar with them by turning their power against them, reversing the flow."

"Well, he's dead. So, we won't have to worry about him now."

"There will be more. I—" His body spasmed, causing his back to arch. His breath was coming in ragged gasps. Then his hands scrambled for the sheath that lay nearby and he pulled it against his chest. The sheath started giving off a slight glow.

"Beware of Kartahn Zeg. Beware the *Qélosan*. Find Nora. And… Emma."

"Emma?" I looked around for her, but she wasn't among the faces around me. "Jack, what happened to Emma?"

"The *bahrantu*—" he started, but he spasmed again and the glow from the sheath spread to encompass his entire body. His eyes were closed, and I couldn't tell whether he was breathing. I strengthened my connection to the magic and looked at him, wishing I'd been able to learn how to heal with magic. I couldn't tell what was happening, but I could tell he wasn't dead. At least, not yet.

"Who or what is a *bahrantu*?" I asked, looking around.

"It is the name for the creatures we fought," Zoriaa answered. Right. The giant scorpions. "They are servants of the *Bahréth*."

"Why would those scorpions—er, *bahrantu*," I corrected, "why would they take Emma?"

Zoriaa shrugged. "Information, perhaps. She clearly wasn't a danger to them, so they wouldn't worry about her putting up a fight."

I thought about that for a moment. "Does Emma actually know anything that would be bad for her to talk about?"

"She knows about Nora and the Sword of Light," she answered. "That's certain to get Kartahn Zeg's attention. If he survives his wounds."

"Speaking of that," Kerbas interrupted. "What was that weapon?" He was looking at Luci. "It barked."

"It's a pistol. A handgun," Lucy told him. She drew one from her shoulder holster and ejected the magazine and the round from the chamber before handing it to him. "It launches a projectile, like a bow, but uses a small explosion as the force behind it."

"Ah," he nodded, looking into the barrel. "The *Félbahlag* use something similar on their ships, but much larger. Not something you could carry around with one hand. What is its range?"

"Accuracy from too far a distance with a hand-gun is limit-ed," she answered, "but with—"

"Guys," I cut in. "Focus. They took Emma."

"Right." Lucy took her gun back from Kerbas. "Sorry. Who's Emma, again?"

"She's a kid from my high school. Somehow, she got stuck here with Nora."

She frowned, "How…"

"I don't know," I told her. "But she's here and those scorpions took her. We have to get her back." I looked around the group and then my eyes went to where Jack was unconscious on the ground. "And we need to take care of Jack."

"If we can get Jack to our healers," Zoriaa suggested, "they may be able to help him. Our griffins are immune to *bahrantu* toxin, but for most, it is very deadly. Without treatment, he may not survive."

"Okay," I nodded, "if you can take Jack to the healers, we can go after Emma." She seemed to hesitate. "What?" I asked her.

"This was before Jack had become the Champion of the sword, and that may change things. But Jack was only given leave to be amongst our people under Nora's supervision," she explained. "She took responsibility for him. Now that Nora has disappeared…"

"Why would he need sup—" I stopped the question before I'd finished it. The details didn't matter right now. "He can't get into any trouble in his current condition." From her expression, I could tell that wasn't enough. "Okay, what if I take responsibility for him?"

"That would probably be acceptable to our queen," she said. "But if you are going after Emma…"

"I can't be in two places at once," I finished for her. I looked at Jack. Not a pretty sight. "Fine," I said, not liking the decision. "Jack's condition is clearly life-threatening. If they're hoping to get information from Emma, they should at least keep her alive for the time being. And maybe they'll have their hands full trying to heal their leader. But we need to get Jack's situation handled fast before they decide they don't need Emma anymore."

I mentally created a priority list for myself, based on who seemed to be in the most danger. First Jack. Then Emma. Then find Nora. I hoped I was right.

A sound drew my attention and I looked up to see that more of the *bahrantu* had gathered at the far edge of the plaza. There were also several mammoths, as well as at least a platoon of armed soldiers. There were way too many of them for us to face.

"Pack it up!" I yelled. "We need to move!"

Zoriaa picked up the sword and slid it into the sheath that Jack still gripped to his chest and Kerbas and one of his soldiers threw Jack over the back of a Griffin. Meanwhile, Lucy, Grace, and I were climbing to the saddles of our *Rorujhen* mounts. The scorpions were running toward us, their tails horizontal behind them. The griffins took to the air, but that left three of us on our *Rorujhen*. Fast as the *Rorujhen* were, the scorpions weren't so easily left behind. Plus, the *Rorujhen* were still a little shaky.

I didn't know where we were going; there was no plan except to run.

# CHAPTER TWENTY-FOUR

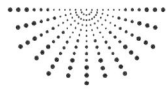

## NORA

*S*lowly, I became aware of a rocking sensation. The nearby cry of a seagull brought me to an upright position. I was in some sort of a rowboat or skiff. The line from the bow was tied to a wharf a couple of feet above my head. I'd spent a few years bouncing between foster families in a coastal city and had picked up some of the terminology hanging out around the docks.

Other memories came to me as well. Bits and pieces of long ago; things that couldn't possibly be my memories. At least, not the memories of Leanora Leland.

The rising sun shone mutely through the morning fog along the shore from the east. From what I could see through the fog, to the south looked like open water. The air was heavy with the smell of salt and seaweed. A gull on the gunwale of the little boat cocked its head at me, probably wondering if I had anything for it to eat.

"I could use something to eat myself," I mumbled as my stomach growled.

Where was I? I remembered the flash of magic as I shoved Emma away from the sundial mechanism. *Emma!* I looked around quickly, but I was alone in the small boat. Had the spell sent her someplace else? Had it dumped her outside the boat? I looked around at the clear blue water. In the morning light, I could see vague shadows of fish moving around, but nothing that looked like a young girl.

Hopefully, my shove had gotten her far enough from the sundial that the spell only affected me. *Cast far.* That's what Nimué's letter had said. If someone monkeyed with the spell they'd be cast far. So that's where I was. Far. Far from Emma. Far from Jack. Far from Zoriaa. Far from Tyr Nya Lu.

As I thought of that, more glimpses of Tyr Nya Lu flashed in my mind. Maybe, somehow, could the spell that sent me here also have jarred loose memories of that earlier life Zoriaa was talking about? Could I really have lived before as Nimué? Maybe I could find out more about it in Tyr Nya Lu. Little good it would do me considering I probably wasn't anywhere close to that now.

But where was I?

I wasn't going to get any answers sitting in a boat. A rickety-looking wooden ladder was hanging down from the edge of the wharf. The air hung heavy with humidity, and I put the hood of my cloak up to ward against it getting too damp and frizzy as I stood up to make my way to the edge of the boat. I stumbled and grabbed for the ladder and heard something *thunk*. I looked toward the sound and saw that it was Nimué's grimoire. I'd had it in my other hand when I'd reached for Emma. As I bent over to pick it up, one hand on the ladder, my shifting weight caused the little boat to move. The sound of the hull hitting the nearby piling was loud in the quiet of the morning. I struggled to regain my balance and retrieved the book.

My next challenge was to get up the ladder while holding the book. I grabbed the ladder and the boat shifted again. My arms flailed and I tried to catch myself on the line holding the boat to the wharf. Unfortunately, I grabbed the loose end hanging down and the knot came undone. I grabbed frantically for the ladder as the boat started to drift.

"Yo-ah! What you try do?" The voice came from above.

There was a heavy thud and someone else was in the boat with me. I barely had time to wrap my arms around the book before I was thrown bodily from the boat to the deck of the wharf. I heard a scurry of motion and dark eyes looked at me from over the edge. A large man climbed the ladder. He had the end of the line in one hand and quickly tied off the boat. He wore nothing but a pair of loose, knee-length pants.

"Try steal boat, yeah?" he growled at me. "Have dem put you in da stocks! No like teeves dese parts!"

"No!" I shook my head. "I was just trying to get out of it."

"Hah! Why you der even?"

"I don't know, I just woke up there."

"Huh." He grabbed me by the collar of my cloak. "You go to law."

"Leave her be," another voice sounded. "She no try steal you sorry boat."

"What you know 'bout it?" the man snarled back. "She untie!"

"By accident!" I cut in. "I grabbed the line when I fell, and the knot came undone."

The second man chuckled. "Sorry boat like sorry seaman. Use slipknot for tie boat? Maybe sorry knot from Baggies, like sorry boat."

I studied the second man as he spoke. He had a lean, muscular build and was probably close to six feet tall. On his otherwise bare shoulders, he wore a short, hooded cloak that was down to reveal golden-brown hair. He wore loose, short pants and had dark brown skin, like the first man, but instead of dark brown, his eyes were a bright green.

"Mind talk!" the first man snapped. "Dem *Félbahlag* boats easy make. She no right sit my boat!"

"Yo-ah," golden-hair flipped a coin at the other man. "Pay back for use."

The first man caught the coin out of the air and looked at it. "Copper?"

"More wort dan Baggie-boat."

The man started to sputter a response but golden-hair cut him off.

"We done. Move off 'for lose patience. Gwan trow you to dat boat you sweet of, may Kaiaru put you bot' to bottom o' da sea."

The man glared at him, one hand moving to the hilt of a knife at his belt as he took in golden-hair's measure.

"Stay clear my boat," he said finally. Then he walked off down the wharf.

I got to my feet. "Thanks—"

"No speak," golden-hair said as he put a hand on my elbow to guide me. "Dis way, fast. Need you not so open, Princess. Too easy, whoeva see."

I went along, thinking that princess had been an odd term of endearment to use for a stranger, but he'd been helpful so far and I needed information. He led me down the street away from the docks and then cut left down an alley. A few twists and turns later we went down a short flight of steps and in through the back door of a building. From the various barrels, it looked like a stockroom for some kind of business. Some of the shelves held racks of cups made from various materials.

I didn't have much time for looking around, though. As soon as he had ushered me inside and closed and latched the door behind us, he went to one knee, cupping his right fist into his left palm in front of him, his head tilted forward.

"Princess Luana Alaso," he said. "I name Corlen Veranu. Been watching you to come. I help whateva need."

That surprised me. He obviously thought I was someone else. A princess, no less. If this had been a scene from some rom-com, this would be where the character would be too embarrassed to fess up to the mistaken identity. I guess that's why I didn't care for rom-coms; I'd rather be embarrassed than dishonest.

"Sorry, Mister Corlen Veranu," I told him. "I'm not your princess."

His head came up quickly and his eyes narrowed. I lowered my hood so he could get a better look at me. Maybe that would help.

"Who—" Before he could finish asking his question, there was a rapping at the door we had come in.

"Let me in! Fast fast!" The voice was female.

Corlen Veranu leapt to his feet and opened the door. A figure rushed past him, and he closed the door behind her. Like me, she wore a dark green cloak with the hood up. She lowered her hood to reveal dark skin on a strikingly pretty face, blonde hair, and piercing green eyes similar to Corlen's.

"I see you on dock," she said to him. "I tink you look me?"

Corlen hesitated as his eyes went back and forth between us. The girl gave her head an impatient shake and she turned to me.

"Who you den?" She eyed me critically. "Red hair like *Fu-Mo Ri* but no tall. Where you come, outlander? Why you here?"

"I'm here by accident," I answered. "I'm just trying to get home, but I seem to get further and further from that happening. I'm Nora. I take it you're the princess?"

"He tell dat already, hey?" She nodded. "I see him rescue stranger wid green cloak, I guessed he tink you me. But how he know bout green cloak? Dat secret. Somebody tell him for reason." She turned back to him. "You come for help me or come for take me back?"

"Course help!"

"Finally find tongue, hey?" She studied him for a moment, then shrugged. "I already risk. Decision done. If you betray, I see you heart cut from chest before day drag me to dis marriage."

Corlen drew his knife from his belt and offered it to her, hilt first. "If you doubt, take heart now."

"Tsk. No so drama. Only loyal man let me do, and then is waste. Put blade nay."

Corlen blinked at her slowly and I stifled a chuckle. Then his eyes turned back to me. The princess also turned her sharp eyes on me.

"Still decide for do you," she told me. "You stranger for me. No good you know I here. If word spread…" She shook her head.

"Loose lips sink ships?" I supplied.

"Dat." She nodded.

"I don't even know where I am," I told her. "I was in Tyr Nya Lu, and the next thing I knew I was waking up in that boat."

"Place of myt and legen, dat," she said. "Only know little. Someting happen?"

"There was a kind of protection spell," I explained. "If you mess with it the wrong way, it sends you far away… Somebody messed with it." I shrugged. "I tried to stop her."

"Den you here?" She tilted her head. "You tink rando you land here where I be?"

"Where is *here* exactly?"

"Dis island Carabora. We in *Kajoran* Archipelago."

"I'm not actually from this world." I frowned. "So that doesn't really tell me anything. But thanks."

"Archipelago go from Danu in west to Félbahrin in norteast."

"So, we're east of Danu? Okay, that helps. Sort of."

"Princess," Corlen cut in. "Need move you safer place. Resistance make good place for hide."

She shook her head. "No go for hide. Stow on *Félbahlag* ship for come dis far. Now need own ship. *Kajoran* ship wid loyal *Kajoran* captain and crew. Dis what you must do for me."

"Ship?" He was incredulous. "Go where?"

"I answer dat when time right," she said. "Dis not time right. Find me ship."

"Dat not so easy, Princess."

"If easy," she quipped, "why I need you? How you name?"

"Corlen Veranu."

"Corlen Veranu, we wait here. You find me ship." She looked

at me. "I tink for now best you travel wid us. Dey look one woman. If dey see two, dey tink okay."

"Princess—" Corlen began.

"Still you here?" She cut off whatever he was going to say. "Tought you gwan find me ship."

"Aye dat." He scowled. "I know pub owner, hey. He leave you be. But maybe not uders come later for drink. You stay quiet. I be back soon as I can."

He went out the door and Luana barred it behind him. In one corner of the room were some rickety chairs and a small table with writing materials and what looked like a ledger. I motioned to the chairs and we both sat down. She adjusted her cloak as she sat, revealing a curved sword tucked into a sash that wound several times around her waist.

"What's your deal?" I asked her. "Who's after you?"

"The *Félbahlag*, of course," she said. "Do you really know nothing of us?"

"Sorry." I shook my head. "I'm just a stranger in a strange land. Wait, why were you talking so differently before?"

"We *Kajoran* have developed our own way of speaking the common tongue. We call it Kadj or Kadj-speak. But since you aren't one of us, I'll speak in a way that is easier for you to understand."

"I appreciate that," I said. The Kadj-speak wasn't too hard to understand, but normal language would be easier. "So why are these *Félbahlag* after you?"

"King Unais Elizondo of the *Félbahlag* took control and subjugated our islands about twenty years ago," she explained. "Not the current one. The last one. King Unais Elizondo the Second was assassinated some years back. King Unais Elizondo the Third is on the Félbahrin throne now. Anyway, I will soon reach my third seventh year. This is very auspicious for the *Félbahlag*—"

"Third seventh year?" I frowned. "You mean twenty-one?"

She nodded. "They have been waiting for this to ship me off

ADAM K. WATTS

to the mainland to marry one of their nobility. Duke Fernen Gabiran. They think this will give them some legal justification for annexing our islands."

"And you don't like him?"

"Like him?" She scoffed. "I don't even know him. But he is a typical *Félbahlag* noble. He already has four wives. I would just be his exotic showpiece, and a tool to control the *Kajoran* people. He would probably never even touch me after consummating the marriage. But first, I would have to be circumcised so that the consummation would not make him unclean in his religion."

"Unclean? How demeaning." Then the rest of what she said hit me. "Wait… Circumcised?"

"A vile practice," she answered. "They mutilate their women in the name of religion."

"That's sick." I shuddered. I'd heard of the practice among some extremist groups on Earth. Evidently, fear of women wasn't just an Earth thing. "So, you took off and they're trying to find you? I'd run away, too, I don't blame you."

She shook her head. "It is not simply about running away and avoiding their plans for me. We must drive the *Félbahlag* from our islands. We will be independent again. If I can manage that, I will show I am fit to be queen. That I am fit to be named for Queen Luana Alaso, the first *Kajoran* queen."

"I take it you have a plan?"

"We have known this time would come." She nodded. "My mother prepared me for it since the day I was born. But the plan is mine, as it must be. The fate of our people is in my hands, and no other's."

"Wow! No pressure, huh?" I tilted my head. "Isn't that a lot of weight to be on one person's shoulders?"

"A queen must be able to bear it; that is her purpose."

I supposed she was right. Not being a queen or a princess, it wasn't a responsibility I had to worry about. That was totally fine with me. I glanced at her. She was about my height. Though she was only a couple of years older than me, she seemed a lot older. It would be easy to let her be the adult and just follow along with whatever she said. I envied the way she exuded confidence and authority so effortlessly.

"You said you wanted me to travel with you?" I asked her. "I'm not sure I want to get involved in your… predicament."

"I understand," she shook her head, "but it cannot be helped. First of all, you know I am here. This is a secret that must be protected. At all costs. Secondly, you have said you are a stranger here. You know nothing of our people or our islands. Even if it were safe for *me* to let you wander off on your own, it would not be safe for *you*. Strangers, especially women, are not well regarded by the *Félbahlag*. You need time to get your bearings. And information."

"I still might be better off on my own than hanging out with revolutionaries."

"Were it not for the *Félbahlag*," she told me, "you would be perfectly safe in our islands. And those days will come again. But that is not today. And I suspect the Great Mother has sent you to me for a reason."

"Then you're not giving me any choice in the matter."

"I am open to suggestions." She lifted her hands, palms up. "If you have a better plan?"

"Not at the moment." I scowled at her.

"Then why don't we go with my plan for now," she suggested. "If you come up with something else, we can discuss it. Yes?"

"Fine." I shrugged. She was right — I really didn't have a better idea. We sat in silence for a few minutes without speaking. Then I realized that if I did ever want to come up with a better idea, I needed more information. "Can you tell me about this place? These islands?"

"Certainly." She smiled. "What would you like to know?"

"Anything," I answered. "Everything."

She thought for a moment. "I'm not sure where to start."

"This is totally new to me," I said. "A few weeks ago, I didn't even know this world existed. You said you were named after the first queen. How did she become queen? Maybe that will give me some context."

"Ah, that was long ago," she told me. "Mama A'iwanea appointed the *Kajoran* people to watch over the land, the sea and the plants and the animals. And she appointed the most worthy to watch over the *Kajoran* people."

"Mama who?"

"A'iwanea is the mother goddess of our people," she explained. "She created this world as a gift to Papa Mohanga, the Sky Father."

Religion. I suppose that could be interesting.

"So you're saying that some goddess appointed your family to rule your people?"

"I am not certain that *rule* is the correct word," she considered. "Perhaps in the sense that a parent rules their children. But a parent is there to teach; to guide and to protect. That is their responsibility. Though this does come with having authority."

"Okay." I wasn't sure what to make of that, my experience with parents being as limited as it was. "So, you have two gods?"

"Oh, no." She laughed. "There are many *awa'ia*, just among the children of Mama A'iwanea and Papa Mohanga. Not to mention other *awa'ia* who came to the world later and served other races."

"What do you call your belief system?"

Luana laughed again. "It is not a belief system if I am understanding you. But the family of *awa'ia* who watch over the *Kajoran* people are the *Noélani*. We follow the ways of the *Noélani*."

"How many of these *awa'ia* do you have in *Noélani*?" I guessed *awa'ia* was their term for gods.

"There are many," she answered. "Some of the strongest of Mama A'iwanea and Papa Mohanga's children are Brother Itara of the sun, Sister Korana of the moon, and Uncle Kaiaru of the sea."

"Uncle?"

"We defer to many of the *awa'ia* as uncle or auntie. At least," she corrected, "of the *Noélani awa'ia*. Except for Brother Sun and Sister Moon. And Mama and Papa, of course."

"Of course." I managed to keep myself from rolling my eyes. "I'm not big on religion," I admitted. "No offense. I just can't get my head around all these people claiming they know what god is and how everyone else is wrong."

"That sounds like the *Félbahlag*." She frowned. "The *Félbahlag* Church of Ah-Shan proclaims that Shan, the three-faced god, is the only *awa'ia*. Though none can claim to have seen him."

I raised an eyebrow at her. "And people can claim to have seen your *awa'ia*?"

"Oh, yes." She nodded. "Once, this was a common occurrence. But — When other *awa'ia* came to this world and created their own people, there was conflict. These races did not respect the ways of *Noélani*, and some were violent and attacked our people. Mama A'iwanea and Papa Mohanga brought all of their children together to separate the *Kajoran* from the other races. The land was split, and our islands were formed. The *Noélani* were spent from the effort, and they have slept ever since, resting. Only Auntie Akajokira sleeps fitfully and can sometimes be roused. She is our protector. But for a long time, the *Kajoran* people were safe. Until the *Félbahlag* came."

That sounded too much like a pat answer for me, but I didn't say anything. She was free to believe whatever she wanted. We spent the next few hours talking about other aspects of *Kajoran* life and culture. She told me about their art, and their music and traditional dances. We also talked about *Kajoran* food, which evidently tended to be spicy. I was getting hungry, though, so I didn't want to think about food too much. Overall, the place sounded wonderful, a tropical paradise.

It did sound like things turned sour when the *Félbahlag* had come in and taken over. They had evidently assumed a patriarchal society so they imprisoned Luana's father, King Aputi, not realizing Queen Palila was actually in charge. They evidently also viewed the *Kajoran* as ignorant savages, except for their ability to produce fine linen. The *Félbahlag* had tried to enforce that all *Kajoran* wear some sort of shirt to cover their chests, especially the women. Those who complied usually wore some sort of sleeveless top. Most preferred the short cape or a wrap like a sarong, but again, the *Félbahlag* objected to the men wearing a sarong. The tropical weather on the islands hadn't required the *Kajoran* to layer-on a bunch of clothing, but the *Félbahlag* evidently had developed some religious objection to bare skin.

Schools had been put up and all *Kajoran* children were required to attend. I didn't have a problem with education, but it sounded like these were religious schools and they were trying to indoctrinate the *Kajoran* children into being like them. It was actually a familiar story to me. It had happened all over on Earth; some country with a technological advantage coming in and oppressing the indigenous population to make them more "civilized" and convert them from their religions while taking advantage of the people and their resources.

# CHAPTER TWENTY-FIVE

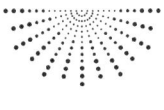

## NORA

*a*s it got later in the afternoon, we started to hear noises above us in the building and we lowered our voices to whispers to keep from being heard. At long last, there was a light rapping on the back door.

"I'm back," it was Corlen. "Let me in."

I'd been stretching my legs, so I unbarred and opened the door. He came past me, followed by two others. The first was a *Kajoran* woman, based on what I'd seen so far of the *Kajoran*. The second was a very tall, slender man with dark hair, muddy eyes, and pale skin reddened by the sun.

Luana jumped to her feet and a dagger appeared in her hand from somewhere.

"*Félbahlag!*" she snarled. "We betrayed!"

"No!" the woman replied. "He safe."

"Princess," Corlen spoke up. "You not betrayed. Dis Captain Lélé Corana. Da *Félbahlag* first mate, Shahz Dega. He one doze follow *Félbahlag* old ways. He no serve dea king an no serve dea religion."

"Shahz ship wid me more dan dozen years," the captain supplied. "He loyal. If we take you, you ship wid him too or you no go."

Luana peered at the man with narrowed eyes.

"You say, *Félbahlag*," she told him. "Why I trus you?"

The man shrugged, humor showing in his eyes. "You should not. There is nothing I could tell you or any compelling reason you should take the risk."

"Senior member my crew," the captain said. "Decide now before talk more. If yes, if no, all good. Part friends and no talk of meet."

"No find better?" Luana asked Corlen. "No find ship no... risky?"

"Fast choice no easy find," Corlen answered. "Captain Corana no risky. Strong choice. Dis Mama A'iwanea blessing dat Captain Corana ship here. Even if many choice, Captain Corana best."

Luana hesitated, clearly unhappy with the situation. "Aye dat," she said finally. "I take you judge on this, Corlen Veranu. No like trus life to *Félbahlag*, but if best choice, best choice."

"Decision done," the captain spoke. "No more talk dis. Good?"

"Aye, dat," Luana answered. Her dagger had disappeared to wherever it had come from.

"Now time my decision," the captain replied. "Where you need go?"

"Good we say after leave on ship?" Luana asked.

The captain shook her head. "Only take on ship if good where you go."

"No sound like loyal *Kajoran*!" Luana snapped.

"Yo-ah. Ship and crew safe, dat on me first," Captain Corana said. "No blind promise. Some risk okay. Limit."

"Me to free *Kajoran* people from *Félbahlag*!" Luana told her. "Take dea boots off our necks!"

"Dat all good," Captain Corana answered. "But no promise ship, all blind."

"Till now I say no one on plans," Luana said.

"Much wise." The captain nodded. "But time now to talk

some."

Luana gave a nod. "After Mama A'iwanea and other *awa'ia* split lands and make *Kajoran* islands," she began, "dey make sleep for rest. Dey tink we all safe den."

Captain Corana shrugged. "Long time gone. Wat den?"

"*Félbahlag* come too many," Luana went on. "An stronger weapons. Stronger armor. We no can defeat. Not jus *Kajoran* lone."

"You look ally other races?" Captain Corana asked.

Luana shook her head. "I go wake Mama A'iwanea. Tell her bout dem *Félbahlag*. She protect. Make *Kajoran* safe."

"How you tink dis?" The captain was dumbfounded. "You tink you wake Great Mother? How you tink you find?"

"Mama A'iwanea give piece of heart to First Queen," Luana answered. "*Kajoran* queen have connection, have bond, to Great Mother. I have Heartpiece. Heartpiece tell me direction. Mama A'iwanea sleep in Lantesia. Can wake her wit Heartpiece."

"Wat you?" the captain asked her. "Dis crazy!"

"Maybe."

Before the captain could respond, a muffled commotion sounded through the floorboards above us and the door at the top of the stairs to the pub rattled violently, followed by heavy thuds as someone tried to batter it open.

"Go to back!" Corlen yelled, shoving a heavy shelf over to fall onto the base of the stairs.

The rest of us were already running out the back door into the alley. There was a half dozen soldiers waiting there. Before I could blink, Luana had taken out three of them, sword and dagger flashing in the late afternoon sun. Two others were down from the blades of Corana and Shahz and the last was running.

Corana turned to Luana. "Our paths one. For now. Go to ship!"

As she spun to lead the way out of the alley, I remembered the spell book that had come with me from Tir Nya Lu. I couldn't lose that! I panicked and ran back into the storeroom. I grabbed the book off the table just as the door to the pub was smashed open and several men charged down the stairs. They were momentarily slowed by the fallen shelf, and I went through the door to the alley, only to find it empty.

I ran to the street and looked for the others. They were halfway to the docks and had run into a larger group of soldiers. I started in that direction and six more soldiers stepped onto the street in front of me. One of them noticed me and I ran between two buildings just as he started to raise a crossbow.

The alley I found myself in cut between the buildings. The far end opened into the jungle at the edge of town and before I knew it, I was crashing between the fronds and leaves. If I could get deep into the jungle, I hoped I could avoid getting caught. The ground quickly began to slope steeply upward and I had to grab onto branches and rocks to help myself along. I could hear cursing as the following soldiers forced their way into the jungle behind me.

I didn't think the hill was very tall and I pushed forward until I reached the top. From the crest, I could see a lush jungle between surrounding hills. The narrow valley floor ahead was lower than the ground of the town behind me.

Pain exploded in my shoulder, and I stumbled forward. I glanced down to see an arrow protruding about two inches from below my collarbone. Something else struck my back and I fell down the slope in front of me. I tried to catch myself despite the searing pain but I was moving too fast. Rolling and falling, each turn was excruciating as the arrows were levered back and forth in my wounds by the ground.

I thought it would never stop. I came to a halt against the base of a broad-leafed bush. I struggled to rise, sure my pursuers would be close behind, but I couldn't even make it to my knees. My vision blurred and I collapsed back to the ground as darkness engulfed me.

**End of Book 4**

# GLOSSARY

*Ah-Shan:* Religion of the *Félbahlag.*

*An-Jhyeh:* Demi-gods of the *Bahréth.*

*Ande Dannu:* (Fae of the Summer Court.) They were *Loiala Fé* who migrated from Daoine to Danu.

*Ashae:* (Sidhe or Fae) *Ashae* are roughly six and a half feet tall, with pointed ears, platinum-colored hair, pale blue eyes, and light skin. *Ashae* are a faction of the *Uthadé.* They split from other *Uthadé* on Danu and migrated to Daoine.

**Avalon:** An island in the Sulosh Sea where stands the ancient *Uthadé* city of Tyr Nya Lu.

*awa'ia:* Kajoran word for god.

*Baensiari:* Title for the protector and keeper of the Sword of Light. The first three *baensiari* were Duanna, Aradi, and Nimué.

*Bahrantu:* Large, scorpion-like creatures that serve the *Bahréth.*

*Bahréth:* Reptilian race from the southern continent of Danu. They stand ten feet tall on their hind legs, bear a spiked tail of another six feet, have razor-sharp claws, a venomous bite, chameleon abilities, emit a call that pains the ears and sends shivers down your spine, and are extremely cunning.

*Bayibaa:* African word for witch.

**Bronsam:** African word to indicate an evil being.

**Caladbolg:** A name for the Sword of Light.

**Carabora:** An island in the Kajoran Archipelago.

**Cheenya:** A traditional hard liquor of the *Wyl-Dunn.*

**Claíomh Solais:** A name for the Sword of Light.

*Daijheen:* From the world of Sheobal. While *Daijheen* can adopt a human form, they are naturally red skinned, have claws, horns, and batwings, and stand approximately eight feet tall. They are sometimes referred to as demons.

*Dannu Fé:* (Fae of the Winter Court.) They were *Loiala Fé* who migrated from Daoine to Danu.

**Danu:** The original home of the *Ashae* of Daoine.

**Daoine:** This is the continent and realm of the *Ashae* and *Ulané* Jhinura. Origin of *Loiala Fé.*

**Daruidai:** An ancient order predating the druids which serves to police the world of supernatural and magical elements.

*Félbahlag:* (Fir Bolg) *Félbahlag* are roughly six feet tall, with slightly pointed ears, brown hair and eyes, and swarthy skin, owing to their interbreeding with humans. *Félbahlag* were a faction of the *Uthadé.* They split from other *Uthadé* on Danu and migrated first to Ireland and then to Greece. Eventually, they managed to return to Ireland. There were natural portals from Danu to

Ireland at this time and it was very easy to walk from one to the other. Nuada and the *Uthadé* wanted to expand to Earth in demanded half of Ireland. The *Félbahlag* refused and fought the first battle of <u>*Métur*</u> against the *Uthadé* on Danu. They lost this war and retreated to a small continent east of Danu. Where they have established pre-industrial technology heavily influenced by their time on Earth.

**Félbahrin:** Home of the *Félbahlag*.

**Fragarach:** A name for the Sword of Light.

*Fu-Mo Ri*: (Fomori) *Fu-Mo Ri* are roughly six and a half feet tall, with pointed ears, red hair, green eyes, and pale skin that tends to freckle. *Fu-Mo Ri* are a faction of the *Uthadé*. Because of their difference in coloring, many *Uthadé* considered them lesser or monstrous, despite a large number of marriages between the two groups. The *Fu-Mo Ri* fought the second battle of *Métur* against the *Uthadé*. Although they did terrible damage to the *Uthadé,* they lost in the end. At least one ship of one hundred men and one hundred women was all that survived, though they may have been joined by other ships. It is thought they may have become pirates.

**Gram:** A name for the Sword of Light.

*Jhiné Boré*: (Dryad or tree nymph) They have dark, greenish-brown skin, black hair, green eyes, pointed ears, and Asian features.

*Jhyeh:* The gods of the *Bahréth*.

**Kadj** or **Kadj-speak:** A type of pidgin spoken by the *Kajoran* people.

**Kajoran:** The people native to the islands of the Kajoran Archipelago.

**Kajoran Archipelago:** A string of islands that runs from the east coast of Danu to the south-western tip of Félbahrin.

**Lantesia:** A mythical city under the Sea of Lantesia off the eastern coast of Danu.

**Laraksha-Vo:** This is the primary *Urgaban* city on Daoine.

*Loiala Fé*: (Fae) They are roughly the same size and appearance as humans but have pointed ears.

**Mireygna:** Legendary *Ashae* mage, possibly a goddess. It is thought she may be three women or sisters, or one woman who can appear as any one of three avatars.

**Murias:** Ancient *Uthadé* city on the west coast of Danu.

*Noélani:* The awa'ia, gods, of the *Kajoran* people.

*Pilané Jhin*: (Pixies) Typically about three inches tall with humanoid bodies and features. Sometimes confused with *Sula Jhinara* (sylphs.) They live in flowers and primarily live on nectar and pollen. They can also be mischievous. Skin may be beige to dark chocolate, or blue or green. Blue and green pixies have butterfly wings, the others have dragon-fly wings. They are also strong telepaths. They are alternately male and female and change over a two-year period.

**Pokorah-Vo:** *Urgaban* city founded by criminal exiles from Laraksha-Vo.

*Qélosan*: A race of beings often thought to be angels.

**Ralahin:** A specific term for magic used by the *Ulané Jhinura*.

**Raven's Nest:** Restaurant owned by Mira and Bavrana in Su Lariano. Managed by Mouse.

*Rorujhen:* This race is similar in appearance to a very large horse. However, they are much faster, are fully sentient, and communicate telepathically.

**Scian of Goibhniu:** These are the two matched daggers that Mira carries. They were created by the master *Uthadé* smith Goibhniu.

**Sheobal:** Home world of the *Daijheen.*

**Shianri:** The estate in the Shifara region which Mira inherited when she killed Vaelir, a White Rider. The word means hearth or home, or even nest.

**Shifara:** The *Ashae* capitol in Daoine. This includes Shifara City and Shifara Castle, each of which are walled and are connected by a causeway.

*Shrolin chalé:* These words of power are infused with magic and can be invoked orally. The literal meaning is "give strength."

**Solaian:** Capitol city for *Ande Dannu* on the east coast of Danu.

**Sulosh Sea** or **Suloshné:** Large lake or inland sea on Danu. It is also known as the Eye of the Goddess because it is roughly shaped like an eye and has an island.

**Su Lariano:** An *Ulané Jhinura* city, home to Neelu. Mira's first home on Daoine. There is an outer town, but this is primarily an underground city built into caves and tunnels under a mountain.

**Tir Nya Lu:**

*Tolkeda:* Holy scriptures of the *Bahréth.*

*Tuatha de Danann:* Human name for the *Uthadé.*

*Ulané Jhinura:* (Sprite) They are generally about four and a half feet tall, so can appear to be human children except for the pointed ears. Using magic, they are able to move very quickly. They also appear to have slightly Asian features.

*Urgaban:* (Goblins) *Urgaban* are typically around four feet tall. They are generally humanoid, but the head is noticeably larger, with a heavy jaw and wide mouth, and their arms are longer. Their pointed ears are also very long. They have pale, yellowish skin and no hair.

*Uthadé:* (*Tuatha de Danann*) Ancient race from the world of Danu. Three factions split from the *Uthadé* to become the *Ashae* of Daoine, the *Félbahlag* of Félbahrin, and the *Fu-Mo Ri.* The remaining *Uthadé* moved to another world and have not been seen in centuries.

**White Rider:** This was an elite group of *Ashae* warriors, all male, who were supposed to be the executors of justice in Daoine. They wore white armor of hardened leather. Higher-ranking Riders used *Rorujhen* as mounts.

*Wyl-Dunn:* (Wild Fae) They were *Loiala Fé* who migrated from Daoine to Danu.

*Yo-ah: Kajoran* word used as an expletive or to get someone's attention.

# ABOUT THE AUTHOR

 Primarily an author of fantasy and science fiction, Adam K. Watts was born in Santa Clara, California, and was raised mainly in the heart of "Steinbeck Country" in Salinas, California. He has always been an artist and has made forays into writing, painting, composing, dancing, performing arts, and digital photography. As a child, his mind was caught by the poetry of Robert Frost; the words from "Stopping by the Woods on a Snowy Evening" and "The Road Not Taken" resonated with him. The ideas of looking into the woods with a longing to enter but turning away out of duty and responsibility, and the desire to travel a path few have seen, have lent his soul the aspect of the seeker. This aspect has been reflected in many of his works; images that bespeak of places that call, of paths that make you want to walk them, and corners that beg you to come look and see what is just around them, or just the wandering wind asking you to walk with her.

He was also shaped at a young age by *Man of La Mancha*, a musical play inspired by Cervantes and Don Quixote. "Tilting at windmills" is a metaphor for pushing back against the machinery of civilization advancing at the price of beauty and the human spirit. He believes that advancement can and should be achieved, but the cost should not be valor or honor or justice. An impossible dream? Perhaps.

"I've been a lover and avid reader of fantasy and science fiction since I was knee-high to a short Hobbit. I have finally escaped the confines of professional non-fiction writing to follow the purpose that has been burning in my heart since I could lift pencil to paper. Those embers, never quite cooled, have been fanned to unquenchable flame and I cannot contain the result. Enjoy!"

To learn more about Adam K. Watts and discover more Next Chapter authors, visit our website at www.nextchapter.pub.

Dear reader,

We hope you enjoyed reading *The Sword of Light*. Please take a moment to leave a review, even if it's a short one. Your opinion is important to us.

Watch for more Tales of the Misplaced releases coming soon!

Best regards,

Adam K. Watts and the Next Chapter Team

The Sword of Light
ISBN: 978-4-82417-123-8

Published by
Next Chapter
2-5-6 SANNO
SANNO BRIDGE
143-0023 Ota-Ku, Tokyo
+818035793528

7th March 2023

Milton Keynes UK
Ingram Content Group UK Ltd.
UKHW011948110923
428497UK00003B/43